RAV...
HOW TO BE F...

"An endearing novel that gives hope to those who know what it's like being different."

— *Kirkus Reviews*

"A spirit-lifting and surprising coming-of-age story."

— *Foreword Reviews*

"I always smile my way through a Julian Winters book. Remy's story of self-discovery is empowering and lovely."

—ADAM SILVERA, NYT best-selling author of *What If It's Us*

"You've been warned: Remy Cameron is coming for your heart. I adored this tender, heartfelt love song of a book."

—BECKY ALBERTALLI, author of *Simon vs. the Homo Sapiens Agenda*

"I don't often swoon, but I swooned HARD for this incandescent book. Julian Winters has crafted a deeply moving story of love, family, and identity that will stay with me forever."

—ADIB KHORRAM, award-winning author of
Darius the Great Is Not Okay

"Reading Remy is like gaining a best friend. Told with empathy, humor, and sincerity, this is an astounding follow-up for Julian Winters. The world needs Remy Cameron, and I, for one, am ready for everyone else to discover just how heartwarming this book is."

—MARK OSHIRO, author of *Anger is a Gift*

"I loved this book so much. What a gift to the world, and to all the people—myself included—who are still trying to figure out an answer to the question, 'Who am I?' Julian Winters' answer should include, 'A fabulous author everyone should read.'"

—BILL KONIGSBERG, award-winning author of
The Music of What Happens

"Winters has gifted us with a bighearted, compassionate, and hilarious book about discovering who we are underneath the person everyone else expects us to be. We are more than labels, and this is more than a book. It's a hug for everyone struggling to find their own identity, and a way to let them know they are not alone."

—SHAUN DAVID HUTCHINSON, author of *We Are the Ants*

RAVES FOR
RUNNING WITH LIONS

Gold Winner, 2018 IBPA Benjamin Franklin Awards | Teen Fiction

Finalist, 55th Georgia Author of the Year Award (GAYA)

#1 Amazon Bestseller | Teen & Young Adult LGBT Fiction

"Funny, wise, and ridiculously romantic. It hit me right in the heart."

—BECKY ALBERTALLI, author of *Simon vs. the Homo Sapiens Agenda*

"A heartwarming freshman novel from an author poised to be a modern Matt Christopher for an older audience."

—*Kirkus Reviews*

"A warm, funny, smart and poignant debut, full of heart and full of hope. I loved the adorably cute relationship that emerges between Sebastian and Emir, I loved the humour, and I loved being reminded what it's like to be a teenager during a long, hot, messy summer, when everything is new and exciting, anything seems possible, and the world is opening out in front of you. I throughly enjoyed it and hope it gets all the accolades and praise it deserves."

—SIMON JAMES GREEN, author of *Noah Can't Even*

"Inspiring and uplifting… an absolute gem of a novel. It's an utterly charming crowd-pleaser with nimble writing, exceptionally well-drawn characters and a swoonworthy romance. I freaking love this book."

—CALE DIETRICH, author of *The Love Interest*

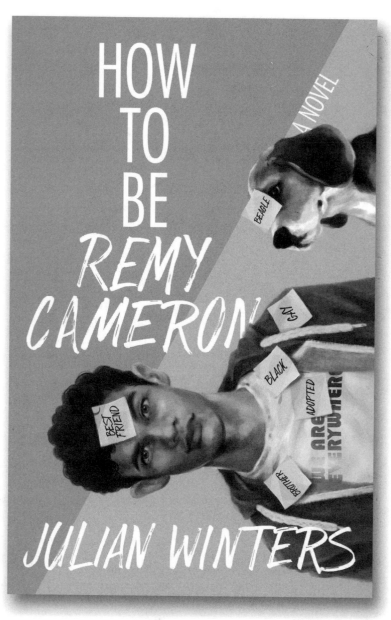

HOW TO BE REMY CAMERON

A NOVEL

JULIAN WINTERS

interlude press • new york

interlude ✦ press • new york

For the ones still trying to define themselves: You're more than the labels they give you. You're greater than the definitions used to limit you. You're one of a kind. Be yourself, always.

"To be yourself in a world that is constantly trying to make you something else is the greatest accomplishment."

—Ralph Waldo Emerson

WHEN I GOOGLE MY NAME, there are over four million search results. None of them are relevant. Unfortunately, being club president of the Gay-Straight Alliance at Maplewood High School and having a major addiction to cold-brewed coffee hasn't earned me a Wikipedia page.

What makes Remy Cameron, well, Remy Cameron?

Is it because I'm one of the few openly gay students at Maplewood? One of five black students? Maybe it's my superior taste in music? Or that I'm still recovering from a bad break-up with a guy, even though it's been way too long to be pining over him? My kick-ass family? I shouldn't use that type of language in an essay, but I just turned seventeen a month ago and adulthood is knocking on my door.

This isn't how I was taught to start an essay.

Maybe my essay should open in the time before I began to question my entire identity because of an assignment for AP Literature...

CHAPTER ONE

"EARTH TO REMY CAMERON."

Let the record show that I'm not completely ignoring my best friend Rio. Yes, I spaced out for a bit. It was a defense mechanism to avoid suffering through her latest music obsession: punk-riot grrrl bands. They're not bad, just not my favorite.

Also, she was droning on and on about one of my least favorite subjects: homecoming. Football games, tiaras and crowns, and school-mandated dances aren't my jam. The pep rallies are usually kick-ass, though.

I'm busy staring at myself in the full-length mirror next to my desk. I turn left, then right. Okay, I'm not as hot as Chadwick Boseman, but that's cool.

I have these large, blue-gray eyes. My dark, thick eyebrows contrast with my tawny-beige complexion. My best feature is probably my hair. It's brownish, like earthy soil after a spring rain, simultaneously wavy and curly. For an entire summer, I had it cut in one of those close-to-the-scalp shadow fades, but that didn't work well with my ears. They stick out like Dopey's in *Snow White*, but I like them.

On my phone, Rio's pixelated face has warped into something resembling annoyance. Or speculation.

"You're not paying attention," she says.

"Do you even care about this kind of stuff?"

Rio puts on her best affronted face. Seriously, there are no Outstanding Performance by a Best Friend awards in her future.

But the slight sarcastic twist to her lips and how her spring-green eyes glint with mischief are the best. I laugh. This has always been us, since we were third-graders jumping off the swings at recess. We have an unmistakable bond that's two-thirds humor and one-third arguing over meaningless things.

"I don't care about homecoming," Rio says. "But I care about laughing at the people who *do* care."

"Like Lucy?"

"Like Lucy."

"It's gonna be a big deal for her."

"Blah, blah, blah, '*as junior class president*,' and all that jazz." Rio blows out a breath to sweep the longer bits of her amber hair off her face. "We should've never helped her with that damn campaign."

"We're her best friends."

Rio puckers her lips. "Freaking promises made in third grade. What did we know back then?"

"A hell of a lot about friendships and *Adventure Time*, clearly."

The screen goes fuzzy, freezing on Rio's eye-roll. She snorts, then says, "But we're older now. This is what adults do."

"Worry about homecoming dances?"

"Bingo, Romeo!"

I force myself not to make a face at that awful nickname. Rio gave it to me in seventh grade when I had a crush on Elijah Burke. It's not quite my most embarrassing moment. Elijah was definitely cute and, by ninth grade, definitely straight too. Picking crushes isn't my strong point.

"You're seventeen now," she reminds me. The background music has softened but it's still raucous and percussion-heavy, all the signs of indie-rock-gone-bad. "Time to make adult choices."

"I am, by choosing to avoid social activities that require me to wear anything other than a comfortable sweater and skinny jeans."

"Are you sure you're gay?"

"Is that a real question? Do you remember freshman year?"

Yeah, no one will forget my freshman year: one of those priceless moments, a true MTV teen melodrama starring me, the guy who comes out in the middle of his student council election speech.

Go, Team Remy Cameron.

Rio's on another rant about her crusade against all things homecoming. She's anti-school-activities, which is so hilarious because she's a "journalist" for the school's trashy newspaper/blog hybrid, *The Leaf*. Truly unoriginal title aside, Rio's content is at least decent.

Not that I make it a habit of reading *The Leaf*. I'd rather listen to music. I don't know, music takes me to a place books never did. I'm only slightly religious, but something about blasting indie-pop moves me spiritually. At least Rio and I both avoid mainstream music: true best-friend solidarity.

"And the freaking spirit week bullshit!"

I watch Rio stomp around her bedroom with one hand waving around dramatically. It's kind of funny. I can't disagree though. Maplewood's homecoming scene is pretty lame. It's all flash with no sass. Every year, I wish things would change. Just once, let the homecoming queen be anyone other than the girl with the most social media followers. And the king could be anyone other than *Insert All-Star Jock Here* guy. Why does there have to be a king and queen? And why does it almost always have to be a "popular" guy and girl?

"It's ridiculous!" shouts Rio.

I nod robotically. My eyes shift over my bedroom.

On my bed, a pile of clean clothes wait to be put away. On my desk, an Algebra II book is open to whatever chapter I don't care about. Linear equations are another thing not very high on my list of fun Sunday activities. Across the carpet is a colorful sea of sneakers.

My bed is tucked against a wall layered in neon-bright Post-Its. Each hanging leaf has a quote or silly doodle or lyric from a favorite song. In the middle of the Post-Its collage is a banner and brochure for my dream school: Emory College of Arts and Sciences. I plan on applying to the Creative Writing Program—if I survive junior year of high school, that is.

My heartbeat accelerates at the thought of not getting in. I force my eyes to look elsewhere.

I have this cool, geometric bedside table from IKEA. It was a pain in the ass to put together, but it's worth it now. I nearly choke when I spot an uncapped bottle of baby lotion on it. Yeah, I better hide that before Mom comes by for her weekly cleaning session.

"And those lame chants from the cheerleaders, holy hell."

"Tell me about it," I say with just enough enthusiasm to keep Rio going. She won't be happy until she gets it all out.

Rio rips into the football team's list of accomplishments. Spoiler alert: there aren't many checks in the W column. "Our school is like a bad version of a Disney-channel movie."

"A very, very bad version. Edited and shortened for content."

"Why do we even go there?"

I shrug one shoulder, but I know why. As candy-coated, made-for-TV as Maplewood is, there's a pulse of something untouchable. Under the layers of suburbia exists a change waiting to happen, a bubble ready to burst.

I hope I'm there when it happens.

"So, it's decided." Rio squints, lips carefully curved. She's thinking. "No homecoming participation for us this year."

"Again."

"Again. Lucy is gonna kill us."

"Kill *you*," I clarify. "I'm anticipating serious bodily harm for myself. A few broken bones."

"Why are you the sole survivor of *The Hunger Games*?"

"Because Lucy likes me best."

"She doesn't," Rio says with a sweet, humorous lift to her lips.

"Okay, okay." I concede. "We're both dead."

"It'll be worth it."

Suddenly it's eerily quiet on her end. Rio Maguire and silence don't go together. They're foreign enemies. It's an omen. My stomach plunges to my knees just before Rio says, "And if we skip the festivities, maybe you won't have to see Dimi."

There it is.

I bite my thumbnail. Mom says it's a terrible habit. I think it's a healthy coping mechanism. I hate this topic. Honestly, who enjoys discussing breakups? Exes? The aftermath of your first real relationship? For months, I've done a spectacular job of avoiding any talk that involves Dimi. Rio hasn't thrown her "I told you so" in my face—yet.

I swallow. "Sure."

Rio's nose scrunches. She's holding something back. "It'd be good to, you know, not see him."

"Definitely."

I see his face every freaking day at school. It's the perfect situation: having to walk past your ex and his friends on your way to homeroom each morning, a sweetly-wrapped "fuck my life" moment I seriously dread.

Luckily, I'm saved from poking at old wounds with Rio. My bedroom door creaks when it's nudged open by a small head. I'll never tire of seeing those big, round, hazel eyes, that gumdrop nose, and large ears. Warmth like the inside of a hoodie spreads through my veins when Clover's tail wags and she pants happily at me. I check the time: 7:15 p.m. Clover is never late.

I turn back to my phone, to Rio's serious face. "Sorry, my favorite girl needs me."

Rio rolls her eyes. "If you say so."

I scratch behind Clover's ear. "No, I gay so."

My weak attempt at humor gets a snort out of Rio. Thing is, this is what Rio and I do: Try to one-up each other with sarcasm. Of course, Rio always wins that war. But it makes taking on all the intense stuff, the topics that we hate discussing, ten million times easier.

"Avoiding things is not very seventeen-year-old-like," she tells me.

"Wrong." I grin at the screen. "It's very seventeen-year-old-like."

The call ends on a freeze frame of Rio's middle-finger in a goodbye salute. I scramble to grab my shoes, a hoodie, and Clover's leash. We're out the door before I have a chance to think about all the things Rio could've said.

I'VE LIVED IN BALLARD HILLS all my life. Our neighborhood is in a little corner of Dunwoody, a fast-growing suburb just north of Atlanta.

Two-story houses with attics and finished basements and brick walkways, painted in a kaleidoscope of pastel colors—tear drop blue, seafoam green, daffodil yellow or cotton candy pink, all identical in sizes and structure with neatly planted trees that reach toward the sky like emerald hands. Even at the start of October, the lawns are immaculate and evergreen.

It's a white-picket-fence wet dream.

I glance past the gloss and finish of my neighborhood to watch the last rays of dipping sun from in front of the house belonging to Ballard Hills' notorious rule-breaker; Mr. Ivanov.

Every holiday, Mr. Ivanov goes to extremes to decorate his front yard. My favorite is his Christmas theme: plastic reindeer and a galaxy of twinkling lights and a giant Santa Claus inside of one of those inflatable snow globes. Robotic elves guard the walkway while a massive sleigh butts up against the edge of his lawn. It's over the top. It's also six levels of dope.

Currently, the yard is a sanctuary of Halloween decorations. Cartoonish ghosts swing from a white oak's limbs. Amid the bushes near the entrance, a strobe light pulses, flickering over a dancing skeleton on the blood-red door. Cotton cobwebs stretch over foliage. It's off-the-wall and has I-shop-at-Party-City-too-much written all over it. The best part is the collection of hand-carved pumpkins staged along the front steps. Their faces vary from witches to vampires, ghosts, and cats. I can't get enough of the Frankenstein one.

"Well played, Ivanov." I grin and hug myself against a rare cool breeze. Georgia's never cold this time of year.

I've never really spoken to Mr. Ivanov. He's a quiet widower who spends most of his time peeking out from his living room curtains at passersby. He has sleek gray hair, the kind of face that naturally scowls, and owns one too many flannel shirts.

Clover barks at my feet. Right. She has a schedule to keep. All my stalling in awe has delayed things.

"No need to get sassy."

Clover cocks her head and blinks a few times, another reminder that my humor fails to impress anyone.

I adjust my earbuds while thumbing at my phone to crank the volume. Nothing beats an easy stroll through the neighborhood after sunset while listening to my favorite band, POP ETC. Clover leads the way. I bop to acoustic guitars and mellow vocals.

The walk is mostly Clover sniffing every bush or small patch of fallen pine needles. She's a beagle with a killer sense of smell. Walking with her is a constant stop-and-go. I don't mind that much. It's not a workout—not the kind I *need*—but, whatever.

I love the view of a neighborhood drifting toward slumber: windows lit like glowing gold eyes, cars of various sizes parked in driveways, street lights illuminating arcs of the road.

Autumn is beginning its annual dance-off with summer. I can smell it. Under the layers of peaches and bug spray is a hint of baked apples and wood smoke. This is the best time of year.

Our favorite stop—*Clover's* favorite stop—is right outside Maplewood Middle School, which is tucked inside the heart of a block about a half mile from home.

I turn away to let Clover do her business in the line of pine trees near the school's wire fence. This spot is a maze of memories. I ripped my favorite green jacket climbing the fence with Lucy. The junior football team used to practice a few feet away. Shirtless Elijah always ignited those nerves in my belly, the sizzle trailing lower until I bit my lip sore. Call it a sexual awakening, though my attraction to guys began a little before those Elijah days.

Maplewood Middle feels like a lifetime ago. It wasn't. When you're in high school, middle school seems like a faded memory, and elementary school feels like an alternate reality, one where you're free as a bird, uncaged and happy.

Cars cruise by. Their headlights shine across the zipper on my red hoodie and my crimson Converse.

"It's cool; nothing to see here," I say to each car. "Just a kick-ass hunting dog claiming her territory."

In the distance, a rabid Japanese Chin yips from behind a fence.

I chuckle. "That's right, Fido, this land officially belongs to Clover Cameron. Shit somewhere else."

Clover harrumphs, signaling her finish. She starts our walk again while I blindly flip a one-finger salute to the other dog. Clover stops for a whiff of a bush—a potential, new kingdom to claim. I wait patiently, jamming to my music.

And then there he is.

His dark hair is tugged into a small topknot. A few strands have fallen to cut across his round jaw. His skin is flushed and shiny; his breaths are uneven. Silver light glints from a single hoop earring in his left ear. His eyes are on the brownish-side of hazel and hypnotic, even at this hour. He's wearing yellow running shoes, no socks, and a half-zipped, thin, gray hoodie. I dig it. I dig him too; at least, my lower half does.

My heart is sprinting toward my throat. I want to fix my hair and check for leftover pizza sauce on my face.

He looks familiar. I can't put a finger on where from.

Our eyes meet. I stop breathing. He smiles, a dimple leaves a comma-shaped dent in his cheek.

Honesty moment: Dimples are irresistible to anyone who doesn't have them. It's not a thing; it's a fact. I'm a proven statistic.

He eases past Clover and me, because my feet and heart and deer-in-headlights face are frozen. Then he says, "Cute."

It's one very basic word but it rotates in my head for seconds—*cute, cute, cute*. I want to say something back. Something cool, memorable. But the thing is, flirting is another weakness of mine. I'm only good at flirting via text. Never in person.

My head turns in his direction. A bloom of pink crawls across his face.

"Dog," he corrects. He couldn't have been talking about me. Not when I look like a Desperately Single Gay Teen in an American Eagle ad for Pride month. "I meant cute dog," he says, stumbling. His Adam's apple does a funky dance as he swallows. "Cute dog and... Okay. Have a nice night!"

Then he's jogging away, leaving behind unsaid words and an unforgettable smile and *cute*.

Clover barks. Or she's been barking, but I can't move. Not yet. I need a few seconds to clear this boy out of my head. He can't stay.

After Dimi and the Summer of Emo-Music Hell, I decided that it was time to just *be Remy*, single and focused and chill-as-eff. No more trips to Boyfriend Land for me.

"Not happening," I say to Clover—and myself.

Clover doesn't give me any crap about whatever just happened. She's too cool. My dad named Clover. "Because you'll be lucky if your mom lets you keep her." It's true; my mom isn't high on animals— small, big, or friendly.

It took a very convincing speech and three hours of pleading until she caved. We officially adopted Clover from a pet shelter into the Cameron clan on a Wednesday when I was nine. She became the young, willing-to-dive-into-danger Jimmy Olsen to my Superman— or maybe the other way around? As far as importance, Clover might top Rio and Lucy on the friendship chain, not that I'll ever *tell* them that.

The sidewalk leading away from the school is cracked and bright gray under halogen street lights. Part of it is covered by a trail of pine needles. But one clear stretch of asphalt stands out in electric green and blue. Fresh graffiti edges up against the soles of my shoes: an intricate maze of arrows and squares, one long stream of artistic chaos.

"Sick," I whisper.

Clover sniffs at it, unimpressed. It's a war of colors and shapes, but I can't dissect its meaning. Unique but unfocused, it's definitely not the work of the Mad Tagger, a somewhat infamous artist in the community. It's just a lookalike, maybe a homage.

I step over it. It'll be gone in a day or two. That's one thing about Ballard Hills: Rule-breaking is only permitted when it's fun and whimsical and *Better Homes and Gardens*-friendly.

CHAPTER TWO

WE'RE BARELY THROUGH THE BACK door and into the kitchen before Clover is whining. I unclick her leash. She trots off. First comes a casual stop at her food bowl. She sniffs vigorously for two-point-five seconds in hopes Mom generously left her table scraps to enjoy. No such luck.

Mom isn't as lenient as Dad about spoiling Clover.

Clover scampers out of the kitchen, no doubt to find her favorite playmate, my little sister, Willow.

"Well, this was fun!"

I can't blame Clover for wanting to hang with Willow. By far, she's the coolest seven-year-old I know, not that I make a habit of planning Lego playdates with other seven-year-olds.

My phone chimes. It's a new Facebook notification. I can't believe my mom makes me keep a Facebook page. I rarely use it. It's mostly for my aunts and uncles on Mom's side to feel as if they're part of my life. Okay, I might sneak on there to read all the cheesy, lame, and artificially sweet birthday messages people post on my wall. Seriously, what is it about birthdays that makes people you haven't spoken to in years suddenly remember you exist?

There's a new friend request. "Free Williams?"

I don't recognize the name or the profile photo, which is a young, black woman with a dark cloud of loose curls covering everything except her smile. It's one of those snarky ones that makes you want to laugh with the person. Her mouth is stained by a wine-colored lipstick. She has bright white teeth.

We have zero mutual friends. Most of her information is private. The bare minimum facts—student at Agnes Scott College, her birthday, last high school—are displayed. She's an anomaly. Yet, after I stare too long, something simultaneously like a warmth and a chill spreads through my blood. She seemed vaguely familiar to me. Maybe she knows me from a GSA event. Maybe it's a mistake. Either way, I swipe away the notification.

After hanging up Clover's leash and toeing off my shoes by the backdoor, I slide across the kitchen's hardwood floor toward the fridge. The walk has built a gnarly craving. Ice cream cake.

Birthdays are a huge deal in our house. We each have strict guidelines to ensure our special day is ten levels of awesome. My number one rule: *ice cream cake only*. Not that there is anything wrong with a thick layer of sweet icing on a sheet cake from Publix, but ice cream cake is my favorite. It always has been. Actual scrapbooks dedicated to three-year-old Remy Cameron's face smothered in melting vanilla ice cream cake exist.

Inside the freezer, in all its boxed-glory, is my birthday cake from Cold Stone Creamery: layers of strawberry ice cream and red velvet cake and graham cracker crumble. My fingers tingle as I reach for it.

"Come to Daddy."

I pause, then cringe. Since my joyous discovery of porn, phrases like that have been outlawed. Once, I almost jabbed Brook Henry for jokingly using that phrase with Lucy. It would've been a short fight. Brook is a swimmer with sweet muscles and godly height and he's fast. I'm kind of a disaster just walking. It'd make a great viral video.

I slice a generous piece of cake, dump it into a bowl, then exit the kitchen. Under my breath, I hum a POP ETC song. Something about the rhythm guitar and upbeat lyrics thrums in me.

Suddenly, my jam session dies. Soft music is coming from down the hall, from the living room. Over a song I don't recognize, I hear my mom's tickled-laughter and my dad's unbelievably bad singing voice.

"O-kay."

I tiptoe toward the living room. If they're having sex, I'm demanding a bigger budget for pocket money at Emory—and a new car.

When I peek in, there's no horrifyingly gross stuff happening on our sofa. Nope. Just my parents. Dancing to music.

Correction: *This is gross.* The music is definitely something '80s. Something about the rains and Africa. As much as I live and breathe for music, I tend to stay in my own indie pop lane or whatever Lucy and Rio force me to listen to. This is a Dad song. His "classics" are '70s rock and '80s dance tunes.

I scout the scene. Most of the furniture has been displaced. The coffee table is angled in the corner. Part of the cream sectional sofa is shoved against the far wall. Any possible tripping hazard has been removed—well, except Dad's two left feet.

Watching my parents is strange. They shimmy-shuffle more than they dance. In the warm light of the standing lamp, Dad's hair looks like a copper crown. Forget-me-not blue eyes follow his feet, probably counting his steps. A serene smile dominates Mom's baby doll face. Locks of blonde hair fall across her pale skin. Under Dad's large hands, she's small and fragile.

This is unacceptable Sunday behavior. It's also kind of hard to look away. My parents are the perfect opposites: muscular computer nerd and peppy wedding consultant.

The song changes. I know this one: Tears for Fear's "Everybody Wants to Rule the World." Dad has no concept of romantic music.

"I love this song," Mom says, of course.

"I *know*." Dad's grin is ridiculous. But Mom laughs into his shoulder.

Sometimes, I wonder if, in ten years, I'll be helplessly in love, so unexplainably consumed by a connection to someone that we'll still have date nights, hold hands for no reason, dance on Sunday nights. Is that sort of thing hereditary? Not that I have to worry. Being adopted cancels out the romantic gene, right?

It's not that my parents' ability to keep the spark alive isn't admirable. But they can have the whole "sappy romance" thing. Relationships are a total buzzkill. So are breakups, especially the crying part. God, I don't miss that part. Bowls of ice cream cake and Clover are all I need, thanks.

No love story waiting to happen here.

* * *

MORNINGS IN THE CAMERON HOUSE are ridiculously fun. I'm not a morning person, at all. I hate being talkative and smiley and joyous anytime before ten a.m., but my family has a way of bringing it out of me.

I shuffle into the kitchen Monday morning with the worst hangover—a two-days-away-from-school-isn't-enough hangover. Thankfully, my dad has the perfect cure—his world-famous French toast. If Bobby Flay is the king of southwestern cuisine, then my dad is easily the emperor of southeastern breakfast breads.

Since I was a kid and could use my baby teeth to mash food around in my mouth, I've been addicted to French toast. No offense to pancakes and waffles lovers, but there's something ethereal about fluffy, cinnamon-y bread fried in butter. Dad is always coming up with new versions, none more phenomenal than his chocolate and banana recipe. Saliva gathers as if my mouth's a wading pool when I anticipate the salted-caramel syrup that goes on top.

"Perfect timing, kiddo," Dad says. With one hand, he ruffles my bedhead-disastrous curls while his other hand flips a thick slice of toast.

It's like watching an artist. Dad doesn't need fancy brioche bread either. I've witnessed him take regular, store-bought wheat bread and turn it into sopping, eggy pieces of nirvana.

"Hungry?"

I grin weakly before zombie-limping toward the breakfast table. Mom is already midway through her first mug of coffee. Sunlight pours from the nearby window to cast a golden veil over her as she absently flips through a bridal magazine. She hums and sips. Before she leaves for work, Mom will demolish another cup.

I pause to hover over Willow. She's sitting on her knees to lean over the table and read the Sunday comics. Of course, Willow's definition of "reading" is just a bunch of mumbling and tracing her index finger over the art. It's very serious business.

Sunday comics are Willow's life, along with Bert, her stuffed Batman doll she's carried around since she was a tot learning to walk. No judgment here. I still have a corner of the blanket my grandma quilted for me as an infant. It's tucked into a drawer in my room though. I'm sentimental, but I'm also a junior in high school.

I kiss the top of Willow's strawberry blonde crown before flopping into the chair next to her. "Mondays are the worst."

"Doctors have found that the reason so many people hate Mondays is because they try too hard to change themselves over the weekend, creating mental and emotional confusion." Over her mug, Mom winks.

"What doctors, Mom? The ones on primetime medical dramas?"

"No." Mom raises a sharp eyebrow. "The ones that say sarcastic teenage boys are more likely to have their phones cut off by Tuesday for being unforgivably rude before their parents have had their proper caffeine fix."

"It's a good thing you don't have one of those teenage boys, right?"

"It is, Remy." She looks at me, her eyes as brown as hickory wood. "At least you'll be the coolest-dressed kid on a Monday."

I smile at my long, knobby fingers. Mom has never had a problem pointing out my awesome fashion sense, even before I came out. Maybe she knew? Was it my obsession with bright colors and cardigans? I doubt it. It might've been my mild crush on Nick Robinson. Very mild. But, let's just say I didn't see *Jurassic World* four times for the dinosaurs.

Thing is, my mom didn't make a big deal about those things. Neither did my dad. Coming out to my parents was tough and scary and kind of a tear-fest. An entire month of losing sleep over what they would think. How they'd react. And if their adopted, black son would just become an afterthought now that, guess what, he's gay too!

But it was nothing like that. *Nothing.* I can't explain what it was about my mom's gentle expression and my dad's fingers combing through my curls and the taste of those first few tears on my lips, but I'd relive that moment over and over just to hear again, "Okay, so what's the big deal?" from my mom in a choked, crying-laugh.

"And how long did this outfit take to put together?" Mom asks.

I shrug nonchalantly. I don't tell her I planned it out Wednesday of last week. Some secrets should be kept. "Guess."

"Too long," Mom says, half amused.

"Yep!"

Today, I'm sporting a loose, black-and-white-striped T-shirt under a thin, purple hoodie with faded olive skinnies and a pair of bright-white Vans. Later, I'll tug a beanie over my messy, short curls. For a first day back to school, I'm killing it.

Mondays can bite me.

"If you're trying to look casually-sharp, mission accomplished."

Her compliment leaves me kind of dizzy. I cuff my hands over Willow's ears. "You're a badass, Mom."

"Thanks, honey," replies Mom. "But I'd appreciate it if, next time, you covered your dad's ears instead. He's at that impressionable age."

"Hey!" Dad yells.

"The truth hurts, babe."

"So does a life without my killer French toast."

I chuckle as I lower my hands from Willow's ears, careful not to disrupt the messy buns on either side of her head. She's got this whole Princess Leia obsession lately. I approve.

"Don't listen to her, kiddo," Dad says. He dishes out plates of French toast accompanied by burnt bacon and runny eggs. Emperor of breakfasts might've been a stretch. Dad flops into the chair next to Mom. "She's still not over Zack Morris. Hashtag Man Crush Mondays."

"Dad, no."

"What?"

"You're not allowed to hashtag anything. Ever."

Dad's laugh is a cross between a bear and a Disney character. It's loud, but silly and contagious.

I scrunch my nose. "And Zack who?"

"Kiddo!" Dad's indignant expression isn't very believable. He and Rio should start an acting troupe. "Have we not taught you enough about the glory of *Saved by the Bell*?"

"Is it on Netflix?"

Mom smacks Dad's bicep when he squawks. Her cheeks are lit like a stop light. "Jesus, Max, please. Hush."

"But he—"

"I know, I know." Mom squeezes his forearm to stop the flailing. They trade a sweet, crinkled-eye look that makes me want to vomit. Seriously. My parents and their heart-eyes.

Across from them, Willow pretends to gag. I grin. Hands down, Willow is my favorite tiny human. I'm not worried about having to be that menacing older brother who threatens bodily harm on some random boy or girl for crushing Willow's heart. Romance isn't Willow's jam either.

We eat quickly around small conversations. My parents talk about TV shows and pop culture. I swear, they're determined to be those "cool parents" who can quote movie scenes and recite the lyrics to every bass-heavy, radio-friendly song. It's funny, but also annoying.

"So," I say, chewing casually until my parents look at me. "I'm thinking of getting my lip pierced for my next birthday."

I'm not serious. Needles and I are not compatible. When I was ten, I begged my dad for two weeks to get my ears pierced, mainly because two boys in my class had their ears pierced and, *hello*, everyone thought they were so effing cool. Then, in the chair with that vicious, skin-puncturing, metal piercing gun six inches from my left ear, I started wailing like a kicked cat and sobbed my way through two scoops of strawberry cheesecake ice cream on the way home with my ears fully intact.

Mom levels me with one of those "not this morning" looks. "And on October second of next year, I'm thinking of taking away your car, grounding you until after college, and making you wear overalls everywhere."

My birthday is October first. Rio always makes a big deal about that. "First of the month, first born, first place loser since the first day you met me."

"Mom! Where's the democracy?"

"Oh, honey, there's no such thing. Ask all the rich, corrupt politicians."

I pucker my lips, but I don't have a solid response. I might have to revoke her badass status, though.

After breakfast, Mom pours her second cup of coffee into a stainless-steel travel mug. "Willow, let's suit up. I have to get you to school and meet up with the future Mr. and Mrs. Gleeson about a venue."

"Almost done, Mommy!"

There's an unwritten rule about Willow. She's incapable of doing anything productive in the morning until she finishes pretending to read the comics. Even Mr. Whitaker, her first-grade teacher, knows it.

I sneak Clover a slice of burnt bacon, but her crunching almost gives us away.

Thank god, Dad clears his throat. "Are they still looking for one of those historically romantic themes?"

"An evening under a blanket of stars and the words of Emily Bronte." Mom's fake, dreamy sigh signifies her disinterest. This is the same woman who dances to lame '80s music with her husband.

"My kind of party."

"Does that mean you'll be attending, Max?"

"Not on your life, Abby."

My parents laugh together. It's synchronized and corny and so them. I scoop up my plate, deposit it in the sink, then dodge my jumpy little sister to get to my backpack and beanie. I pocket my phone and keys.

"Hey," calls Mom before I get too far, "don't forget you're picking Willow up from school today. No chillaxing with Lucy and Rio."

The squeak of my shoes echoes on the hardwood floor as I spin around. "Mom," I say, sighing, "I take back that badass title. You've been demoted."

"To what?"

"A basic, wannabe hipster."

"Score!" Dad curls an arm around her noticeably tight shoulders. "At the bottom of the uncool chain with me, where you belong."

Mom's lips are pursed. I don't have time to humor her. I'm already late. I drop a quick kiss on the top of Willow's head before jogging for the door. If I'm lucky, I'll make it to school before the first bell.

CHAPTER THREE

"You are the paragon of lame, Remy Cameron."

I'm still not fully functioning. It's not ten a.m., I haven't had any caffeine, and it's a Monday. Everything in my brain is haze and mist while I yank my unnecessarily thick anatomy textbook from my locker, shove my bookbag in its place, and eagerly turn around. It's hard to be anything but giddy when Lucy Reyes is in front of you.

Dramatically academic insults aside, Lucy is one of my favorite sights in the morning, especially Monday mornings. She's always busy on weekends and I miss her large, rich-brown eyes. I miss the way her inky black hair falls around her face in this ethereal-but-badass-villain kind of way, and the way she always smirks as though she's got your number and is ready to call you on it.

Lucy's the living, breathing definition of *cool* as she manages to angle her skateboard into the locker four doors down from mine. It's not even supposed to be *her* locker. Our assigned lockers had us on different ends of the hall, but at the beginning of the semester, Lucy used her ultimate killer instinct to gamble Luke Henderson out of this one in a game of cutthroat Spades. Card games and Lucy are a hazardous combination.

I sigh at her. "SAT Prep words before nine a.m.? Uncalled for."

Lucy flashes that trademark quirk of her lips. "I spent my weekend preparing."

Yeah, I'm aware. Lucy has nothing against social politics and Saturdays chugging iced macchiatos, but weekends are for the books.

Studying is her priority. Lucy's one goal is getting into a highly-respected university—Ivy League if she can. It's not that I don't value her choices. I just miss my best friend on weekends, when we're not weighed down with homework or trying to stand out in the traffic jam of students clogging up Maplewood's hallways.

"That's beside the point," says Lucy, waving a dismissive hand. "Rio says you're not going to the homecoming dance."

I mumble, "Traitor," while tugging down my beanie.

It's my own fault. Secrets never last long between us. Not that time Rio stole my Scooby-Doo fruit snacks in fifth grade. When I split my pants in sixth grade. Rio's brief crush on our freshman math teacher, Mr. Nichols. Lucy's dad picking up in the middle of the night and leaving.

Sometimes, sharing is important. However, this isn't one of those rare moments.

I shrug lazily. "I'm not going."

"Yes, you are." Lucy's mouth pinches; her eyebrows lower. It's scary. She could easily star in a horror franchise with those eyes.

"Not happening, Lucy."

"It wasn't optional. Or shall I remind you…" A grin splits my face when Lucy launches into her Class President speech. I have to be real—it's all kinds of phenomenal. Maybe because Rio and I helped her perfect it.

"I'll think about it."

Lucy huffs, arms folded. I'm not bothered by her dramatics. I shoulder my locker closed. A fleet of freshmen scampers past us when the bell rings. Bunch of rookies. They're all probably still trying to figure out the lay of the land: which hallways to cut down to get to class on time, how to avoid the mob of foot traffic on the east wing stairs.

"Is this about—"

"No," I hiss, cutting Lucy off. I look around; this stinging heat spreading through my ears. "It's not." I can't say anything else. I hate how Lucy and Rio talk around the one subject I never want to discuss.

My eyes prickle with hot dampness, blurring my vision.

Lucy pins me with a stare. "You're deflecting."

"Is that your professional opinion?"

Lucy can roll her eyes all she wants, but we know she's the "mom" of our trio. It'd be hard for her not to be. She's the oldest of four children of a single mother who works all the time.

"You're the embodiment of lameness, Remy Cameron," she says, tossing an arm around my shoulder.

We walk to class like that, not saying what's really on our minds.

THE ONLY REASON I SURVIVE the first half of the day is that Jayden graciously slips me a can of Red Bull in homeroom. Oh, and the spike of adrenaline I experience in world history after Mrs. Thompson threatens us with a pop quiz three minutes into class. It never happens. Mrs. Thompson makes Bellatrix Lestrange from *Harry Potter* seem tame. A lot of Maplewood students—and faculty—will be thrilled when she finally retires, by choice or by force.

Mercifully, lunch is right after world history. Our table of friends is the holiest random group of students ever. It's as if someone took a handful of Skittles, M&M's, and SweeTarts, shook them up in a bag, and then tossed them on a table. We're a motley collection like that movie Dad loves, *The Breakfast Club*, except there are nine of us at a long table close to one of the main doors but farthest from the lunch line. We're cool, I guess. Maybe subjectively?

I don't care. I honestly love this bunch of weirdos.

I love being squished between Rio and Lucy and tossing super-greasy tater tots into Jayden's waiting mouth. I love how his girlfriend,

Chloe Parker, has one arm tucked around his shoulders while she talks about last Friday night's game. I could care less about football, but she's the school's quarterback—Maplewood's first-ever female quarterback, actually—so I listen anyway.

"Oh, tell us more," deadpans Jayden.

"Shut up, dork."

Jayden's head tips back, and he laughs. "I hear about this stuff all the time."

"Um, hello." Chloe arches an eyebrow. "You're a cheerleader. And my boyfriend. Be supportive, okay?"

Jayden smacks a loud kiss on the cluster of freckles along Chloe's cheek. She's not easily embarrassed, not like me, but, when Jayden pulls back, pink blossoms across the bridge of her nose. She turns to tell Lucy something.

Yeah, they're *that couple*, like my parents. It's the quarterback and the cheerleader. If I hadn't known them both since middle school, I'd probably find their relationship ridiculously gross. It is, some days, but I'm willing to tolerate it for the sake of friendship.

Also, I was probably just as bad with… *Not going there*, a tiny voice in my mind says.

"Oh my god, don't record me eating," groans Rio, holding a hand over her mouth.

"This is for official business."

"Instagram is officially bullshit." Rio crumbles a napkin and tosses it at Alex.

Alex and Zac Liu document everything on their phones. They're hardcore social media junkies. Technically, they're not supposed to have their phones out but have been granted special permission from Principal Moon as co-managers of *The Leaf*. I swear that blog is just a circle of hell where students rant about sports, the weather, their least favorite teachers, and whatever other useless crap they can get away with.

All the serious posts come from Rio. She's the only one with the guts to dig into Maplewood's dark side. Not that a place like Maplewood has some seedy underbelly of shame and crime and sex scandals. I mean, she's not blogging about what—or *who*—went down at Andrew Cowen's last party. The most illegal thing going on around the halls is students buying weed from Alex and Zac.

"Newsflash," says Lucy, slouching low enough to rest her head on my shoulder, "Mondays suck the hardest. I'm already tired."

I prop my chin on her head.

"Too much overachieving is detrimental to a teen," says Jayden.

Lucy flips him off.

"Oh my god, stop with all the advanced-placement terms," I groan.

"Says the nerd in AP Lit." Rio snorts.

"Hey," I retort, waving a ketchup packet in her face, "We both know I'm taking this course to get into Emory. Any other AP class would've been a total failure of our educational system. There's no way I should be in advanced *anything*."

"I concur," Sara says.

Sara Awad is exceptionally gifted with her sarcasm. I'm jealous of that talent. I'm also jealous of how she's always so well put together. Perfect eyeliner frames wide, sparkling brown eyes. A long nose and sharp cheekbones contrast with crescent-moon dimples and rare sightings of acne. Today, her pale-rose hijab juxtaposes perfectly with her light-blue top, like the beginning of a sunset against a late-summer sky.

"Thanks, Sara," I say.

"I'm always here to validate your basicness."

Damn, she's *good*.

I haven't known Sara as long as Rio, Lucy, Jayden or Chloe. She came as a package-deal with the Liu twins. She's not an asshole, just guarded. I guess we all are. We're not consciously trying to be this table of Diversity Rocks in Maplewood's ocean of suburban realness. Maybe a hint of solidarity brought us together? Maybe it's because we mesh well.

I mean, it's not as if a giant sign over us says, "Sit here if you're anything other than *Insert Stereotypical Teen*!" There are plenty of other kids—from all kinds of backgrounds and races—that sit elsewhere. We fit together because we *like* each other, not because we fill the Check Other category.

Sara cocks her head at Lucy. "You look pretty good for a zombie."

"Thanks." Lucy winks, popping a tater tot in her mouth.

Sara drops her chin; her cheeks are slightly red. I think I'm the only one who notices. I'm also confident that I'm the only one who knows Sara's secret.

She has a crush on Lucy.

That's the other reason Sara sits with us at lunch, why she's the first one to our table every day, always positioning herself right across from Lucy. She claims it's because she brings her lunch from home since everything served in the cafeteria is harmful and processed and against her family's beliefs. Some of that is true. Most of it is bullshit.

It's Lucy, plain and simple. Almost every student at Maplewood with good eyes and hyperactive hormones has a crush on Lucy. But Sara's crush is different. I can't figure out how. I just know, just as I know Zac is possibly gay or bi or curious. That was a little easier to detect. Zac had this familiar look in his eyes any time he watched Dimi and me holding hands or kissing or teasing each other. It's the same look I have whenever I watch a Zayn Malik video on YouTube. That longing, I-have-a-boner-for-this look.

"I miss Mr. Riley's bio class," says Alex. It's easier to tell them apart, now that Zac has these adorable, rectangular-frame eyeglasses and Alex, for whatever reason, has dyed the tips of his spiky hair electric blue. "Best naps ever."

"You slept through biology?" Chloe asks.

"Who didn't?"

"Um, hello." I raise a hand, waving it in front of Alex's pinched face. "Mr. Riley is the coolest!"

"You're required to say that."

"I'm not."

"*You are*," Alex and Zac say together. Freaky twin assholes.

Sara reaches across the table and pats my hand. "As GSA president, you're contractually-bound to speak positively about Mr. Riley."

Frowning, I pull my hand back. Yes, Mr. Riley is the faculty advisor to GSA, but that has zero weight on my opinion. He's one of those teachers you can't help but like. He tells the worst jokes, dresses like a recent college graduate applying for his first real job and talks to students like people instead of this colony of ants marching toward their demise.

But, for whatever reason, these conversations always lead back to me being the loud-and-proud leader of the New Gay Millennium. It's as if coming out at fourteen defined my destiny from then on. *Hey, there's Remy Cameron, the Chosen Gay One*, as if I'm Harry Potter, except, instead of the cool scar and endless sexual tension with Draco, I was given a rainbow patch and all these expectations. I'm pretty sure other students came out before me. Maybe they weren't as vocal, but they existed.

Glaring at my tater tots, I mumble, "He's still cool."

"So," Rio starts, her voice has that tone she gets when she's peeved but slightly protective. "Are we done talking about the living legend that is Mr. Riley? Because I, for one, want to talk about the Mad Tagger."

I sag next to her. Rio is top-notch at subject changes.

"I'm working on this story—"

"Pending approval," Zac points out.

Rio cuts her eyes just enough to shut Zac up. "I'm working on this story," she repeats, firmer, "for *The Leaf*. Whoever the Tagger is, a lot of drama is gonna go down when he's caught."

A few nods and mumbles break out around the table. We're all in our own thoughts about it.

To me, it's not that serious. The Mad Tagger is simply someone having fun with art and graffiti across Maplewood's campus. It started at the beginning of the school year: nothing big, spray paint on sidewalks, chalk on brick walls, loopy writing in silver Sharpie over old posters. It's usually *Alice in Wonderland*-related content—hence the Mad Tagger name. It's harmless but kind of wicked stuff.

No one knows who the Mad Tagger is. A student? A teacher? An angry alum? It's this mystery that keeps building and building. I stopped chasing clues a month ago, but Rio's obsessed.

"I love his art," says Jayden. Amused crinkles form around his eyes. They're as clear blue as an afternoon sky.

"It's a complete waste of time." Chloe sighs. "Whoever it is could be doing something positive for the school. Start a club. Join a sport. Something *legal*."

"Spoken like a true jock and a detective's daughter," teases Jayden.

Scowling, Chloe punches his shoulder.

"I dunno," Lucy says, sitting up again. Her hair falls over one side of her face, but she pushes it back. "Brook likes it."

Of course, he does. I barely hold down a laugh. Lucy and Brook are another of Maplewood's premiere couples.

And, on cue, in walks the tallest, coolest, happiest dude ever. The electric-shock of fluorescent lighting in the cafeteria refuses to do this guy justice. Brooklyn Henry should be on the cover of *Italian Vogue* with his classic swimmer's build, all broad shoulders and seriously narrow waistline. Defined muscles show under his clothes. He has large hands and toned legs and smooth, umber-brown skin.

Brook waves, then stares at Lucy. His smile is always half-cocked when he looks at her. It's as if she's the moon—no, as if Lucy's a freaking gathering of stars at the edge of the universe.

Rio nudges me. "I think I'm gonna barf."

"Me too."

I don't mean it. I like Brook. He's a senior and swim team captain and cool with the entire planet. None of us were friends with him before the Lucy thing. I mean, yes, he and I had spoken, shared amicable nods in the halls, but nothing else. People automatically assumed we were friends, that we hung in the same church group or after-school programs. There was a mandatory connection in everyone's minds. *Two male black students at Maplewood? Of course, they're best friends.* Why does race automatically equate to instant bonding? Also, why does the same thing happen when it comes to sexuality, and religion, and age? Am I only meant to be friends with other black, gay, or seventeen-year-olds?

"Sup Awesome Squad," says Brook.

Awesome Squad? Holy hell. If Lucy is the unofficial mom, Brook owns the dad role. His jokes and corniness teeter on the edge of unbearable.

I'm so blinded by Brook's magical charm that I don't notice the guy standing next to him until Brook says, "Everyone remembers Ian, right?"

A shaky hand waves, then out comes a voice that's three-fourths unsure and one-fourth nasal and sweet. "Hello… Awesome Squad?"

I blink a few times, then stare. It's hard not to.

It's him. The boy from last night. The boy with the hazel eyes and unforgettable dimple and *cute*. The boy who might've starred last night in a brief, dizzying dream that my right hand vividly remembers.

"Ian!" squeals Chloe.

"The Parkster," Jayden says, as if he's one of those stoner skateboard kids. For the record, Jayden falls firmly into that Looks Sexy But Is So Lame category. He was born to be geektastic.

"Wow, welcome back." Lucy sizes Ian up.

I do the same. Again, it's impossible not to. Recognition finally kicks in. *Ian Park.* I vaguely remember him, except, the Ian Park I recall was nothing but round cheeks and long arms with a short torso and a horrible bowl-cut hairstyle that belonged on an eight-year-old, not a sixteen-year-old with a goofy smile.

Now, well… He's different. Maybe it's the black-rimmed glasses that slope down his narrow nose? Maybe it's the hair, which is longer in the front, hanging down to his jawline. It's almost the color of a moonless sky, but it has the reddish undertones of a total lunar eclipse.

My teeth hold my lower lip in a vice grip.

"How was Cali?" Jayden asks.

Ian mumbles something, bobbing his head.

"Didn't you move to Irvine?" Chloe asks.

"Arcadia," replies Ian.

"The asshole didn't want to come back," Brook says, laughing. He winds an arm around Ian's long neck to tug him closer.

My eyes dart to the distinct shape of Ian's Adam's apple. The sharp curves of his collarbones peek from beneath a white T-shirt. The

Dimple creases his right cheek when his mouth quirks. And then those eyes find me.

"Yeah, so, I'm Remy. I mean, sure, you remember me." *Does he though?*

Heat spreads like an infection under my skin but my mouth is on autopilot. "Or maybe you don't? Because we weren't friends." My ears catch fire. "I mean, we weren't enemies. We just—you know, you're a year older and I'm like… I wasn't cool enough. But now I'm so effing cool. Mad cool. They redefined cool when I came around and…"

Out of nowhere, my voice fails. No, it squeaks like the hero dying in a video game. My throat tightens around every vowel and oxygen has stopped reaching my brain. "So, yeah, I'm Remy Cameron." I try to sit taller, but embarrassment takes me down like a freaking bowling pin. "President of GSA and absolute lame."

Painfully awkward seconds pass. Our table is silent. It's as if the entire cafeteria is holding their breath.

Ian stares, eyes glazed.

"Uh…" My beanie is shoved in my locker. I'm not allowed to wear it during school. I feel every imperfect curl as my trembling hand runs over my hair. "Has anyone tried the fresh soft pretzels today?"

"Have *you*? You probably need something to replace the foot currently occupying your mouth," whispers Rio.

I want to kick her under the table.

Pinkish flush has taken permanent residence in my cheeks. I hate that it's so visible. My light skin makes it impossible to hide physical mortification.

"Uh, no," Brook says, a thick eyebrow raised. "Thanks for the recommendation, though."

"Sure."

Choked laughter echoes. I don't have to raise my eyes to know it's Sara and the Liu twins—assholes, all of them. Tomorrow, I'm creating a Google sign-up sheet for new lunch companions.

Brook shoots me one more "what's up with you" look before falling into a conversation with Lucy. A cacophony finally fills the cafeteria again—trays dropping and bantering and a table of choir geeks singing an old Whitney Houston song. A brush of warmth, like the fingertips of a sunrise, skims my back and I start.

It's Ian.

He leans down close enough to whisper, "I remember you, Remy Cameron." A mini-grin parts his lips. Then he's nudging in next to Brook.

I slump in my chair. *Okay, good* is vibrating against my jaw but it never makes it out of my mouth. It stays there, buzzing against my teeth. And I slowly start to drown in all the discussions happening around me.

Pretending the last five minutes never happened isn't an option. Right?

CHAPTER
FOUR

Ms. Amos is talking. Actual English words are coming out of her mouth, but she might as well be speaking a brand-new alien language. I can't string together vowels and vocabulary and sentences, which is a shame because AP Lit is my favorite class of the day.

Today, AP Lit is like forty-five minutes of watching *Llama Llama* reruns.

I'm daydreaming. Specifically, my mind's replaying Ian's face on a constant loop, in perfect high-def quality. The clarity is incredible. I picture his pale-gold skin. His scrunched nose and owlish eyes when I barely took a breath while rambling at him. His thick lower lip, the little tweak of his mouth after he whispered to me.

The images fade to fuzziness after a while, like sitting in the first row at a movie theater. One neon thought lights up my mind: Ian's hot. Every shifting cell in my body is aware of it. Blood rushes to my face—and somewhere beneath my navel too. Then the train derails. *No relationships. No boyfriends.*

I focus on the front of the classroom. Ms. Amos is pacing. Besides Mr. Riley, she's my favorite. She wears colorful print blouses with slacks and always has a twitch at the corner of her mouth, as if she's trying not to smirk at something moronic a student said.

Bonus point: Ms. Amos used to be a lecturer at Emory. On the wall by her desk is a series of framed essays she's written, photographs of her with famous authors, articles in *The Atlanta Journal-Constitution*.

"Let's talk about our new book." In her hand, Ms. Amos holds a book with a red cover and weird stick figures. "It's by Tennessee Williams."

Ford, a senior football player, clears his throat.

"Wasn't he gay?"

I swear, Ford is homegrown, southern realness. He's freckled-face with buzzed blonde hair and electric blue eyes. He has a hard-on for plaid shirts and boots. A future Chick-Fil-A Employee of the Month.

"He was remarkably talented. A legendary playwright. A dedicated brother who loved fiercely." Ms. Amos's mouth begins to curl, and she has a glint in her eyes. "And if you'd like to discuss his sex life, then, yes, Mr. Turner, he was gay. I'm sure you can find further reading about that on Wikipedia, if you're interested."

A fuzzy melody of coos and snickers echoes in the room.

Ford's chapped lips curl into a venomous sneer. Lucy would say Ford's the paragon of assholes. You don't gain extra points on the SAT for that, but I'd award ten points to the House of Reyes.

"We have a lot to learn from writers of any gender, race, sexuality, individuality," Ms. Amos continues. "One of my favorites is Benjamin Alire Sáenz. A wonderful example of a diverse writer and poet creating classics."

Our AP Lit classroom faces the main lawn, and the view is unobstructed by trees and foliage. Bright, October sunlight washes across the pride etched into Ms. Amos's face. I love this part—when she dives headfirst into topics that excite her.

"Gay too, right?" Ford's chuckle is like a cat choking on kibble.

Ms. Amos narrows her eyes; her mouth is pinched as she waves him off.

Ford and I both sit at the front of the class. Three desks separate us. He leans past Sara to leer at me. "Perfect authors for GSA, right, Remy?"

Another harmonic strum of laughter fills the classroom. None of this is new. Ford's been a dick since middle school and probably before then. Destiny determined Ford's douchebag legacy a long, long time ago. His popularity only stretches to the small universe of football jocks without a real brain. No one on the baseball or basketball or swim team respects the guy. I think Chloe only tolerates him because of some loyalty to the pigskin gods.

Ms. Amos drops the book on Ford's desk. "And what could we learn from you, Mr. Turner?"

"How to pick up girls?"

Sara hisses something. In my blurred peripheral vision, Chloe's raising her notebook as if she might assault him—death by a Five-Star.

"You think so?" Ms. Amos challenges.

"Haven't had many complaints before."

Their exchanges turn into white noise in my ears. I've heard this before. Ms. Amos says all the proper, teacherly things. Ford retorts with all the typical dude-bro-sarcasm. It goes nowhere.

Unfortunately, my mind does. *Ian, Ian, Ian…*

"Hey," Chloe whispers, and I do my worst attempt at not startling. She says, "You're daydreaming. Where is your mind hiding?"

"Nowhere. Its favorite place."

She ruffles my hair. "I doubt that, Remy. Someone like you is always somewhere. Always."

The bell rings. Sara's out of her chair first and turns to Chloe. "Let's go. We can catch Lucy if we hurry."

Groaning, Chloe grabs her notebook and stands.

Ford hovers over my desk like a thundercloud waiting to unleash a hailstorm. "It was a joke, Remy." Funny, nothing in his artificial smile says that was humorous.

Chloe punches his shoulder. "You're gonna be the *joke* by the end of practice today."

"Wait, come on—"

"You're screwed, Turner."

Like a whipped puppy, Ford follows Chloe and Sara out the door, begging for mercy.

All the rush of escaping class has dissipated. I gather my things slowly—pens, a highlighter, notebook. At the front of the room, Ms. Amos stares at me. She doesn't say anything.

I pause. "Sorry if I wasn't like..." I wave a hand around; my mind can't produce real words. "...*here* today."

A hint of forgiveness flashes in her eyes. That doesn't calm the wave of nausea in my belly. I disappointed Ms. Amos by not being as vocally active in class today. I hate disappointing people I admire. I hate that I might've let her down.

"Have a great day, Mr. Cameron."

"Thanks."

Once I'm outside, I exhale so heavily, my lungs hurt.

Lucy's right—Monday's suck so hard.

* * *

WILLOW SCRAMBLES PAST ME THE second I swing open the front door. Her sneakers squeak on the hardwood floor. For the entire drive home, I've been trying to figure out her wardrobe choices. I'm on the fence. To match her Princess Leia puffs, she's wearing a ZAP! comic book-style shirt, a ballerina tutu, and orange and black socks to go with her purple high-tops.

"Mom let you go to school like that?"

She drops her backpack in the hallway. After a quick twirl, she throws a hand over her giggling mouth. Her two bottom front teeth fell out two weeks ago. "Yes!"

"Okaaay," I sing as she rushes off. Willow is a hell of a lot more confident at seven than I am at seventeen.

I barely have my backpack off before Clover's charging up to me. I drop to my knees. Clover climbs into my lap for face-licks and sniffing.

"I missed you too."

Mondays may be awful, but Clover makes up for it. My nose is pressed behind one of her ears. She smells like Dad's just let her in from the backyard: like grass and that butterscotch-y aroma pine sap gives off. Her fur is still sun-warmed.

And then my nose wrinkles at new scents—acrid, smoky, burnt spices. "Dad!"

In the kitchen, my dad leans over a charred dish in a metal baking pan. He looks as if he's mourning over poor Dobby's dead body.

Small confession: I've never actually read the Harry Potter books. But I've seen all the movies and all the internet memes, which sort of counts, right? I mean, it's not full Potterhead status, but I hate long books. This is something we don't discuss with Lucy—she's a diehard fan and mostly a Ravenclaw according to the Pottermore sorting quiz she's taken *nineteen times.*

Next to Dad's elbow, the iPad is playing the Food Network. I grab a pear from the copper-wire fruit bowl at the center of the kitchen island, where Dad continues to grieve. I hop onto a bar stool opposite of him. "What is that?"

"According to Ina Garten, it's a French apple tart."

I sniff—the sweetness of the apples is altered by scorched crust. Ina's cheery voice mocks us from the iPad. Her recipes are a death wish for amateur cooks.

My mouth puckers. "Looks like something Clover upchucked after eating Mom's roast beef."

"Be quiet," says Dad with a sideways grin.

I only tease him to keep that look in his blue eyes bright and effervescent. "What have we said about trying to replicate Food Network recipes, Dad?"

Chin lowered, Dad mumbles something back.

"Come again?"

"Not without notifying the local authorities first."

It's not that my dad is lacking in skills at the stove. What he does with bread and eggs and sugary toppings is a religious experience. But he's also under-baked birthday cakes and burnt cobblers and made things that were supposed to resemble pies look like Willow's soiled diapers.

Thing is, Dad's constant kitchen experimentation is a result of pure boredom. He's a stay-at-home tech advisor for a software company. It was easier when Willow was a baby, when Mom had this itch to get back into the wedding business. The decision to relocate his office from a swank downtown Atlanta office building to a back corner of the house was all his. Managing drool and pacifiers and constructing impenetrable baby gates kept him occupied while he waited for the next techno-challenged college brat to accidentally crash their laptop with a virus from watching free porn.

"So," I say as I wave my pear at the crispy would-be tart, "what's this about?"

"Uncle Dawson and Aunt Sandra are coming to visit." He nudges the blackened tart with an oven mitt. "You know your aunt insists on something home-cooked."

The pear's skin breaks easily under my teeth. I chuckle and chew at once. Thanksgivings are always a hot mess of bad dishes starring

Aunt Sandra's under-seasoned green beans. The entire Cameron clan is talentless in a kitchen.

"Is Gabriel coming with Uncle Dawson?"

A loose curl rests against Dad's wrinkled forehead. Our hair is similar, except his curls are smooth, while mine become defiant when I let them get too long.

Maybe it's because we're not... Nope. Reel it back in.

"I doubt Gabe wants to suffer through another car ride with Sandra and her Christian rock playlists."

Pear juices dribble to my chin when my mouth curves up.

Aunt Sandra is one of those church-every-Sunday-morning southerners, one of those pray before *every* meal, "God bless you" when you sneeze, can quote Bible scriptures on the fly religious types. It's not a bad thing. Religion isn't a bad thing. Even as a kid, I knew having something to believe in was important. A deity, the universe, whatever. But it's the people who use religion for status and power over others and not for comfort and hope that betray its purpose. Aunt Sandra isn't holier-than-thou either. I've heard her swear at least three times behind the wheel.

"Maybe Gabe can endure?"

Dad laughs. "Your uncle loves Gabe too much to test those waters again."

He's right. Gabriel, Uncle Dawson's partner, is a faithful Catholic who can only handle so much Christian rock. The ninety-minute drive from Athens to Dunwoody is pushing it.

"Dawson will be thrilled to spend time with you," Dad says. "That is if you're not too busy being a social surf king."

I roll my eyes. What even is a social surf king? Thankfully, I didn't inherit my dad's sense of humor.

I love Uncle Dawson. He has a history of being amazing. He was the first person to hoist me on his narrow shoulders to celebrate my coming out. It was as if he was doing it for both of us. He was taking his first breath as an openly gay person with me, a moment he didn't get to have when he came out in his early twenties. I was happy to share.

"I'll try to make myself available, Dad," I finally say.

"Good. Are you gonna post about it on your SnapBook, Insta-Tweet, or whatever?"

"Dad…"

"Let me guess. There's a rule against notifying the world you're hanging with family, right?"

"Pretty much."

We laugh. I love laughing with my dad, love how the depth of his chuckle infects me. Its low rumble manifests way down in Dad's chest before it springs free like a dolphin cracking the ocean's surface.

Tossing a dishtowel over the charred dessert, Dad leans on his elbows, his chin against pinkish knuckles, before he asks, "How was school, kiddo?"

My body mirrors his slumped appearance. My muscles put a lazy effort into a shrug. "Another Monday." It's the easiest answer. My thoughts still drift like abandoned satellites. In the deepest, darkest parts of my brain, Chloe's words echo.

Someone like you is always somewhere.

Someone like me. What does that mean? Someone gay? Someone whose sexuality will always be the punchline of stupid jokes from assholes like Ford? I can take the heat. Coming out at fourteen was scary and heavy and exhausting, but that was three years ago. I've adjusted. Plus, being queer is freaking boss.

"Kiddo?"

I blink at my dad. My jaw moves with nothing coming out.

Willow comes running in, yelping and sparing me additional fatherly questioning. Bert swings from one small hand as Willow leaps into Dad's open arms. They twirl and giggle.

"Well, hello there! How was *your* day?" Dad asks.

Willow rambles excitedly.

Chin propped on my knuckles, I watch. Dad's energy carries a different kind of charge when it comes to Willow: a Ferris wheel's lights against a blue-black blanket of night's sky, neon signs hung in dimly lit restaurants.

The differences between Willow and I are slight. We both laugh as though helium fills our lungs. We love cartoons when we're sick. Mom swears the only time we didn't cry as infants is when she'd sing to us. And photo evidence proves Dad had no clue how to put a onesie on either of us or how to brush our hair so it didn't stick up the wrong way.

But Willow has Mom's strawberry blonde hair. Dad's wide, earnest eyes. Her smile is a charming mix of theirs. I don't have any of that. Denim-blue eyes, light-brown skin, and thick eyebrows don't match my parents' features.

I stand. "I'm gonna take Clover for a walk."

Clover's so smart. One word and she's scampering into the kitchen, tail wagging. She's an adorable manipulator.

"Kind of early, isn't it?"

I shrug. "Maybe she's taking *me* for a walk."

"Maybe, kiddo."

"Maybe."

Dad returns to fawning over Willow and her wild stories about beating some snotty-nosed boy at a swinging contest during recess.

I click on Clover's leash. She leads me out the door.

Lilac skies greet us, stretching toward infinity with pinkish clouds swimming lazily. Early evening heat curls around me. Pinprick beads of sweat tickle my hairline. Ballard Hills is easing into a peaceful hideaway of minivans and sedans finding their homes in driveways.

Clover waddles like the queen of the neighborhood.

"Have you come to greet your loyal subjects?" I say to her.

Clover ignores me when a red car zooms by.

Before Willow, it was just me, loud, anxious, adopted Remy Cameron. Doctors told my mom she couldn't have children. I don't know the medical term, maybe because I never asked, but whatever it was meant my parents found me. I didn't need to know why my mom couldn't have children, not after I was seven, when they explained what adoption meant. Maybe that's because I had so many other questions: *Why did that lady give us a funny look at the grocery store? Why do kids at school say I'm not yours? Why do I color pictures of us with different crayons?*

Then, unexpectedly, my sister came along. No one explained that to me. Willow was a freaking, right-from-the-Bible phenomenon. My parents had their very own miracle, and I felt like a bookmark, a placeholder. It was a sad, heavy thought for a ten-year-old. But then I'd catch Dad smiling at me over a plate of French toast. Mom would ruffle my hair with one hand while cradling Willow. I'd always get the first gift at Christmas because, according to Dad, "You're the firstborn, so you go first."

Firstborn. I'm their first child. I don't know, but my smile is always cheek-achingly big at that thought.

Clover takes us down the usual route to Maplewood Middle, where she does her business; over the freshly clean sidewalk where the Mad Tagger imitator's work has disappeared; around the corner, as if she's chasing the slowly setting sun. It's my favorite time of day—when the neighborhood is my own personal Narnia fenced by towering trees and rows of pastel homes. And my mind settles.

I feel normal again.

I feel like Remy Cameron.

CHAPTER FIVE

"HE STRUCK AGAIN!"

I'm at my locker switching books between classes when Rio walks up, all rosy cheeks and owlish eyes. I hum nonchalantly at her. I can tell she's about to burst with whatever gossip has her bouncing from foot to foot, but I stall. My fingers hover over a pack of Reese's peanut butter cups. Snacks are a must to survive third period.

Finally, I turn to her. "Who?"

"The Mad Tagger, duh!"

Today, Rio's theatrics are Tony-worthy.

I nudge my locker closed, then lean against it. "What makes you think it's a 'he'?"

"Poor penmanship."

"That's gender-profiling and a little rank, don't you think?" I ask, my left eyebrow arched. "You have a second-grader's penmanship."

"That's irrelevant evidence." Her dismissive hand flaps in front of my face.

"Evidence?" With my teeth, I tear into the orange Reese's wrapper that's preventing me from enjoying a mouthful of epicness. "What is this, *Law and Order: Maplewood High*?"

"This is a *criminal* case."

"Your outfit is a criminal case." Slowly, I size her up. "What're you wearing?"

Rio's jacket has rose patterns spewed all over it. Underneath, she's wearing a cream blouse with a crooked red bowtie. It fails to go well with her high-waisted jeans and a pair of red flats that look right out of a high school production of *the Wizard of Oz*.

"It's called fashion." Rio rolls her eyes.

"It's called my dead grandmother's living room couch."

"Let's keep it real." Rio pokes a thick finger into my shoulder. It hurts. Unfortunately, I'm more bone than muscle. She says, "You're not exactly Mr. Trendsetter Maplewood High."

A scandalized noise escapes my throat.

"How many times have you worn that shirt this month?"

I wrinkle my nose at her.

Full disclosure: This is my favorite shirt. There is absolutely nothing wrong with my baseball tee, with its red sleeves and WE ARE EVERYWHERE printed across my chest in rainbow lettering. It's cool as eff. Yes, I might've worn it last Wednesday, probably the Monday before that, and enough times during the summer that my mom hid it from me so she could wash it. Now it's soft and slightly faded and still mega-queer.

"Shut up," I say with no heat.

Before Rio's painfully obvious retort breaks her pursed lips, the bell rings.

Jayden runs by. Even in a rush, his chestnut hair stands perfectly still in a cool pompadour. "Head ups!" he yells over his shoulder, "Sara is looking for you. Serious business."

I sag against my locker. If it involves Sara Awad, it's either about a social event or Lucy.

Rio nudges me with her hip. "Yuck. You stink of popularity."

"You do too."

"Only by association, my little social pixie."

We follow the flow of bodies to the east wing. It's not overcrowded today, but the hallways reek of cheap deodorant and perfume that's supposed to smell like jasmine but reminds me of drugstore candles.

I'm halfway to class, to breathable air, when someone brushes my left side. My body reacts immediately: muscles charged like the aftershock of lightning, pulse fuzzy like footsteps in a heavy snowfall, skin numb like after an overdose of Novocain. I smell only the expensive body spray, like crisp leaves before they change colors, like a love sampled but never savored, that I desperately miss.

Dimi walks with a small pack of soccer teammates marching behind. His laugh crawls under my skin, warm and strident.

I can't move. Wait, that's a lie. My shoulders pull forward, my chest sinks, as if I can hide in the middle of the hall. My heart beats and thumps and cracks against my ribs like a rioting thunderstorm.

He doesn't even notice me.

"Are you okay?" Rio's gripping my elbow with her thumb in the crook as if she's testing my pulse.

"Yeah," I manage to get out despite a heavy tongue. "No biggie."

Rio's a true friend. She nods and doesn't make a single comment about how pale I am, how my breaths are irregular.

"We'll talk about this Mad Tagger business later."

"Sure," I reply, an obvious lie.

She doesn't comment on that either. Only a glimmer of annoyance passes through her eyes, then disappears. "He's a nobody," she whispers.

I count backwards from ten, a little trick Mom taught me when I used to get off rollercoasters with clenched fists and blurred vision. Then I say, "Relationships are for losers."

It's a shame that I'm the biggest loser to ever lose.

I'm in danger.

It prickles hotly up the back of my neck, tingles in my fingertips. I pretend today's lunch of questionably authentic chicken fajitas are a lot more appetizing than they taste. I watch Principal Moon scold a freshman for texting during school hours. But disaster is looming, and it comes in the form of Sara when she plops down at our table. I haven't been avoiding her—much. It's not as if we share any classes outside of AP Lit. Sara is a borderline super-genius and I'm an average student. *Very average.*

"Nice shirt," says Sara, civilly.

I pause mid-sip from my peach soda, carbonation bubbling on my tongue, then look around. Jayden is curled in on himself, laughing. Chloe's red-faced, demolishing her second Capri-Sun pouch. Zac, animated hands and all, is leading the discussion about whatever MTV teen saga was on last night. I'm not keeping score.

Sara's staring from across the table. O*kay*, so she *is* talking to me—perfect.

It's not that Sara and I aren't friends. We are, on some level. It's just that all our conversations depend on someone else starting them. Then we chime in, agree or disagree. Our social interaction hinges on a third party initiating what we're too awkward—or indifferent—to do ourselves.

After a swallow, I say, "Thanks?" Usually I'd be proud to show off my wardrobe—it's kind of my thing—but this feels like a trap. Compliments are the bait.

"New?"

Rio guffaws.

"No." I squint at Sara. The ruthless fluorescent light gleams off her ceramic braces. Her plastic grin is the lure. Mouth twisted, I say, "What is—"

"So," interrupts Sara, elbows on the table, hands bridged for her chin to rest on, "when is the next GSA meeting?"

"Monday."

"Monday?"

I nod slowly, waiting for her to reel me in. Then, I add, "We welcome new members promptly at four if you'd like to...?"

Sara answers with a middle finger. We exchange glares—fireworks and lightning and nuclear bomb explosions. It was a foul thing to say, to be honest. I'd never intentionally out anyone, not that I know anything about Sara's sexuality. That's not the mission of GSA. It's not on my agenda either.

"Perfect," says Sara with a forced grin. "The homecoming committee and I would love to drop by."

"Homecoming committee?"

This is why I suck at games like Monopoly. I lack strategic skills. I'm not cutthroat. I'm the first person to buy all four railroads and Mediterranean and Baltic Avenues. I'm bankrupt and in jail after my fourth roll of the dice.

"What for?" I ask, biting into my fajita. My earlier assessment that lunch was anything resembling edible was incorrect. I chug half my soda just to get it down.

"I have my reasons," replies Sara.

"Such as?"

"I'd love to see more diversity in this year's events. True representation from all aspects of our school." Though it sounds as if it's borrowed from an ad for "It Gets Better," Sara's calculated speech seems almost genuine. She leans closer. "Maybe we could get a few members to run for homecoming court?"

Ignoring the hint in her voice, I poke at the imitation fajita. Is she referring to *me as Homecoming Prince*? Because, if so—no way.

"Come by if you want."

A hint of sadness tugs at the corners of Sara's mouth, tightening the creases around her eyes. Then it's gone as swiftly as it came, and she's steely, confident, no-bullshit Sara again. She turns away to start a new topic with Zac and Alex.

I shrug it off. It's one of those "no hard feelings" things Sara and I do. We orbit in the same galaxy, just around different planets.

At the other end of our table, Brook has one arm lazily slung around Lucy's shoulders. Limp, ketchup-covered fries are hovering near his mouth, but he's busy chuckling at something Jayden's said.

Next to him is Ian.

Facts: Maplewood is filled with cute guys. Nerdy types, jocks, the I-know-I-am-but-pretend-not-to-be cute types. They're everywhere. And the struggle is real because they're not *guys like me*. I do my damnedest not to bring any extra unwanted attention to that fact that I'm gay. That means no ogling other guys, especially if they're potentially straight.

But my eyes can't help noticing Ian. He's his own category of cute, a to-be-named category. His glasses never sit perfectly on his nose. His skin still has leftover bronze from summer and California sun. Today, he's wearing a denim jacket, unbuttoned to reveal some unrecognizable anime character on his T-shirt.

I only know maybe five anime characters. Lucy is the high authority on those things. But I'm so focused on his shirt, I'm startled to find him staring back at me. It's warming like midafternoon sun across downtown Atlanta. It pushes into my skin like confident fingertips, playing my nerves like a perfectly-tuned piano.

"Yeah. So. Nice shirt." It comes out so bad. My tongue is stone-heavy behind my teeth. What a perfect time for our table to go dead-silent!

Ian's eyes lower. "Thanks."

"Oh, shit," says Lucy, hand flying to her mouth. "Victor Nikiforov from *Yuri!!! On Ice*. Sick."

"Language, Ms. Reyes," Mr. Riley says, loftily, as he passes. He's usually cool about students swearing, but also spectacularly good at putting on a show when authorities like Principal Moon are around.

She's in a corner of the cafeteria, watching over us like a high-fashion jail warden.

Cheeks pinking, Lucy turns back to Ian. "Dude, you're into Y-O-I?"

"Who isn't into YOI?"

Hello, me! YOI? I don't know if they're still talking about anime or a communicable disease.

"Jesus Christ, no. No, no, no," protests Brook. He jerks a thumb in Lucy's direction, then says, "You better not be writing fanfiction like this one. It's not cool."

"You wouldn't know cool if it slapped you," Lucy argues.

"It's not *you*."

"Shut up." Lucy's hardcore smiling. That girl is so far gone for Brook, it's wild.

Ian and Lucy start talking about anime and characters and fanfics like two long-lost friends. Lucy Reyes, president of the Anime Club, all-around legend when it comes to being smooth and confident around others. These are two things on the *Things Remy Is Not* list.

I glare at my fajita. My stomach shrinks. Death by Inedible Lunch Scum is a gnarly way to end this midday misery.

CHAPTER SIX

Ms. Amos is leaning against her desk. Her mouth is twisted into a dramatic smile, one far too smug for any high school teacher. It's unfair. With the swipe of her red pen, she can change our academic futures—seriously, it's probably one of those inexpensive ones from Target. She shouldn't be given the right to torture us with silence and deep stares and awkwardness at the beginning of class.

"I've made a decision," she finally says.

Someone mumbles, "Retirement," coughing into his hand.

No one laughs.

Andrew Cowen is a senior, Brook's teammate, and hosts the ghost of a failed sitcom-dad in his scrawny, six-foot body. He and Ford share a special throne in Douchebag Hell.

"I guess you'll find out next year when you repeat my class, Mr. Cowen?" retorts Ms. Amos. Andrew slumping in his chair only broadens Ms. Amos's grin. "Thanks to Mr. Turner's colorful excitement over tapping into the works of Tennessee Williams, I've decided to move up an assignment I was saving for after the Thanksgiving break."

A symphony of sighs and groans unites everyone, including me. *Screw you, Ford Turner.*

"Please." Ms. Amos cocks a hip and winks. "Contain your glee."

I thump my forehead against my notebook. *Jesus.* The last thing I need is more work in a class I'm barely passing.

"You'll be composing an essay. A very personal essay." Ms. Amos crosses to the other side of the room. "The subject is simple: 'Who am I?' Write a thought-provoking—and, yes, I realize that'll be terribly hard for you, Mr. Turner—essay about who you are. What defines you?"

Ford sniffs, chin cocked.

Ms. Amos walks back to her desk. "Are you defined by your race? Religion? By your music tastes?"

A student with a choppy haircut and a questionable face-piercing throws up devil horns and starts headbanging. Behind me, Chloe snorts.

"Are you defined by your privilege?" Ms. Amos stops in front of Ford's desk.

"Since I'm *privileged* enough to take your class, I guess not," replies Ford.

Ms. Amos ignores him and steps over to Chloe's desk. "Are you defined by your strength?" Then, to Sara, "Are you defined by your family's history? Your clothes?"

A painful lurch, like the aftershock of an earthquake, moves through my chest when Ms. Amos stops at my desk. "By your name?" To the room, she asks, "By your sexuality?"

From the back of the class, a jock says, "Well, Remy might be."

How very unoriginal. It's as if I can see these things coming, these ridiculous, homophobic jokes that I know will always follow me. But I can't ever predict how my body will react. Will I tighten up in anger? Will I freeze up in fear? Will I blush with embarrassment?

Ms. Amos, unentertained, folds her arms across her chest. "Are you defined by how many days you'll spend reviewing your life choices after being expelled for bullying? You remember our zero tolerance policy, correct, Terrance?"

Silence blankets the room. If only it was quieter behind my ribs.

"Take this assignment seriously. It's worth thirty percent of your grade," Ms. Amos announces.

"That's basically pass or fail," Ford says, choking, as his freckled face goes blotchy red.

Ms. Amos nods; the corners of her mouth curl more deeply. "All essays must be typed, double-spaced, and submitted to me the week before Thanksgiving break." She's back at her desk, leaning. She's short, five-foot-nothing; her feet swing, and the toes of her shoes skim the floor. "Also, there'll be oral presentations of your essays."

In my peripheral vision, I spot Ford discreetly poking his tongue into his cheek. *Of course.* He's imitating a blowjob. Talent like that will look good on his college applications.

Behind him, Hiro Itō hisses, "Knock it off."

Ford sniffs.

Hiro gives me a small shrug. He's a senior and super popular in the gamer crowd. I suck at video games; I've got no true hand-eye coordination skills. But Hiro and I have a silent respect for each other. We share a singular passion: disdain for bottom-feeders like Ford.

"You can use any art medium you want for presentations: music, photographs, visual media, PowerPoint, whatever." Ms. Amos's relaxed shoulders expand. Pointedly, she says, "Help us understand who you are."

The class is filled with mumbling. A few students are furiously taking notes. Sara's rubbing her temples. Yeah, my brain is ready to skydive right out of my skull.

When Ms. Amos returns to rambling about Tennessee Williams, I slump so far down in my chair, I nearly split my chin on the desk. *This. Is. Perfect.* An entire essay on who I am. Essays aren't among my favorite things. I was banking on studying extremely hard for the final exam to pass.

I need this class to boost my application for Emory. Average student and GSA President aren't enough. AP Literature is my golden ticket. Ms. Amos's affiliation to Emory is the key that unlocks the gates. But an essay that determines my final grade?

I'm freaking doomed.

* * *

AFTER SCHOOL, MAPLEWOOD HIGH'S STUDENT parking lot is like a scene out of an apocalyptic film, one of those gorgeously shot movies starring kids from Disney Channel spinoffs. The suburbs of Dunwoody are too pretty for George Miller-style adaptations.

Tucked under a blanket of pale-blue sky, the gray of the parking lot is broken up by bright yellow parking lines and sparse clumps of green grass that lead to the woods nearby. The only cars left belong to sporty students or band geeks or detention-dwellers—and slackers like me.

Curbside, Lucy's next to me; our asses are numb from sitting so long. The late afternoon sun stretches its golden paws over the far side of the cracked pavement. The sweet afterglow of midday heat lingers. Georgia in the fall is a different kind of beast. It's humid and thick and sweaty as if it were still June, and at the same time the air still tastes a little like September: sweet-tart McIntosh apples and spicy butternut squash.

As if reading my mind, Lucy says, "The Gwinnett County Fair."

I hum contently.

We share a look that says we already miss sharing funnel cakes with Rio, with our mouths covered in powdered sugar, on a cool September evening.

In the distance, I can hear the marching band: snare drums and trumpets and that swell from the brass section. They're trying something new, a cover of a Gorillaz song. It's sick. My foot taps against the ground with the drumline.

The first big pep rally of the year is Friday. My anticipation is high.

Sneakers pound against the ground. The cross-country team trots by. They all wear tiny athletic shorts and loose shirts. I hide my grin in the crook of my elbow. Some of the guys are just—I don't know—something about sweaty hair and tinted cheeks, focused eyes and syncopated breaths.

I cross my legs, hoping no one notices the little twitch in my jeans.

Lucy whistles. "Hot."

Infinitely embarrassed, I elbow her.

"You don't think so?"

"What? *No.*"

"Liar."

"Whatever," I mumble, shaking my head.

Lucy returns to coloring the toe of her Converse with a red Sharpie.

My phone sits on the sliver of asphalt between us. I have one earbud in. POP ETC pumps into my veins. "Backwards World" comes on and I think, *How appropriate.*

Across the lawn, to our left, I spot Silver ducking behind the main building. No doubt he's headed to have a cigarette out of teachers' view.

Silver is a mystery, an undiscovered planet. He's a quiet loner, unlike his older sister, Darcy, who is Maplewood High's resident religious dictator. Popular and sparkly and influential, she's president of the Godly Teens First Organization. Yep, GTFO. I don't know why no one's voted that name off the island yet.

Silver's real name isn't Silver. It's a nickname other kids gave him for his pale-blond hair, stormy eyes, and nimbus-cloud skin tone. I've never said much to him though we're both juniors. Something about Silver seems untouchable. Students adore him for his looks but fear him for his silence.

Watching Lucy from the corner of my vision, I bite my thumbnail. "What do you wanna be when you grow up?" I hate that phrase: "When you grow up." I'm seventeen, a quarter-inch short of six-foot-one and have a long-standing love affair with cold-brewed coffee. I'm probably not *growing* anymore, not physically. I'm cool with that. But Ms. Amos's essay has me on edge.

"Grow up?"

"Yeah. Grow up," I repeat.

Lucy's lips twist into a smile. "You mean once you get past this immature dickhead phase."

"Is it really a phase, Lucia?" I tease.

Despite the dark curtain of inky-black hair falling below her brow, I can still see Lucy roll her eyes. "I don't know. You first."

"An actor." I reply with the conviction of a true thespian—which means none at all.

"You definitely have the dramatic part down."

"Hey!" I nudge her shoulder until Lucy almost tips over.

"We both know your dream is to go to Emory and become some world-famous writer."

My stomach twists into eighteen knots. I'll never make it to Emory without this essay. I did a little research after the AP Lit class: part of the admissions requirement is an essay, a personal statement. They want to know who you are.

So freaking perfect.

"Don't you ever think about these things?" I ask.

Lucy's shoulders pull tightly when she's lies. It's the first sign. "Sometimes." Lucy's a thinker and a planner. "I wonder if my dad imagined being a father at twenty-two. Did he want it? Or was it something he involuntarily settled into?"

I nod, but she doesn't see. Chin tucked, she's glaring at her shoes. "A lot of adults do that—settle for what they become." There are sad wrinkles beside her mouth. "They lose that thing you need to fight."

"What's 'that thing' they lose?"

Lucy tips her head skyward. Floating islands of clouds hide the sun. "Who knows, Rembrandt."

We sit in silence. The late school bus chugs in, its motor rattling. Detention-dwellers hop on like convicts minus the orange jumpsuits.

Silver emerges from behind the school and pops the collar of his dark denim jacket. His profile is sharp: long, thin nose and photogenic cheekbones, downward tilt to his bitten-red lips. He was born for the runway.

The marching band has quieted to just the woodwinds playing a somber tune.

I clear my throat. "I want to be a guy Willow looks up to. A role model. Besides my parents and Clover, my little sister is all I have."

Lucy's foot nudges mine. Her half smile is a reminder that Willow's not *all* I have.

"I want her to know she can be anything."

"Me too." Lucy's index finger pokes my shoulder. "I want to make my sisters proud."

She's the oldest of four girls. Her father stuck around long enough to realize he was settling, four daughters later. This bond Lucy and I have burrows deeper than liking the same movies or long hugs or laughing. We're both children of abandonment, I guess. We don't talk about that, but it's there like the roots of a tree, like a sunrise. It's there, even when people aren't talking about it.

Maybe all of this is too heavy for today.

"We should hit up Chick-Fil-A," suggests Lucy. "Brook's almost done with swim practice. I'm dying for an Arnold Palmer."

"Gross!" I frown. "First of all, hell no to Chick-Fil-A and their anti-queer agenda. The GSA would disown me."

"True that."

"Also, sweet tea?" I make a gagging noise.

"Oh, come on," Lucy says, tugging my right ear. "How long are you going to wage this vendetta against sweet tea?"

It's not a vendetta; it's a lifelong commitment. Sweet tea is the devil's juice. I know it's a southern tradition, but it's sadistic. Iced tea shouldn't be sweetened. It shouldn't even exist. The tangy-sugary mixture of sweet tea and lemonade in an Arnold Palmer is against what I represent.

"It's downright disrespectful."

"Remy, *seriously*."

"It should be outlawed."

Lucy sighs. "We live in Georgia."

"Exactly! Everything should be made of peaches."

"There's *peach* sweet tea."

I frown at the sky. "What has this world come to?"

Lucy's laughter is contagious, and it infects me like a wild fever, shifting from my belly to my chest in hyper speed.

"Anyway, I can't." I reach for my phone. "I'm supposed to meet Mom and Willow."

A text notification from Mom awaits me. Under that is a Facebook reminder: *Friend request from Free Williams.* I forgot all about that.

But I don't have time. I swipe away the Facebook notification, already anticipating a lecture from Mom for being late.

After dusting off my jeans, I help Lucy to her feet.

"It's cool. I'll just hit Rio up," she says. "We'll grab milkshakes. She's always down for those."

"Are you trying to make me jealous?"

"Maybe." Lucy grins as if the lie is puckering her lips. "Is it working?"

"Hell yeah!"

Lucy's fingers wrap tightly around my elbow before we reach my car—full-on death grip. I wince, trying not to squeal like a trapped puppy. She's pointing toward the doors outside the gym.

I suck in a shallow breath. The universe truly loves me. Ian, shoulders pulled forward, chin lowered, eyes the ground while the swim coach talks to him. Coach Park, Ian's dad, has been a staple at Maplewood High for a decade, continuously leading the team to championships or at least runner-up status. He's quiet and stern and slightly intimidating.

My eyes are drawn to Ian. He's a spot of blue ink against a gray canvas, a prism of rainbow light in a sea of ordinary, a promise and a bad decision.

"He's cute," whispers Lucy. "That likeable kind of weird."

I lick my suddenly dry lips. My heart twitches, then turns into an entire drumline inside my ears. But I don't know why. It's just Ian. Of course, that's not how my brain works, or my body. My fingers tingle, and my lips are itching to smile. On all future job applications, I think I'll add *'has zero chill when looking at cute, potentially dateable people'* under the Other Skills heading.

"No new relationships, Lucia," I remind her—and myself.

"Are you remixing Drake?"

I exhale dramatically.

"Fine." Lucy pouts. "Let that jerk-face Dimi ruin your future love life. Kill your barely existent sex life in the process."

I should've never told Rio or Lucy about losing my virginity: massive, unforgettable mistake. Not the sex part, though, that was— actually, I don't want to think about that part. I don't want to waste anymore brain cells on Dimitar Antov.

"You can date again." Lucy's hand slides up to my shoulder, squeezes. "It's legal."

A lump the size of Mars clogs my throat. "Yeah, whatever. I'm late." I wave and jog to my car. I'm desperate to get away from conversations that lead nowhere, nowhere except frustrated sobbing and a playlist of tearjerkers and bad acoustic cover bands. I don't want to go there.

* * *

FACT: I MIGHT BE THE coolest high schooler in all of Georgia. Of course, cool is defined by being the only high schooler grocery shopping with his mom on a school night, but whatever.

Willow is here too. She's the epitome of badass with a beanie pulled to her eyebrows, rainbow tutu, mini Doc Martens, and a Jack Skellington shirt. Her outfit alone scores more cool points than I do in a month.

She shuffles side-by-side with me through the frozen meals aisle at Whole Foods Market.

"Hey," I say, the word drawn out by my smile, "dope outfit, Twinkle Toes."

It's an old nickname. When Willow was first learning to walk, she took every step on her tiptoes like a prima ballerina. Mom still has video of it on her Facebook page.

Eyes scrunched like cartoonish horizontal commas, Willow cocks her head. Her laugh is buried in Bert's cape.

"Maybe we could do lasagna from scratch?" Mom suggests. She's pushing an empty shopping cart down another aisle. "Uncle Dawson might like that."

"Uncle Dawson likes pulled pork sandwiches and coleslaw," I say flatly. "He lives on a diet of oven-baked pizzas or whatever Gabriel makes."

Mom snorts. "Those Cameron men—all terrible cooks."

"Was Grandpa a bad cook too?"

"Oh, the worst!" Mom's expression is endlessly fond. "The first time I met your grandparents, Grandpa made undercooked meatloaf and mashed potatoes. Instant food poisoning. I was sick for three days. Your dad thought that was the nail in the coffin of our relationship."

"Not his George Michael obsession?"

Mom's head tips back as she cackles. Strands of rose-gold hair brush her cheeks. Her eyes shimmer with the kind of magic memories create.

I've seen the photos. Dad's wardrobe of leather jackets and skin-tight Wranglers and one of those cross-shaped earrings. Proof that the badass gene obviously skipped a generation when it came to Max Cameron.

"That was slightly worse than Grandpa's cooking," Mom concedes.

Grandpa died when I was two years old. I don't remember much about him: his voice, deep and melodic, his grayish beard, his scent of spearmint gum and fresh-cut grass.

In Dad's office, pinned to a corkboard stuffed with Post-It reminders, is a Polaroid. It's of Grandpa and me. My tiny hand is trying to curl around Grandpa's thick, freckled forearm. The tip of his nose is pressed to the crown of my head.

Dad always swears Grandpa's life changed for the better when I was adopted. "He finally stopped missing your grandmother. He'd come to visit all the time. Walk right by your mom and me to get to you." Dad's eyes are sad when he adds, "And he'd hold you for hours, singing lullabies with made-up lyrics while you slept."

I wish I could remember. But the euphoric rush that comes from knowing I shared something with Grandpa makes up for that. I can't recapture all those moments but I'm thankful to have been loved so deeply by a man who wasn't my own blood. I miss him.

"Angel hair pasta?" Mom suggests.

My nose wrinkles. "Why bother? Neither you nor Dad cooks."

"Correction: your dad makes scrumptious French toast."

"The best!" Willow announces to half the dried pasta section.

In a gleeful whisper, Mom adds, "He's talking about a pumpkin spice recipe."

"Oh my god, my family has become the definition of basic," I lament, mouth curving upward. "We're never gonna recover."

Mom rubs a hand through my curls. She's almost as tall as me, but she still stands on her toes. I don't jerk away. It's all nice: the pressure of fingertips on my scalp, the warm smile written onto Mom's lips, Willow's tiny hand clutched around my middle and ring fingers, laughter pouring out of us like clouds cracked open to release a storm. That's how laughter can feel—like rainfall after a drought.

The only reason I'm here is to prevent Mom and Willow from overflowing our pantry with granola bars and Nutter Butters. But it feels bigger. It's as if I'm a part of something, an irreplaceable piece to a puzzle.

And, right on time, the universe steps in to remind me I'm not a part of *something else* anymore.

First, it's the voice—rough but somehow soothing like thick, raw honey. Then, it's the hands—strong with long fingers, made to touch and catch and break. My favorite argyle scarf hangs loosely from square shoulders. The tight Maplewood Marauders soccer team T-shirt stretches across a chest built for my head to rest on during lazy Sundays so worn-soft cotton cuddles my cheek while we binge unsolved-murder documentaries—Dimi's favorite.

Life is so ironic. It's so damn hilarious, because instead of my head pillowed against Dimi's chest, there's a hand with spidery fingers. Pinkish knuckles lead to a thin wrist that's attached to a guy with blonde, perfectly-styled bed-hair.

Sex hair.

I swallow the acid building at the back of my throat.

This guy has half-scrunched periwinkle eyes, freckled skin and a crooked smile that should be awkward, but isn't. It's freaking charming. He's the worst kind of reminder that Dimi *is* a part of something else—someone else, *Jules Littleton.* I only know his name because I haven't gotten around to unfriending Dimi on social media. That's not because I have wicked cyber-stalking skills. Well, maybe that too.

Jules is a freshman at Georgia Tech and has Lacoste model status. It kills me to think that way. But Jules is five steps ahead of me at adulting. He's not "clingy" or "desperate."

Dimi's words, not mine. It's how he defined our break-up. "You spend more time with me than your friends. You're always… *there.* Always need to hang out. Or text. It's like—you and me and nothing else."

The way he said it, with a choked voice and halfhearted tears, crawled into my chest, coiled around my heart, burnt the oxygen from my lungs. I was the reason we didn't work. I wrapped myself so tightly around Dimi that neither one of us could breathe.

But I still miss Dimi: the forehead kisses and the smell of his pillow, his stupid pillow, his loud snoring after sex—

Unpopular opinion: I don't miss the sex that much. Maybe I wasn't any good at it? Who is at sixteen? I was always awkward and uncomfortable. I never knew where my hands should go. Was it normal to nearly give your boyfriend a concussion when he went to kiss your neck, but you were aiming for his mouth? We laughed more about how quick and clumsy it was than we worried about how supercharged it should've been.

On reflection, I probably did it more for him than for us—for me. But still, why we do miss the people who hurt us?

"How does one bake a spinach quiche? Are they *baked*?"

I can barely follow Mom's voice. It's cottony fuzz in my ears. Thumbnail under my teeth, I watch Dimi and Jules. Dimi's soccer-calloused hand palms Jules' nape. Dimi's lips peck Jules' temple while they stroll through the produce section.

"Earth to Remy." Mom again.

Dimi is taller than Jules. He beams down at him, at his *new boyfriend*.

And there it is—my heart and emotions doing a flash mob routine in my chest cavity. Thinking of Dimi is like holding an open palm to a dancing flame. You know it'll burn, then scar, and then become this throbbing ache beneath your skin every time you see something luminous and warm. But the curiosity remains, the constant *what if* any time you're near the flame, the fast-beating heart under layers of warning. But what if Dimi and I had...? What if?

"Honey?"

I snap around to my mom. I'm blinking too fast. Pressure builds behind my eyelids, a dam threatening to break. Am I that person?

The one that's going to cry in the middle of Whole Foods over a guy? A stupid, insensitive, ordinary guy?

"Hey," Mom says, too carefully. "Are you okay?"

Guilt hooks my chest. I avoid gazing at Dimi. My brain refocuses: deep, easy breaths. But it's too late. Realization spirals across Mom's pinched brow and crinkled nose and tight mouth. She's spotted Dimi.

Tears nearly prick past my eyelids. Pathetic. I'm the opposite of Georgia-Tech-genius Jules Littleton.

"Well." Mom has replaced worry with a flashy smile. "I have an idea."

I blink at her, then Willow. It's the first time I've noticed Willow squeezing my fingers tighter.

"How about some Cold Stone ice cream before we go harass your dad into watching a movie?" Mom suggests. She's on my other side. Our shoulders touch; her warmth calms. "It's never too early to watch *It's the Great Pumpkin, Charlie Brown.*"

She and I share twin smiles. Summer storms. Cold Stone Creamery is unquestionably the best. And Charlie Brown holiday movies could cure bird flu, I swear. It's just—it's perfect. My mom is the closest thing to a divine being on Earth.

CHAPTER SEVEN

Rio is standing at the top of the concrete steps that lead to the main pathway to school on Monday. I march up to her and cut off my awesome morning playlist. Her eyes are focused on the ground beneath her.

A maze of graffiti decorates the concrete. It's a series of blues, greens, and reds. Two giant arrows squiggle in opposite directions. At the end of one, where the arrow's tip points toward Maplewood's main building, is a blue pill and words outlined in thick, black Sharpie: "This way to Wonderland, Alice." The other arrow, running down the steps toward the student parking lot's exit, is a red pill: "This way to Adulthood."

"She's done it again."

I grin. "It's a 'she' now?"

"Obviously."

Rio twists and angles her phone to snap as many high-def photos as possible while other students step over and around the graffiti. A group of freshmen art geeks gawp from a distance. Three cheerleaders, ponytails swinging in tandem, scoff at it.

"How do you know it's a she?"

Rio's sigh exits through her nose. "This stuff is too brilliant to be the work of a dumb guy."

"It could be a they or a them, you know," I point out. "They could be non-binary."

"True," concurs Rio.

I love that about her—how she doesn't make a big deal about sexuality or gender. It's so normal for her to switch pronouns. She never blinks an eye at anyone who's anything other than straight.

It wasn't difficult coming out to Rio, not entirely. Coming out to anyone is always awkward. But Rio only lifted her eyes from the book she was reading, leveled me with a long stare, then said, "I think your shirt's inside out." It was, but that's beside the point. In the middle of the school library, I came out to my best friend. And she didn't flinch. Rio didn't have one of those accidental expressions that says, "Holy shit, I need to keep calm, my friend is super-gay."

Rio just… carried on. It's as if her face said, "Remy Cameron is gay, and the sky is still blue."

"Either way," says Rio, squinting at the concrete, "they're getting sloppy."

I shrug my backpack higher on my shoulders, then cross my arms. I'm waiting. I know it's coming: Detective Rio Maguire's full synopsis. She never disappoints. "It's obviously done after hours, possibly at night. After any faculty has left. Someone who knows the campus inside and out, where the cameras are."

"Definitely not a freshman," I point out.

She squints at the handwriting. "This person loves colors, so it's not Veronica Hanson."

"Too goth?"

"Too everything." Index finger tapping against her chin, she offers, "An art student, maybe?"

"Zac?"

"Not *that artsy*." She snaps another photo. "The newest pieces look rushed, as if they didn't have time to fully realize their vision. Someone on a short schedule." Her wavy amber hair is piled messily on top of her head, spiraling down onto her cheeks. "Maybe someone who has to catch Marta to and from school?"

I stiffen my jaw. Atlanta's public transport bites.

"Brook?"

Unlike most of Maplewood's students, Brook doesn't live nearby. He's been using his aunt's address for school records. Luckily, he hasn't been caught. He doesn't have a car either. On the weekends, he borrows his mom's minivan to take Lucy on "dates," also known as trips to Savage Pizza and the AMC 24.

Rio says, "Not really his style. Ford Turner?"

"Lacks the intelligence to pull this off," I say through my teeth. "And the style. Plus, he has a mode of transportation: his pickup truck."

Of course, Ford freaking Turner owns a pickup truck. And a collection of John Deere snapbacks. I don't know why I'm bothering to clear that jerk-face's name, but I tack on, "He wouldn't have to rush anything, even with long football practices," because I want any subject involving him to die quickly.

"What about that one guy who's obsessed with Adult Swim?"

I choke on laughter. Tiny tears catch on my eyelashes. "Magnus Olsen?"

Magnus worships *Rick and Morty* and wears *Aqua Teen Hunger Force* T-shirts everywhere. He's an art geek, especially into papier-mâché and ceramics. And his handwriting is immaculate.

"Not a chance, Rio."

She continues to list suspects on her fingers. Juniors, seniors, Mrs. Richardson, one of Maplewood's most loyal and loved custodians.

"No way."

Rio says, "It's possible," with a bullshitting smile.

I almost call her on it, but my heart crawls up the ladder of my ribs at the same pace as Ian climbs the steps, two at a time.

He skims by us in a breathless rush. I inhale a whiff of clean sweat and bleach—*chlorine*.

What's wrong with me? I should just talk to him. We practically sit together every day at lunch. Ian's next to Brook, who is adjacent to Lucy, which, by the laws of physics, puts me in Ian's breathing space. I mean, it's not as if we have *assigned seats*, so I could sit next to Ian. And, you know, *talk to him*.

Ian's five feet away and bravery is such an easy thing to grab before eight a.m. "Cool," falls out of my mouth, accompanied by a choked, "hair." It's a perfectly acceptable, almost legendary compliment. Usually, I'd be proud of such fine vocabulary usage, except it's a chillier-than-normal Monday morning. Most of Ian's hair is hidden under a beanie. The longer bits catch on the soft wind, teasing his low, flat cheekbones.

He pauses mid-step, looking around. Evidently, I didn't make it apparent I was talking to *him*.

"I mean, like, it's *long*." My mouth has lost control. "And you do that thing where you tie it up—"

"Topknot." Rio, the traitor, coughs in the least discreet way possible.

"Yeah, topknot-thingy!" Mortification clearly has no side effects on my tongue. "It's really cool—your hair. Not that your hat—um, beanie?—isn't cool. It is! Your beanie is so awesome."

Ian's beanie is plain and black. Not even one of those retro woven ones: ribbed and ordinary, very I'm-trying-not-to-look-commercialized.

I feel detached from everything, except my heart. My wild, rampaging, rave-music-loud heart.

Confused and eyebrows wiggling, Ian says, "Uh, thanks?" I love his voice. Chill and a little nasally.

Ian's fingers curl white-knuckled around the strap of his messenger bag. His hands are nice. A splash of sunburn-red spreads across his nose. He swallows; I do too. Then he says, "Sick shoes."

I beam without thinking. Then he's jogging toward the mass of bodies clogging the school's entrance. I turn to Rio. Her smirk is lethal and unwanted.

"Keep your filthy comments to yourself, Rio Maguire."

Rio's hands are up, palms out in surrender. "Nothing to see here." Damn liar. "I won't say a thing to Lucy." Another disgusting, dirty lie. "This entire conversation will be filed under evidence for the prosecution's use at a later date."

"No more marathons of *True Detective* for you."

In a monotone narrator's voice, she says, "The suspect was a six-foot, curly-haired, innocent-looking, young black male with blue heart-eyes the size of Saturn, and…"

I stomp away with a one-fingered goodbye to my *former* best friend.

* * *

THE SQUEAK OF A NICE pair of classic slip-on Vans against Maplewood's terrazzo flooring isn't the best soundtrack to a Monday afternoon, but whatever.

I'm running late. This is all Ms. Amos's fault. Well, sort of. This AP Lit essay has spiked my adrenaline, sent my heart into a permanent residence at the bottom of Knotted Stomach Lane. It's thirty-effing-percent of my final grade. It's the "hello future" or "sorry, you're too basic for us" decision-maker in my Emory dreams.

Welcome to junior year in high school, where college is suddenly the only topic on everyone's brain. It's all Lucy talks about. Rio has already started application essays. Chloe has all but guaranteed an athletic scholarship. Jayden is a shoo-in for some Ivy League institution. And I just… don't want to be left behind.

That's why I stayed after class to talk with Ms. Amos. "Remy, don't overthink things," she told me in the world's most calm voice. Being scarily serene while discussing every major assignment with a student must be a pre-requisite to becoming a teacher. She gave me a few tips. I jotted them down. But it was nothing mind-blowing. She didn't unlock any major secrets to life—*my life*.

Now I'm late for GSA. My body is pretty much all long legs and arms but I'm history's worst runner. Sprinting toward Mr. Riley's classroom, I must look like a drunk giraffe. Sweat dampens my eyebrows. Stuffed with books, my backpack weighs me down. Room 302 is so close.

"Watch it!"

I swerve; the rubber soles of my Vans squeal like tires losing traction on a wet highway. I barely avoid slamming into Darcy Jamison ten feet from the door. She has an armful of poster board, Sharpies, and… jars of glitter?

Gasping, I say, "My bad, Darcy."

Darcy immediately rejects my breathless apology with squinted eyes, pinched mouth, and scrunched pug nose. She sizes me up like some fairy tale wicked queen in a pale pink cardigan, knee-length skirt, and perfectly-knotted blonde ponytail. Then, her eyes trace over the infamous poster tacked onto the outside of Mr. Riley's door.

"The FRIENDLY, SUPPORTIVE, & FUN Gay-Straight Alliance welcomes ALL!" The corniness of that slogan needs to be addressed during the meeting's agenda, like, yesterday.

"Yeah, so." My throat stops working when her death-glare falls on me again. I palm the back of my neck; my eyes shy away from her gaze.

Without another word, Darcy stalks off. No shocker. She probably has important GTFO stuff to do.

Mr. Riley's classroom is all set up for the meeting. The beakers and Bunsen burners and periodic tables are stashed away. Members fill a semi-circle of chairs. The meeting hasn't started yet. Were they waiting for me?

I drop my backpack next to Mr. Riley's desk, then eye the tower of Krispy Kreme donuts parked on the edge: three dozen glazed. The singular reason people can't deny Mr. Riley's epic status—the guy is incredible at providing snacks.

"You're sweating." I turn to Mr. Riley. He's leaning against the white board where smudged blue dry-erase marker lists all kinds of biology terms I certainly don't miss from last year. He has these animated brown eyes. They make you grin and blush and want to throw up. Mr. Riley is crush-worthy. Students from every grade whisper about him in the halls. He's young, and quite possibly single. I can sum up the dreaminess in one feature: the dimples.

Dragging the sleeve of my hoodie across my brow, I say, "AP Lit," as though it's an explanation.

Mr. Riley nods, eyebrows considerably raised. He gets it. Ms. Amos may be a great teacher, but she's notorious too.

"Did I miss anything?"

Mr. Riley shrugs. "Social awkwardness and my killer stand-up routine."

"So, nothing." I say, deadpan.

"Funny," says Mr. Riley. "We could take our show on the road."

"Are you the warm-up act?"

"Does your mom write your material, Mr. Cameron?"

"Ouch. Savage, Mr. Riley." I chuckle. Suddenly, everything that was weighing me down from AP Lit fades. My shoulders are lighter, and my breaths deep and steady.

Mr. Riley always lets me lead our meetings. He takes the role as faculty advisor seriously, but he understands no real conversations will happen if he's the one doing all the talking. I go through the usual introductions, agenda, the club's purpose—all the presidential stuff. I'm not on auto-pilot, but most of this is formality.

It's not exactly a packed room. Majority of the members have been around as long as I have. Slouching, with easy expressions, they nod along—except Rebecca. In her wrinkled "Queer Is Cool" T-Shirt, she pays more attention to the donuts than to me.

Two new freshman faces watch everything with nervous stares and twitchy mouths. Their hearts are practically visible through their shirts. I offer a relaxed smile and make perfect, genuine eye contact until their shoulders unwind.

I love that one of the seniors brings up ideas for Atlanta Pride, which is later this month. One of the sophomores rehashes a conversation about her favorite lesbian character being killed off in the latest CW teen drama. We always get a little loud over that.

Here's the thing, TV producers: Stop killing off the LGBTQ characters. That handsome, perfect-haired male lead who spends half the series hooking up with whatever beautiful girl is available can die, too, or his annoying, bro-friend sidekick. The queer character doesn't have to be the sad storyline. We don't exist to give your bland main character purpose.

Our small group is awesome. It crosses my mind that one day this club might not be necessary. One day, we queer teens will feel at home amongst our peers. We won't need somewhere to unload about coming out or sexuality or negative reactions from family and friends, because being queer won't mean being different. We'll just be teens. Nothing else.

"Now," says Mr. Riley, standing next to me, one hand on my shoulder, "we have a special announcement from Sara Awad."

Sara and her homecoming minions appear out of nowhere. They invade the club's circle. Sara doesn't acknowledge me. That's cool. I step back, trying to become invisible, and watch.

"Thank you, Mr. Riley." Sara is polished grins and excitement and careful wording. Her speech is practically flawless. But beneath the after-school special presentation, is a hint uneasiness in her posture. The corners of her mouth twitch a bit too much. It's as if Sara's trying not to expose herself to a crowd she *wants* to know but, for whatever reason, *can't*.

Mr. Riley once said, "It's your job to be supportive of those who *want* your support. Not those who *look like* they need it. Assumption is dangerous. You could alienate a potential ally with it." He's right.

The other homecoming committee members are tense. As if the wrong breeze could blow and they'd no longer be straight. It's so stupid. We're the Gay-*Straight* Alliance. There are actual heterosexuals in this club. There's Tony Gibb, whose younger cousin is bisexual. Lacy and Macy, inseparable best friends, are obsessed with yaoi graphic novels and shipping boyband members. Ross shows up for the free snacks. And Paige is a school-social-club junkie.

Sara continues to ramble: "And think of the doors it will open if one of you runs for…"

I can't believe this. She's pitching homecoming court ideas to the club with an honest-to-god PowerPoint presentation. I zone out.

The science wing is on the second floor. From the windows, I have a sweet view of the football team's practice field. Chloe is easy to pick out. She's the only player with a ponytail and a killer undercut. Also, she has the best arm. She tosses bullet after bullet at players: long and short distances, never missing. Upfield, Jayden practices with the cheer squad. Everything about him is perfect: his movements, smiles, and enthusiasm. His hair is sprayed, gelled, and deep brown.

Sara's still talking. *Homecoming, yay!* It's quite easily the most boring five minutes of my day, which is really saying something, since I regularly doze off during world history.

Outside, Jayden nails a double back-handspring. He'd make a great GSA co-president. Though he's never had an official boyfriend, Jayden is openly bisexual. Before he and Chloe quit starring in their dramatic rendition of *We're Friends Who Kiss at Parties*, Jayden got a lot of attention from guys at other schools. He's never shied away from it. He's not an attention-seeker, but I've seen the consuming blush that spreads across his face when the right guy sizes him up. But Jayden's more than Chloe and ogling guys. He's a proud cheerleader. He's louder and prouder about his two moms. He's never attended a GSA meeting, though.

"It's not me," he once said. "Also, the LGBT agenda seems to be geared more toward the L and G while erasing the B and T. Get it?"

I did. It's easier for the world to see things in black-and-white: lesbian and gay, but not bisexual. Not transgender. Or any other parts of the spectrum. Nothing other than girls who like girls and boys who like boys. I stopped inviting him after the third try.

"Well," Mr. Riley says, and I flinch back into reality. "That was quite the presentation, right?" He starts a slow clap. Only Rebecca joins him in a total-suck-up move to get closer to donut time.

All the other students are wide-eyed and goldfish-mouthed, including some of Sara's underlings. A strange silence has sucked the air out of the room.

Mr. Riley tries again. "We're all a little more excited about homecoming, thank you, Sara."

Nothing but quiet and awkward expressions, and then, out of nowhere, Sara says, "Go Marauders!"

I blink three times. This is happening. Sara's shoulders are straight, her chin is lifted, her practice-perfect smile shows off her braces. She's not even fazed by the stunned stares directed at her.

"Okay." Mr. Riley rubs his hands together and puts on his best rally-the-troops face. "Maybe we should have some snacks before we discuss ideas for our next monthly LGBTQ book. Kenny! You have a great one for us, right?"

Kenny, all blue-green hair and light-brown eyes, nods happily. Kenny, our resident bibliophile, has wildly unoriginal taste. I'm betting it's another David Levithan book.

Students shuffle to the donuts. The homecoming committee exits. Briefly, Sara hangs in the doorway. Her perfectly composed expression has faded into something gray and blank.

Do you want to stay? hangs on my tonsils. I never ask. She looks relieved. We exchange uncertain stares before she leaves.

CHAPTER EIGHT

"HOW MUCH DO YOU THINK hired assassins cost?"

Lucy lifts a flawlessly-plucked eyebrow at me. I don't blink.

Yes, this is the conversation two best friends have on an ordinary Thursday, after school. We're in my car. I'm supposed to give her a ride home, but I'm stalling. She hasn't complained.

Lucy hums. "Are we talking ex-CIA? MI6? Rogue FBI operatives?"

"All of the above."

"Why?"

I slouch in my seat. "I'm confident Sara hates me. Just curious if she can afford to have me murdered."

"And you think it'd take trained assassins to do that?"

"Hell yeah!" I try, and fail, to flex a bicep. I'm pathetically toneless in the muscles department. Gym class is an unacceptable block of sweating and being awkward because I can't catch a ball. I get more exercise trying not to be tardy to homeroom every morning.

I'm still reeling from Sara's appearance at the GSA meeting. Our friendship is such a mystery. There are days when we laugh at the same jokes, share wide-eyed looks at something epically outrageous one of the Liu twins has said, smile knowingly at Lucy's anime rambling. I remember one lunch break that we spent dissecting Darcy's wardrobe choices.

But there's also a thin wall separating us, one created by some unknown force. Maybe it's because I've raised my eyebrows more than once at the way she looks at Lucy. Maybe it's because I'm out to everyone. Or maybe it's because, no matter how close people think they are to each other, there are always things unsaid, always vulnerabilities we don't feel safe enough to share. But I wish I *knew* her the way I did Lucy, or Brook, or even Alex and Zac.

"Andrew's annual Halloween party is coming up," says Lucy, as if the last minute never existed. I can't blame her.

I don't say anything about her scuffed-up crimson Converse on my dashboard. My dad gave me his old, midnight-blue Toyota Corolla for my sixteenth birthday. It doesn't even have Bluetooth; just an auxiliary port to plug my phone into. POP ETC is softly playing, a catchy tune that's all claps and acoustics. Lucy's shoes wiggle back and forth to it.

"You're going, right." It's not a question.

"Nope," I tell her.

"Why not?"

"Trick-or-treating with Willow." I pop a mini-Reese's peanut butter cup in my mouth, savoring the slow melting of chocolate before the healing burst of peanut butter hits my taste buds. "It's tradition."

"I forgot." Lucy sighs.

I reach under her legs for the glovebox to pluck another Reese's from a wrinkled bag.

"You could always come afterward."

"Maybe."

"Maybe?"

"It's possible." I pop another candy in my mouth.

"Okay, what's the deal? Is this a Code Orange?"

I nearly choke. *Code Orange* is a nickname Rio and Lucy gave any situation involving me coping with feelings or anxiety by consuming mass amounts of Reese's. It started somewhere in middle school.

"No?"

Lucy *tsks*. "We're just gonna pretend you're not devouring your emergency stash of Reese's?" She waves a hand at the half-empty bag. *When did that happen?* She whispers, "This can't be good."

It's not. In my lap, there's a mound of crinkled gold wrappers. In the rearview mirror, I can see melted chocolate smeared on one corner of my mouth. I wipe it away with my sleeve.

"AP Lit is going to ruin me."

"What?"

"We have to do an essay," I grumble.

"But you love writing."

"Short stories. Awful poems. Haikus about Dev Patel's face."

Small confession: I might've gone through a hardcore phase where Dev Patel was all I thought about. It was Mom's fault, forcing me to watch *Slumdog Millionaire*. Twice! Of course, a few late nights scrolling through Google while my right hand did some interesting things beneath my navel was all voluntary.

"It's so stupid." I grip the steering wheel to prevent my hand from reaching for another Reese's. I have restraint—very little. "How can I write an essay about… me? I mean, Jesus, what do I know about how the world sees me, Lucy? I'm…" *Adopted*. I don't say it, though. "I don't know shit."

Liquid fire slides down my throat. All the words, they unhinge my jaw and hollow out my chest. I have no clue where this comes from. But it's true. Fear's a tornado, touching down in my brain, leveling all my carefully built walls. I'm not sure I can handle the pressure of defining *who I'm supposed to be*.

"But you're you," Lucy says, matter-of-factly.

"Gee, thanks."

"It's not that deep, Rembrandt."

Isn't it? In my phone, I have three different maps of possible routes to get home on Friday evenings after classes are done at Emory. I could make the drive in forty-five minutes, an hour max. In time for Dad's French toast dinners and Clover's evening walk. I'd be there to help Willow with her homework or watch endless reality TV with Mom.

One failing grade in AP Lit could ruin all of that.

"Do you know what you need?"

"More Reese's?"

"No."

"A new brain? To stop shopping in the *Where's Waldo?* sweater collection at American Eagle?"

My wardrobe choice didn't go unnoticed at lunch. Personally, I think my comfortably snug red-and-white-striped waffle sweater is the epitome of trendy. My friends—ex-friends—said I looked like a candy cane. I'm already working on a Craigslist ad for new lunch associates.

"All the above," Lucy says. "And a trip to Zombie Café."

I drum my fingers enthusiastically on the steering wheel. In my very unbiased opinion, Zombie Café is the coolest coffeeshop amongst the many littering Atlanta's landscape. It's not quite as hipster as Aurora Coffee in Little Five Points or as polished—and problematic—as the fleet of Starbucks clogging up every corner of metro Atlanta, but it carries its own brand of chic. Ever since my mom let me have my first foamy sip of a cappuccino at thirteen, I've been in love.

"You're a gift, Lucia."

"Remember that when I come to claim your firstborn."

She clicks in her seatbelt and I pull out of Maplewood's parking lot.

ZOMBIE CAFÉ IS PURE PERFECTION. It's whimsy and precision, bright but controlled, euphoria melting into modern construction.

It's everything I loved before I knew the sweetness—and bitter pain—that one word could create.

"Welcome to Zombie Café, where the undead live again and the boring people join the zombie parade after one sip of our Cold Body coffee!"

Okay, it's not perfect. The café's slogan is a mouthful, but when it's shouted from the one barista behind the bar, prepping and pouring drink after drink, I'm impressed.

The interior of Zombie is my second favorite part, from the big, comfy armchairs to the handwritten chalk menus behind the front register. An entire wall is a floor-to-ceiling mural of a happy zombie drinking coffee, a green sun, and cartoony skulls with heart-shaped eye sockets. Inside the zombie's exposed chest cavity is a map of Atlanta in swirls of peach and bumblebee yellow. Novels donated by customers stuff a bookshelf next to a table stacked with classic board games.

By the door, a giant window overlooks Roswell Road. It's the epicenter of the church of college hipsters—a mecca of laptops, iPads, and headphones on round tables. Another wall, opposite the coffee bar, is exposed brick with customers' autographs scrawled in silver Sharpie.

I gaze over the unpolished hardwood floors and the zebra-print rug where children sit with smoothies. This place feels lived in.

"What graveyard gods do I need to thank for a visit from my two favorite delinquents?" asks Trixie, the barista behind the bar.

"We might be delinquents," says Lucy, "but we tip well."

"True story."

Trixie is the best. I don't know if that's her real name, but she's got enough sass and old-school, punk-rock greatness to pull it off.

"Cutting extracurriculars to visit me, kids?" She maintains eye contact while managing to steam, pour, and lid drinks. It's all second nature. Trixie's worked at Zombie since it opened ten years ago.

"Maybe," I say.

"Maybe?" Trixie's grin is infectious.

"Possibly."

"Where else would we spend our afternoons?" Lucy asks, playing nonchalant in the worst way.

"Bullshit." Trixie's mouth cocks; her eyes narrow. "I call bullshit."

Yep, Trixie's a rock goddess in ripped flannel. We're just her loyal subjects.

"This guy," Lucy finally says, jerking her thumb at me, "needed a break from a junior-year-stress meltdown."

Trixie starts another drink, nodding.

I'm too embarrassed to remind Lucy that snitches get stitches. I do need a breather from thinking about Ms. Amos and AP Lit and Emory. I just don't need that broadcast to the small collection of frat bros fist-bumping and drinking iced Americanos at the bar.

"Are you going to turn into one of those seventeen-year-old emo kids?" Trixie asks. She has a half-pixie-cut, half-Mohawk going on. It's dyed licorice red. She's wearing an Indigo Girls T-shirt and has a severe case of mascara overload. Trixie *is* emo.

"What? No."

"Oh, Remy. It's happening. Trips to Hot Topic. Black coffee and tragic poetry." Trixie looks horrified. "Alt-rock music!"

"Trixie, what the ever-loving fu—"

Lucy's wheezing with laughter. "The dark side hasn't claimed him yet!"

I give her the evil eye. I *might* be contemplating ways to torture her at a later date. I ignore their silly banter; my eyes scan the café.

It's not too busy today. The usual college students inhabit their digital islands while a sprinkle of parents wait for afterschool activities to end. The early-in, early-out work crowd savors their last gulp of caffeine. A little girl dances to a song I don't know the words to. I tap my foot along because I love discovering new music, because I love this café, this hole in reality where I exist with no expectations.

Huddled in a pear-green armchair is a boy in a Zombie apron. Sunlight reflects off his full-rim eyeglasses. He's drawing something odd and colorful on a chalkboard in his lap.

I freeze, caught in a time loop.

"New guy," explains Trixie. "Started two weeks ago. He's a little weird, but a cool kinda weird. Like you, Remy."

Like me. No, not like me at all.

"Like Remy," Lucy repeats, her tone nauseatingly snarky. "Basically, he fits right in." Before I can speak—or breathe like a *normal human*—Lucy adds, "We know him."

It's Ian.

"I've noticed," says Trixie with a very unsubtle eyebrow-lift meant for me.

Trixie is freaky perceptive. But maybe my cheeks are warm. Maybe my heart is loud enough for the entire café to hear. Maybe I'm staring.

"I..." Words die tragically on my tongue. This whole outing was a bad idea. I need to be at home, focusing on the essay that decides my future.

Ian hasn't noticed us yet, so we could slip back out the door...

"We should get our drinks to go," I suggest. Panic grips my larynx. It's almost unreal how high my voice gets when I say, "I have an essay to work on! And you probably have class-president-nerds-of-anime-skater stuff to do."

"I don't." Lucy's tone is defiant and gleeful. "Also, hell no, we're staying. I need a break. *You* need a break."

"*Lucia Reyes*." My voice is borderline teenage-camper-running-from-a-chainsaw-killer shriek now.

Ian lifts his head, and his eyes go immediately to me. Is it possible for a six-foot, skinny black guy to hide behind a six-year-old dancing queen? It doesn't matter because Trixie, the menace, says, "You have some friends here, newbie!" while waving Ian over.

This is Armageddon. This is where the wannabe-hero chokes on his own heart and dies from an epic rush of blood surging to his lower half. My boner is warp-speed fast—damn you Jayden and your corny addiction to sci-fi movies—at the sight of Ian pushing his glasses up his nose. They slip back down. His mouth, a soft-looking rose, tilts up on one side. He waves as if his hand is uncertain whether to be enthusiastic or chill. It's kind of manic.

"Take a break, newbie," Trixie yells. "Sit with your friends. I'll hold down the fort." She shifts to us. "The usual?"

"Yep," Lucy says for both of us. Obviously, I'm under some sort of Harry Potter spell. *Ianistoocuteous.*

"Usual for you too, newbie?"

Ian's head bobs, a jerky motion that unsettles his glasses again. He quickly adjusts them.

I am spellbound. I'm still in that thick fog of "what the hell is happening" when Lucy hooks her arm in mine and leads us to Ian's little corner of the café. She collapses into an armchair while I begin to map out all my potential exits—diving through Zombie's giant front window looks like something I could survive, if I was Chadwick Boseman. Lucy raises a sharp eyebrow at me. She expects me to sit, between her and Ian.

"Remy."

"Lucy." My voice cracks, because clearly puberty is a lifelong process.

She clears her throat.

I sit with a heavy exhale and flopping limbs.

Ian watches me. Sunlight kisses tiny specks of dust, a steady stream of glitter around us. Gold beams sweep over loose strands of hair that fall into Ian's glasses. I want to brush them back for a clearer view of his eyes. My fingers twitch on my knees.

"What're you drawing?" Lucy asks Ian.

"Just some promotional art for the café."

I angle for a better view. Ian's art is amazing but also familiar—not in a bad way, but as if I've seen it before and been awed at the skill level. He's sketched a funky manga-style owl in liquid chalk. Above its head is a speech bubble like in old-school comics: "UP OWL NIGHT!"

I can't keep from snorting into my hand. Seriously? It's ridiculous.

"Lame, right?" Ian's lowered head doesn't hide his mortified grin.

"Are you kidding?" Lucy smacks his shoulder. "You've got mad skills, bro."

A smear of pink blotches Ian's skin from cheeks to nose. "Cool." He sighs. "I didn't come up with the slogan. It's for some new nitrogen-gas-infused cold coffee."

"Hasn't Starbucks been doing that for, like, ever?"

Ian flaps a hand in front of Lucy's face. "Ours is different!"

Lucy raises a doubtful eyebrow. "How?"

"They're putting sugar crystals on top!"

"Oh, no."

"Hell, yes," says Ian, covering his eyes in embarrassment.

I'm kind of mad he's hiding his eyes and part of his face behind his big hand. But not mad enough to admit that out loud. I'm too cool and uninterested. I'm also spectacular at telling myself lies.

I stare at Ian's shoes: loafers and no socks, much more interesting than Ian's stupid face.

"Let's get this party started!"

Trixie arrives with a tray of drinks. She's a savior. For Lucy, an iced latte macchiato, not because she likes them, but because they're aesthetically perfect for her Instagram feed. Trixie hands me a cold-brew coffee with thick vanilla cream swirling through it to create a marble effect. It's called the Cold Body.

"It's strong enough to raise the dead," Trixie told me the first day she slid it into my hands. I agree. It's also perfect for all-nighters during final exams.

Trixie passes Ian a big, round ceramic mug. "And the green stuff." She wrinkles her nose.

Ian excitedly accepts it.

I don't know if it's the coffee or the brief of addition of Trixie to our little circle, but courage strikes a flame in my throat and I ask, "What's that?" before I chicken out.

"Matcha latte." Ian takes a careful sip. "I hate the taste of coffee."

"But you work at a *coffee shop*."

"Irony and I are old friends," says Ian. He nudges his glasses up. "It's just a job."

"Watch it," Trixie says warningly but with a rare smile. She flicks his ear, returning to her post behind the bar.

I turn back to Ian. "Just a job?"

"My dad is big on the whole 'a busy mind keeps trouble away' motto," says Ian. "I'm not involved in any after-school activities, something he's not too happy about. Clubs or sports look good for college and all that."

My friends have all had jobs, mainly during the downtime of summer or holiday breaks. Rio worked part-time at Jo-Ann Fabrics.

Zac and Alex got fired from Pizza Hut after only two weeks—apparently getting high behind the dumpsters slows down production. When football season's over, Jayden picks up shifts at one of his moms' auto shop. Brook maintains his job at Regal Cinema year-round.

The café's speakers are streaming soft music. I don't know the song, but the melody sinks its teeth into my veins. My foot taps along to the hand claps.

"What's this?"

Lucy doesn't answer. She's sitting sideways, legs dangling off the chair's arm. Her head is tipped back and her eyes are closed; the day is finally catching up with her.

But Ian stares at me as if I'm an alien.

"What?"

"You don't know this?"

I shake my head.

"It's Kim Carnes," Ian says, awed. "You really don't know 'Bette Davis Eyes' by Kim Carnes?"

"Sorry. Should I?"

Ian's lips part, as though he might say something. He shakes his head. "No. Sorry." His glasses edge down his nose as he stares into his drink. "It's just on a lot of my playlists. I have this thing for '80s music. The songs from that era are so legendary."

I can only count about ten '80s songs I know, mostly thanks to Dad.

"My dad likes classical. But my mom…" Ian's voice softly fades.

Either it's curiosity or the ridiculous spike of caffeine from the Cold Body, but whatever it is, I stretch my foot out to nudge Ian's.

He bites his lip. "When I was younger, I'd sneak down to the kitchen at night. She'd always be there, dancing by herself." His fingers, long and thin, drum along to the backbeat. "Always to '80s music. She'd dance and dance—" Ian pauses.

I tap his foot again.

"So happy and free. My mom's never like that during the day." Ian's looking across the café. He's drifting like a cloud skimming across the moon. "Sometimes she'd catch me watching and grab my hands. I'd dance with her."

We exhale together. I'm there, in the kitchen, spinning under the light as if it's a disco ball. Laughter squeezes my lungs. Soft hands hold mine. Tears soak my eyelashes. I can't catch my breath and I keep hearing a raspy voice talking about a woman with Bette Davis eyes.

"The next day, my mom would pretend it never happened."

I swallow. Ian's still spaced out, on another planet. My heartbeat matches the fading song—*rat-tat… tat*. Warmth curls around my bones and latches on. I can't stop thinking about my parents and the rains of Africa and dreamy looks I've never shared with anyone, not even Dimi.

"Wow. Deep," says Lucy, startling both of us.

I take a giant gulp of cold brew, then wince at the bitterness.

Ian has a green mustache from his latte. "There are theories on word vomit. Studies that say the human brain expels so much information that the mouth cannot process and edit said info before its conveyed verbally. Real scientific stuff."

"Fascinating," says Lucy, deadpan, but with a lift to her lips. She motions toward the bar. "I'm gonna go chat with Trixie about hosting our next anime club meeting here. But, please, you two carry on with this—uh, word vomit stuff."

She isn't discreet when she winks at me. I know what she's doing. I also know that once she's disappeared, it'll just be Ian and me, staring at our drinks in awkward silence. I try to convey that to Lucy with a look. It doesn't work.

"So," I say, exhaling.

"So."

"Well."

"Yeah."

And here we are—two boys with nothing to say.

Another song comes on. I don't recognize it, but I like it. Something about letting love open the door? Yeah, no. I'll pass on the love part, but the melody and words are catchy. I'll probably download it when I get home.

I try not to focus so intensely on Ian, but it's difficult. Rainbow fingers from ink chalk pick at a rip in his jeans. The pinkish-tangerine afterglow from the sunset skims over his face and hair. Plush lips rest against the rim of his mug. The café lights glint off his earring. Ian is a visual maze and I'm lost, that is, until he looks me right in the eye.

"POP ETC!" I shout.

His eyes widen; his mouth goes slack.

After I reteach my mouth to work, I say, "Music. They're a band and they make music. Epic music. POP ETC is my all-time favorite band."

"Cool," Ian says, slowly.

I drain the rest of my cold brew in one swallow. That seems like a good way to die—better than from the unbearable mortification assaulting my nerves.

"I need to get home." I stand, shoulders tense. "I should spend some quality time with my sister."

"Walk your dog?"

I grin. "She's cute, right?"

Ian's eyebrows lift, and I see a subtle twitch at the corner of his mouth. "She's cute," he agrees.

My heart tickles the roof of my mouth, which means I'm close to messing this up. He waits. I swallow, then signal Lucy. She shoots me a look. I don't care. Ian cannot become a priority. He can't be an *anything*.

Thankfully, his eyes are lowered, and the noise from the dude-bro group that just strolled in distracts from the fact that I trip over my own feet speed-walking to the door.

CHAPTER NINE

FRIDAY MORNING, I WAKE TO the intoxicating aroma of Dad's banana and blueberry French toast and a chirping notification. Yawning, I grab my phone. I unlock the screen and blink a few times at it.

Two Facebook friend requests: Free Williams and Ian J. Park.

I don't hesitate to approve the request from Free just to have only one profile photo on the screen. There he is—his face peeking out from a pit of rainbow plastic balls like those at indoor family theme parks—scrunched eyes and enormous smile and hair everywhere.

Fact: I'm a master of self-control. I wait an entire twenty-two seconds—enough time to stretch, rub the drowsiness from my eyes, and have a stern conversation with my lower half about the eagerness it's experiencing at the sight of Ian's lips—before accepting the friend request.

What happens during my extra-long shower afterward is not a lack of will power. I'm simply scratching a very needy, annoying, satisfying itch. That's all.

* * *

CHLOE AND JAYDEN ARE PASSING as I knock my locker shut with my shoulder. They're a DreamWorks version of high school sweethearts—hand-in-hand, big heart eyes, glitter above their heads.

Chloe's wearing her jersey. Jayden's in full cheerleader gear. That means one thing: Game Day.

They're following a slow-build of hallway traffic, the usual morning horde of student zombies. But Jayden's going the wrong way; our homeroom is at the opposite end of the hall.

"Is the pep rally starting early? Or are you two skipping homeroom for a little…" I waggle my eyebrows. "…extra *study time*?"

Grinning, Jayden flips me a middle finger.

Over her shoulder, Chloe says, "You haven't heard?"

That the quarterback and superstar cheerleader are getting it on? Yeah, that's not news. I don't say that to Chloe, though. She scares me. "Heard what?"

"The Mad Tagger has struck again, my dude." Jayden's eyes are bright with excitement. "Tattooed the main gym's doors. Savage! We're going to check it out."

"It's serious business," says Chloe. "Principal Moon is yelling about canceling the pep rally."

"Total anarchy."

Jayden's obvious hyperbole aside, scrapping the pep rally would suck. I wouldn't want to miss the extremely dope performance our marching band always gives. But I could live without the counterfeit school spirit. All the "we are family" unity Maplewood suddenly puts on as if half the school wasn't at war and having meltdowns on social media last night.

"She's talking about scratching homecoming too." Chloe frowns.

"If the Mad Tagger doesn't turn themselves in, we're screwed." Jayden shakes his head. "It's so rank."

I lean against my locker. Jayden and Chloe get lost in the tidal wave of crimson and steel, also known as red and gray, our school colors. School freaking spirit—*go Marauders!* I go the other way.

Since Rio didn't meet me at our usual spot, I suspect she's at the gym too. Rio and her Mad Tagger obsession is another thing I don't comprehend.

"Hey!" Mr. Riley catches up to me in the sophomore hallway. I swear his wardrobe choices always scream "Look at me! I'm cool! I fit in!" Today he's in a bright orange polo, wrinkled-just-enough khakis so he doesn't appear like one of those adults that wake up early to iron, and product-stiff hair. He wears glasses, too, but those wire-thin ones that don't look prescribed.

"Sup, Mr. Riley?"

"How're things going?"

I shrug. I don't really have a good answer for that one. *Fine? Perfect? My future is screwed if I don't pass AP Lit?* "Okay."

Mr. Riley gives me that look I hate—the skeptical one that's always accompanied by a raised brow.

"You haven't been too involved lately. Slightly disinterested."

"I dunno. A lot on the brain," I say, rubbing the nape of my neck. The student traffic around us is thinning out, but I still feel as if everyone's watching us, watching me. "I have a meeting with Mrs. Scott today."

"Ouch."

"Yeah."

"That's like a death sentence, isn't it?" Mr. Riley's face crinkles like used wrapping paper.

I chuckle.

"You know," Mr. Riley's voice dips in that "I'm the adult" tone I've heard in way too many family sitcoms, "GSA is always here for you. Whenever. We're not just a poster-friendly support system for coming out and safe sex talks and navigating social situations. It's about each of you as *people*. We're a team."

Yes, thanks Mr. Riley, that didn't sound like an online slogan, not one bit.

I love GSA. It's a home, a safe space. But is that all I am? And is the club making the impact it used to, before being gay became the "cool thing"? I can't ask Mr. Riley any of these things. Not because he won't listen, but because I'm afraid it'll disappoint him. Disappointment is the perfect motivator for silence.

"I was thinking," says Mr. Riley, dimples on full display. I don't melt into a babbling mess the way I do for other nameless guys. "We should have a Halloween get-together for the members. A place for queer students and allies to be themselves."

I bite my lip. Mr. Riley is about my height. Our eyes are level. There's a quiet plea in his, and I don't know how to respond.

"It's not easy for them to feel normal when the mold of 'normal' presented to them isn't like their own. It's unfair. They should have an outlet to dress up and dance with people like them."

I roll those words against the roof of my mouth. *Like them.*

Nothing against Mr. Riley—I don't really know his orientation or background—but there's more than a mold to break at Maplewood. While our high school is progressive in that it has a female quarterback and Lucy is a Latinx junior class president and Brook is our school's most decorated—and loved—athlete, in other ways it is very, very conservative. The unspoken truths echo in every hallway.

The jocks dress in drag every October and it's considered hilarious, but students like Oliver Nguyen can't wear something nice and fitted from the women's section of Hot Topic because he's gay. Sophomore girls can wear lookalike outfits of their favorite boyband member, but Lara, who's lived near Maplewood her whole life—her parents are freaking legacies—can't come to school on a Monday in a button-up, bowtie, men's khakis, and boots without receiving a dozen funny looks, without the word "Butch" scribbled onto her locker.

I can be GSA president. I can share the same circle of acquaintances as the frat-wannabe crowd. And I can still draw attention for wearing a rainbow Pride shirt one day out of the year. The whispering kind. The kind of attention that suddenly makes everyone forget I'm the same Remy Cameron that came out freshman year and became the punchline of their jokes:

"What's he wearing?"

"Oh, my god, did you know he was the 'girl' in his relationship with Dimi?"

"Did he just say 'fab'? What. The. Hell."

Mr. Riley is still giving me the look. I can't avoid it.

"Okay," I say, shuffling my feet. "It might be cool."

"Very cool."

The bell rings, and I'm so thankful for an escape, a way out of this conversation and out of my thoughts.

"Think about it. Please."

"Sure thing, Mr. Riley."

His mouth tightens; his eyes are bright but weary. "We'll plan later?"

"Fantastic."

Mrs. Scott's office should be on the cover of *Counselors Monthly*, if that's a thing. It's that kind of vibe. Framed posters with quotes about preparation and goals and dreams stare down from beige walls. Rainbows and kittens and cliffsides with picture-perfect blue skies mock you from the wall behind her desk. Everything is tailored to inspire: green furniture, tan carpeting, and a desk covered in bobbleheads and Funko POP! action figures.

Mrs. Scott is clicking away at her computer. Her green-gold eyes are laser-focused. She's humming something that belongs on a smooth jazz radio station.

"Well, Mr. Cameron." She starts every conversation with eye-contact and a pageant-worthy smile, probably a tactic she learned from *Counselors Monthly*. "I see we're on course to follow our plan."

Ah, yes. The Plan. An outline created by Mrs. Scott freshman year to map out my high school career—and the rest of my life—because every student knows where their life is headed at fourteen, right?

The Plan consists of carefully chosen classes—none of which I enjoy—to bulk up my college applications. It's simple: Graduate, go to a "respectable" college, get a six-figure salary, marry a lawyer, have three perfect children that I'll be too busy working to raise, retire unhappily, then die. Maybe it's not that intricate, but it feels that way.

"And how's AP Literature with Ms. Amos going?" She cocks a sharply-penciled eyebrow at me. "You know that is the key to our success and getting into Emory College."

I love how, when adults are discussing a teen's future, suddenly it's a partner project. Everything is "we" and "our," as if Mrs. Scott will be attending community college and struggling through a food service job with her assigned students who barely survive high school. There is no "our" in high school. It's every student for themselves. High school is *The Hunger Games* without all the elaborate costumes and ridiculously attractive "teens."

"It's okay," I finally say.

"Okay?"

"Perfect!" I lie. My throat squeezes around every letter. "We're on track for greatness."

"Are you sure?"

No. I don't have the heart to tell her. "I'm going to pass."

Mrs. Scott nods once, preening. She turns her unnecessarily large flat-screen monitor in my direction. Multiple tabs are open across the browser, all for colleges. Sometimes, that's how my life feels: like twenty open tabs in a web browser that I peruse, but never fully commit to. My stomach drops as I sink lower into the chair.

"It's the only class you have as a legitimate argument to get into Emory. President of Maplewood's celebrated GSA and perfectly acceptable grades in standard classes is a fine talking point, but not enough," Mrs. Scott says.

"I know."

"Well, just in case, I've been looking at alternatives. There is no Plan A without a Plan B, C, D, and so forth." What page of *Counselors Monthly* did she get that one from? "We have so many wonderful choices for you! Prestigious universities; great support systems. All customized for you, Mr. Cameron."

All customized for me. How much is Mrs. Scott being paid to sound like an ad for an online university?

She clicks on a tab. "First, there's Morehouse." She goes into a calculated speech that sounds as if it belongs on the front page of a brochure. *Rich history! Location! Culture!*

"And then we have Morris Brown…"

I squint at her. There's a theme happening here.

"And if those two aren't in your wheelhouse, and you're willing to travel," Mrs. Scott clicks the next tab, "we have the University of Pennsylvania." Really? "Maybe San Diego State University?" Next tab. "Look at that campus! Glorious."

Yes, because I've incessantly voiced my need to move to the west coast.

"Or Ithaca." *Click.* "All these colleges rate high as institutions that have wonderful ties to the LGBTQIA…" She lists every letter

on a finger, as if she's trying to make sure she doesn't miss one. "…
community!"

Click click click. "Excellent academic institutions that have environments created to support students whose identity falls under the
LGBT umbrella."

"Umbrella? Is it raining queerness?"

Mrs. Scott laughs in that movie version of Dolores Umbridge
way—quick and uneasy. "These are great places to consider, Remy."

Whenever Mrs. Scott starts using student's first names, it means
she's trying to calm a storm. The thunderclouds are already hovering
over my brow.

"Friendly environments. Top colleges for you because—"

"I'm black? Gay?"

Meticulously, Mrs. Scott fixes a stray bobblehead. Her plastic smile
is pasted on her rouge lips. "Smart. Creative. Courageous."

"Courageous? For being black? Gay? Or both?"

"Remy." She exhales through her teeth. Crinkled eyebrows pinch
the skin just above her nose. Folding her hands, she says, eerily calm,
"College isn't easy. Movies makes it look that way. All the parties and
friends and relationships; but being out on your own is tough. New
environments take adjusting."

"Adjusting," I repeat.

Mrs. Scott straightens her shoulders. "You'll need a support
system. People like you with similar backgrounds. Who know who
they are."

I want to laugh—or scream. "Mrs. Scott, I'm black. I'm adopted.
My parents are white. I came out when I was fourteen and still don't
understand why that's supposed to be a big fucking deal."

"I'm sure, as someone pursuing a school for creative writing, you can
find more inspired language to use other than *that* word, Mr. Cameron."

And there it is. The change in tone. Suddenly, we're not a "team" anymore. Mrs. Scott is the adult and I'm the… the kid.

"My point is, how many people out there have a similar background at Emory or Morehouse or *fu*—freaking Stanford?" My hands tremble against my thighs. "Are there statistics for that? A club for the adopted, gay, black kids from the suburbs?"

She sighs again, lips pinched.

"I'm seventeen." My voice squeaks. Damn it. "Am I supposed to know who I am?"

According to Ms. Amos and Emory and the entire universe, I guess so.

"You'll figure it out, Remy." Mrs. Scott's expression has returned to a cellophane, TV-ready gleam that probably wouldn't comfort a baby deer. "Until then, these are just alternatives to Emory. Helpful starts."

I tip my head back, glare at the ceiling: tiles and tiles of mineral fiber, hundreds of dots sectioned into perfect squares. Is that how Mrs. Scott imagines life after high school? Hundreds of clueless adults sectioned off in their squares?

"This printout will help." She shuffles a few papers, pinches one, then passes it to me. "President of GSA will look great on your applications, especially at *these* colleges. Talk it over with your parents. I'm sure they'd agree with me."

I hope my parents would agree Mrs. Scott's "suggestions" can go to hell.

"Now," the rainbows-and-power-of-positive-thoughts return to Mrs. Scott's voice, "let's focus on that AP Literature class, shall we?"

CHAPTER TEN

FRIDAY'S PEP RALLY IS COOL but controlled. Principal Moon ensures order is maintained, openly eyeing every student during club speeches and the football coach's lame attempt at sparking interest in the team's potential. What Principal Moon lacks in height, she makes up for in personality and directness and one of those "I'm in charge" bob hairstyles. A mini-Angela Bassett, she always looks poised to take anyone on, toe-to-toe.

Next to her, Lieutenant Parker surveys the students in the bleachers as though he could get one of us to crack during an interrogation. Chloe's dad loves wearing Ray-Bans and blank expressions. I don't know him too well. His work commitments keep him from attending any of her games, but his appearance at our pep rally means this whole Mad Tagger business is getting serious.

It seems as if he and Principal Moon are secretly creating a lineup of suspects. Lucy and I sit together, sharing Twizzlers and betting on who's already being marked for questioning.

"Andrew," I suggest.

"Andrew, as in Brook's friend Andrew?" Lucy snorts. "Not a chance. Too nerdy."

"It's always the nerdy ones."

"It's always the religious zealots or the scorned exes or the bored, rich kids who never heard the word 'No' from their parents."

"So, three-fourths of Maplewood?" I wiggle a licorice mustache at her.

"Basically."

"Darcy Jamison?"

Lucy rolls her eyes. I do too. As hardcore as Darcy is about God and Jesus and wearing skirts that have hemlines below the knee, she doesn't seem to have one corrupt gene in her body. A mean streak? Definitely. But not enough to disfigure school property.

"Ford Turner?"

I stare off into space, trying not to cringe. His name makes my skin crawl. "No," I whisper, but my brain screams *Hell yeah, the classless asshole is a suspect!*

I watch Jayden and the cheerleaders rally the crowd. The freshmen seem into it. The sophomores are bored, heads down, thumbing away at their phones despite the zero tolerance for usage during school hours. We're sitting with the juniors, who are either talking to each other or stupendously baked, depending on how many of them caught Zac and Alex between classes.

The seniors are the real hurricanes. They boo the underclassmen, roar at the introduction of the football team, and toss merciless jokes at our vice principal. When the announcements about homecoming start, they split time between doing the wave and flirting with each other. Friday nights around Maplewood are good for three things: sports, parties, and the next episode of "Who Hooked Up in the Pool?" to be aired in the hallways on Monday mornings.

"It's Jayden, I'm telling you," Lucy says. She's braiding three Twizzlers into a friendship bracelet. My best friends are all mad talented.

"Obviously."

"That hair is hiding secrets."

I recline. My eyes wander again. In the sea of seniors, I wonder where Brook is? Is a certain someone is sitting next to him?

Lucy thumbs at her phone. "I can't believe Rio ditched us."

"You know she doesn't do mandated social activities like this."

Lucy says, "I invited her to the game."

We are both aware Rio's not going. She never does. Rio and loud crowds and trying to find justifiable reasons for two hours of sports don't gel. But something about Lucy's optimism makes me nudge her and wink.

"She'll be too busy trying to uncover the *real* Mad Tagger."

"Maybe she needs our help?"

"Yeah." I sigh wistfully. "Because we've obviously figured out who it is."

"Maybe it's you." Lucy's grinning.

"Clearly. It's always the cute gay ones."

"Who says you're cute?"

"Who says I'm not?"

We settle in for the marching band's epic Bruno Mars medley. That's all pep rallies are about, anyway: percussion and trumpets and losing ourselves in the groove of music we all know the words to.

AFTER SCHOOL, I SKIP THE game. I'm not in the mood to drive to an away game. School activities are usually excuses for more time with my friends, but not today. A loop of the meeting with Mrs. Scott has taken over my mind. A Technicolor, bobblehead nightmare, it replays like a gruesome YouTube compilation of country singers covering pop-rock songs.

The voiceover in the chaos of Mrs. Scott and her college recommendations is, "Who are you, Remy Cameron? Who the hell are you?" The narrator sounds eerily like Voldemort.

It leaves me feeling very un-peppy. I don't want to ruin the game for Brook and Lucy. Rio's locked herself away in *The Leaf*'s

offices—also known as Mr. Ahmed's Creative Writing classroom—to
work on her Mad Tagger piece.

That leaves me and the mostly empty student parking lot—well,
me and one student leaning against an atomic-blue Honda Civic. It's
an older model, but with subtle, newer modifications. A messenger
bag lies at his feet. He's wearing a denim jacket with his hair tucked
under an ordinary black beanie. I hesitate to approach him.

It's *just Ian.* Just a guy that's friends with Brook, who sits with us
at lunch, who likes matcha lattes, who thinks my dog is cute. We can
talk. How hard is that? We're Facebook friends now and that's big…
to grandparents and the government, but whatever.

"Cool car," I say when I'm close enough. "It's very—"

"Please, don't say Asian," says Ian, smiling. "Don't be *that person.*"

I blink a few times, stunned. "No." I shake my head. "It's very retro,
like your music. Like you."

Ian squints. He's not wearing his glasses. Why am I noticing *that*
instead of what the hell just came out of my mouth? He probably
thinks I insulted him.

Retro? What the actual—

"I mean, you're not old school or outdated or…" I pause, rubbing
my curls. "You're not. Retro is cool."

"Is it?"

"So cool," I say. "You're dope."

"Am I?"

"You are." Sweat tickles my hairline. "You're like, way cool."

"I'm not even marginally cool."

"You are! Cool hair. Cool car. Cool clothes." Like an idiot, I tick
everything off on my fingers. He's not even looking at me. His chin
is tipped up; sunlight bronzes his cheeks as he watches the clouds
edge across the blue like ivory glaciers.

My stomach bends and knots like a Cirque du Soleil performer. I lick the dryness from my mouth.

Ian's eyes lower. "Cool clothes? They're sort of—"

"Retro!" A laugh eases through my throat like honey. "You look hot in them." I don't even flinch. My mouth clearly has no chill, so I continue. "Wow. This is terrible. And offensive. The epitome of disaster."

Ian's mouth rises on one side. "Word vomit."

"There are research studies on that, right?"

"Extensive." Ian cocks his head. "I can send you a few links."

It's still warm for October. The breeze swirls between us bearing scarlet leaves and promises, with hints of apples and smoke. The sky is the perfect shade of blue. I love it. This awkward hush between Ian and I doesn't exist when our surroundings are filled with such unpredictable magic.

"Hey," I whisper, then clear my throat. "Do you wanna, like, go somewhere?"

"Somewhere?"

"It's the weekend, and we're two lame teenagers hanging out in a school parking lot."

"Speak for yourself." That solo dimple creases Ian's right cheek. "I'm not lame. I have it on good authority that I'm retro and cool and... hot?"

I look away. Fire prickles beneath my cheeks.

"Come on." Ian's fingers squeeze into my shoulder. "We can just, uh, drive."

"No destination in mind?"

"Somewhere for cool people like myself and lames like you, obviously."

My laugh is carried by the cozy-warm breeze. It's loud and geeky and I don't want to take it back.

OUR RIDE TO SOMEWHERE IS the easiest thirty minutes of silence I've ever experienced, mostly because it's filled with Ian's eclectic collection of '80s music. His phone is plugged into the aux chord; the interior of the car is filled with a steady flow of synthesizers and guitars and awesome.

"This is?" I ask.

"The Bangles," he replies, fingers drumming along the steering wheel.

"And that last song—"

"The Smiths."

I nod along, watching him sing under his breath. He's off-key but doesn't care. Ian's in his own world. I love how music does that—takes us to the middle of a packed arena with a spotlight and a microphone, even if we can't sing the ABCs without our voices cracking. Music doesn't just seep into our souls; it wraps careful fingers around our nerves and presses new life into them.

The windows are cracked open. Fresh air with the scent of orange leaves circulates through the interior while music escapes into the neighborhoods we cruise through. The sky is a canvas of melting pinks and blues. Clouds are brushed gold by the sinking sun. It's The Magic Hour.

A song kicks in, all acoustic guitar and bass. "I know this one!" I thump my palms on the dashboard. "George Michael!"

Ian's soft dimple reappears. He drives a manual transmission and shifts gears like a race car driver. I'm not coordinated enough to text and walk simultaneously. Watching Ian pump the clutch with one foot, using the other to gently press the gas pedal while his right hand eases us into a higher gear, all while he talks about music, is nirvanic.

"Careful," warns Ian, "you might become cool around me."

"Knowing who George Michael is isn't cool. It came with my gay card."

For the first time in a long time, I flinch. I don't know why. After the first six times, coming out became as basic as telling a stranger my name. It became a joke: "Hi, my name is Gay and my sexuality is Remy Cameron." Over and over, I've had to acknowledge my sexuality as if it's a warning. The thing is, you always have to come out. Every day. To new people, to people you've known forever, to people who keep trying to ignore it.

I'm this.

I'm that.

Yes, I'm still Insert Anything Other Than Straight Here. And maybe that bothers me a little some days. But I've gotten used to it. Until now. Now it feels like the first time I've acknowledged my sexuality as this thing that could possibly matter. I don't want it to be a big deal, but it's a *big* deal.

Ian's expression is neutral. His eyes stay on the road, but I watch him earnestly. "I haven't actually..." His words fade, cheeks reddening. "I haven't received my card in the mail yet. I just became a subscriber."

In GSA, we have monthly talks about coming out: how to be supportive, language and tones and how to offer encouragement in face of something scary and new. But those words fail me in this moment.

"Okay."

Ian inhales sharply, the skin around his eyes seems tighter.

"Hey," I whisper. My hand itches to touch his shoulder, to squeeze, but there are boundaries I've been taught not to cross unless invited. "It's cool. So, you're new to coming out—"

"I'm not out. Not too many people know, especially around here," interrupts Ian. His white knuckles are stark against the black steering wheel. "I'm new to realizing I'm gay? Or admitting it to myself? I dunno. I don't want that to be the spotlight people shine on me at Maplewood. Not now."

The music is softer. I don't know which one of us turned it down.

"I'm not saying it's bad or anything," Ian continues. "It's cool that people can come out. Be themselves. That the process is easy—"

"It's never easy," I blurt. I stare out the window, watching burnt-orange leaves dance over gray sidewalks. "Not even when you're fourteen and so sure of yourself."

Fourteen is a strange place to deal with sexuality and hormones and math. I managed two of those things—I still suck at math. And, really, who comes out as a freshman? In the middle of student council elections, no less.

Hi, Remy Cameron does. Happily. At least, I was happy for three fleeting seconds after I announced to the entire freshmen class in the auditorium, "Hello, I'm Remy Cameron. I'm running for class vice-president. And I'm gay. Any questions?"

I worked all night on that speech. And, holy shit, did I get a bunch of questions. None of them were about my proposed plan for better lunches, a mandatory state-wide recess for high school students, or Charlie Brown Day during homecoming's Spirit Week.

But there it was. Remy Cameron—the only black student running for student council, the only one wearing a bowtie and paint-speckled Vans with no socks, the only openly gay member of Maplewood's freshmen class.

We're back to silence, Ian and me. More music spills into the streets; the early evening wind seeps into the car. Our silence is heavy as a thick winter sweater. Can we roll back time five minutes? Is that possible?

"Sorry," Ian finally says. "Word vomit thingy."

"No, it's cool," I say, my knees pressed to the dashboard. "Like you. And it's…" My voice evens out, happier. "…cool that you've sent in for your gay card. The official laminated version is usually a little late."

"Fashionably late?"

"Look at you! Did you join the Facebook group already?"

Ian chuckles, and it's carried by whatever chilled-electronica anthem is on the radio.

We're stopped at a red light when he asks, nervously, "Do you think they'll turn me down?"

"Nah, the club isn't that exclusive." Laughter crawls into my mouth, vibrates in my nostrils. "Unlike everyone else, we're all about letting people be themselves. Retro losers like you included."

We crack up together. I crank the music as we finally reach Somewhere.

CHAPTER
ELEVEN

SOMEWHERE IS A SHOPPING PLAZA dominated by a Chipotle Mexican Grill, a rank Payless ShoeSource, and a Kroger grocery store. Small shops are stuffed between a travel agency, a sketchy dentist's office, an inauthentic New York-style pizza place. Aged gray exteriors with pops of color meant to attract wandering shoppers bleat: nothing exceptional.

"So, this is where the cool people hang?"

Ian's cheeks are lit like a rose-colored neon sign. "All the cool people come here."

Every parking space except for the ones outside Kroger is empty. "Obviously."

In the middle of Post-Apocalyptic Plaza is a small shop owned by a short, old Taiwanese-American man with a thin mustache and crinkles around his smile. He greets Ian with a hug and focused attention. Ian introduces him as Mr. Tsai. We shake hands.

I wander around while they catch up. Sweet and floral scents mix with a hint of cleaning product. Behind the counter, a girl with pink-streaked hair that matches her bubblegum reads a graphic novel. Her seafoam fingernails tap along to the music playing overhead. The menu lists drink after drink in hypnotic colors and cool fonts.

"Bubble tea?"

Ian sidles up on my left side. "Boba," he says. "Ever heard of it?" I shake my head.

He orders for us: matcha milk tea for himself, banana for me. Bubblegum Girl seems uninterested, but she gives Ian a shy wave as we leave. I raise an eyebrow—not one of those "He's Mine" ones—and her eyes quickly drop back to her graphic novel.

"My imo..." Ian pauses. We're walking aimlessly around the plaza. "...my Aunt Jilynn is bomb at making boba. She's got serious skills."

His eyes track passing cars, all fleeing the cracked pavement for the main road. He stirs his tea with the thick straw that's meant to capture all the tapioca balls at the bottom of the sea of green. The balls are this chewy-soft burst of tea when you mash them on your tongue. It's strange, at first, but a nice contrast to the sweetness of the milk.

Ian says, "She's hella cool. She's fluent in Korean and speaks some Chinese too."

The wind whispers a hello around us. I listen to Ian's voice. I love this part—unlocking little mysteries in someone new: their likes and dislikes, their secrets and joys.

"My Korean is out of practice." He says it with regret, as if that's something bad.

I nudge his elbow. "I wouldn't know."

"Aunt Jilynn notices everything," he tells me.

"Are you out to your family?" I ask, because I'm curious, because I want him to know I'm trustworthy.

Our lazy stroll stops in the middle of the parking lot. The sky is ripe peach, minutes from turning dark. Halogen lights click on, framing miles and miles of dark asphalt in waves of pale silver. The air has a perfect October bite to it—chilly but not uncomfortable. It's hoodie weather. A coat of Chipotle's spicy scents wraps around us.

"My parents know." Ian, all denim and soft hair peeking from under his beanie, stares at the gray outline of the moon. "That was interesting."

Simultaneously, we sip more tea. I give him space to elaborate.

"Dad doesn't say much about it. He doesn't seem bothered, though." His eyebrows drop; his teeth gnaw at his straw. "My mom prefers not to talk about it. It's how her family is. They're the old school, hard-working family. Head down, never do anything to attract attention. But I don't think that's who she is on the inside."

"Who is she?"

"The woman who dances to Prince by herself."

"I get that."

Ian lasers me with a doubtful stare.

"Seriously!" I try not to choke. "It's not easy, even with a family supportive as mine."

"Yeah?" Sarcasm has fled his voice, replaced by hope.

"My Aunt Sandra is a hardcore, church-every-Sunday, thou-shall-not southerner." I chuckle around my straw. "She's not the biggest queer-rights cheerleader. That doesn't mean she doesn't love me though. I know she does."

Ian's eyes are unreadable, but the slow-motion lift of his lips says enough. He understands.

We stay still. The moon doubles in size, or maybe it's the way my eyes try not to focus on Ian's mouth, and his eyelashes, and the way his hair catches on a breeze to sweep across the bridge of his nose. I'm trying not to focus on the sad, pathetic jolt of my heart. But something is happening. I can see it, highlighted in Technicolor-brilliance that nearly blinds me.

Ian's hand twitches by his side, so close to mine. And then he says, "Can I hold your hand?"

"What?"

He flinches. Louder, he asks, "Can I hold your hand?"

"You're actually *asking me*?" I'm confused. "I mean, people don't usually do that."

"I do."

Obviously. But I just blink at him a few times. I'm surprised.

"My halmeoni…" He stops, sucking in a breath. "That's grand-mother in Korean." He says it so proudly that I grin. "She taught me you should always ask for consent to touch someone, to hug them or hold their hand, anything. She didn't like being touched by strangers, not even hugs."

"But I'm not a stranger." Wait… am I a stranger? Does he see me that way?

"I know." The magic dimple reemerges. "But you're also someone who deserves to be asked if it's okay to hold your hand."

Deserve. It's the only word in my head. It tastes fuzzy but sweet like a slice of mango against the roof of my mouth. But I don't answer Ian's request with my voice. I reach out. He reaches back. Ian holds my hand.

My tea forgotten, I ask, "What's next?"

That wild, weaponized smile of Ian's emerges—locked, loaded, and I'm its target.

"I'm gonna die!"

"Not today!"

"Okay, but I'm gonna need immediate medical attention and one of those lifesaver bracelets and an unquestionably hot doctor to revive me!"

Under the shine of artificial lighting, we race each other in rickety Kroger grocery carts. The parking lot is a proverbial snooze-fest on a Friday night. Most of suburbia has found something better to do than shop for instant ramen noodles and half-priced energy drinks.

There aren't many obstacles to dodge other than the occasional parked minivan with its armor of bumper stickers. Every cart we commandeer has at least one wheel that sticks. Their carriages aren't meant to carry the weight of a bored high school teenager. And the pavement has far too many cracks for the velocity we're zooming at. It's not the safest idea, but it's the most recklessly fun activity I've ever done on a Friday.

"Car!" I screech.

"Emergency evasive maneuvers engaged!"

"What the hell does that mean?"

Ian grins and banks left. The cart tips, but we don't crash. We find a new path void of grandmas in big luxury sedans.

Wind whips against my face. We take turns howling like wolves at the top of our lungs. The intensity of the moment, of the night, of the *freedom* super-charges me in an unexpected way.

I never want this to end. Of course, it does, when a college-aged Kroger employee stomps up, barking. His face is filled with acne scars and the shame of minimum wage. He never gets close enough. We sprint away, laughing at the indigo sky; our sneakers pound the pavement. Our hands are twisted and twined until we reach Ian's car.

ANOTHER SONG: THIS ONE ABOUT dancing in the dark. It sums up my feelings right now. It's *everything*.

Lingering between my car and Ian's, we're tucked away in a corner of the school's parking lot, hovering in the night's shadows. Ian's car idles with the passenger window cracked enough to enjoy the heavy-synth and percussion.

"Bruce Springsteen," he tells me.

I bite the smile I'm barely hiding from him.

"It's Bruce Springsteen," he says, this time without the squeak but with equal jitteriness, as if the adrenaline from shopping-cart racing still bubbles in his cells. "Big tune. I really like it."

"Me too."

"Me too."

Seriously? Crayon-eating first-graders have better communication skills than us.

We should probably move. The flashlight-wielding rent-a-cops the school hires to watch over the grounds on weekends might spot us. Lucy texted me twenty minutes ago—the football team picked up an anemic victory. That means the team bus could roll in any minute with loud cheerleaders and adrenaline-junkie football players. My friends are meeting at a diner to celebrate the win. But my feet have decided this is where I should be.

"So."

"So," I repeat, breaths shallow. I rock back and forth on my heels. Ian mimics me. We can't hold each other's gaze for long. It's so cheesy, so like a middle school crush, back when liking someone was more fun and less traumatizing.

"I'm just gonna…" Ian jerks his head in the direction of his car, but the rest of his body doesn't cooperate. "If you're good, I mean. It's late. I don't have a curfew, but—"

"Word vomit," I tease.

Ian's nasal laugh riffs better than Bruce Springsteen's voice. My fingers itch to touch his hand, to test whether it's sweaty and hot enough to burn my skin. I want to ask his permission first. I want him to say yes with his eyes, mouth, his whole damn face.

"Yeah." He exhales and sags. "Word vomit."

He finally moves, but not to his car. He steps into my space. He's taller than I am, barely. I've been here before. With Dimi. With a guy at someone's sweet sixteen birthday party when I was fourteen and newly out of the closet and clueless about kissing a boy. I can handle this kind of awkward. He's right there. His breath is minty from his gum. His lips are wet from the quick brush of his tongue between breaths. I'm just waiting for him to ask...

But the kiss doesn't happen. Ian backs away, wide-eyed, shoulders tight. His shoes scuff on the pavement. A hint of lingering courage hooks the corners of his mouth up.

I'm not disappointed. I want to kiss Ian, to make him a permanent entry in my short list of kisses. But I'm also not going to be that guy who forces Ian out of the closet to his peers in the bus I can hear rattling up the road. Coming out should be organic, not a life or death situation.

I'm okay with an almost kiss. I'm also okay with Ian stealing my phone to program his number into my contacts. And I'm okay with the warm pressure of his fingertips against my knuckles for seven seconds too long after he hands my phone back.

I'm okay with all the above.

CHAPTER
TWELVE

WHO AM I? I'M REMY Cameron. I'm president of the GSA, an older brother, a best friend. I'm black, gay, and adopted. But none of these labels define me.

I am…

My fingers hover over the keyboard on my laptop. My headphones pump out POP ETC, dulling the noise in my brain. Beams of sunlight from the window dance across my knuckles, catch on my phone screen, reflect a rainbow across my vision. I'm close to full-blown Code Orange mode. Three crinkled Reese's wrappers lay by my elbow, soon to be joined by a fourth, then a fifth. The cursor on the screen doesn't move.

"Shit." *Delete, delete, delete.*

Why am I struggling? I've written papers before and poems and song lyrics. Before high school, that's all I ever did—write, write, write. It's how I got my feelings out. On the page, I felt alive.

Why is this so hard? Maybe it's because I know what this essay means for my final grade? Because I don't want Mrs. Scott to be right? Also, to get into Emory, I need recommendation letters. I'm positive Mr. Riley will write me one. Some of my other teachers too. But Ms. Amos is the goal. A respected former lecturer at Emory? There's no way they'd reject me with a letter from her. All I have to do is write a freaking essay about who I am.

I know who I am. *I do.*

My fingers pound the keys, a loud, uneven tapping like the opening of an EDM song gone wrong. I scowl.

> Who am I?
> I'm Remy Cameron, world's biggest underachiever, with zero clues about who he is. I'm destined to fail this class and never get into Emory. Thanks for the opportunity!
> The End.

"And that's how my high school career goes down in a blaze of glory," I whisper.

Clover's head pops up from the pile of blankets on my bed where she's been napping. It's a lazy, quiet Saturday. I can't hear Willow, though I know she's somewhere playing with action figures or constructing a kingdom from used cereal boxes. Mom's doing wedding things; Dad's doing lawn things.

My phone lights up—Rio's on FaceTime.

"My life is a disaster," I say instantly.

"That's old news," Rio says. "It's a gay-saster."

"That was horrible."

"Gay-tastrophe."

"You're not even trying today." I sigh.

"You're right." Damp hair that's starting to curl hangs in front of her face like a jungle of red vines. She scoops it away, her skin pinkened as if she's just showered. "How goes the Essay of Doom?"

Lucy and Rio tried several titles—my favorite being Category Seven Graduation Killer Essay, but they thought it was a mouthful—before settling on the Essay of Doom. I'm still not sure why. Maybe it's because Rio's parents are huge Indiana Jones junkies and Lucy has a secret thing for Harrison Ford, which is kind of gross.

"I remembered to put my name and date on it."

"That's more than deserving of a passing grade!" Rio says, rolling her eyes.

"Tell Ms. Amos that."

"I'd rather eat glass. Ms. Amos scares me."

"How is Mad Tagger hunting?"

"Horrible." She drops her phone to twist her hair into a knot on her head. I have a fuzzy view of the K-pop poster-collage tacked to her ceiling. Her only weakness besides bad indie rock is K-pop. "I need a break."

"Same."

"The usual spot?"

Since we were eleven, Rio and I have made a habit of walking to the playground at Maplewood Middle. When I needed to get my mind off whatever crush I was navigating poorly or when Rio needed somewhere else to be rather than her very empty house—her parents are traveling journalists, thoroughly dedicated to their job and not their daughter. We'd skip the merry-go-round for the swings or lay out in the middle of the grass and squint at the clouds until we could turn them into cartoon characters. It's our remedy.

"Sure." I peek over at Clover, her head tilted in anticipation. "Looks like Clover could use a breather."

"Yeah. The funk of a teenage boy's room probably isn't healthy," says Rio. "The rankness of dirty socks and unwashed boxers and seme—"

"Rio!" I squeal, hiding my face. When I peer through my fingers, she's shrugging.

"Good. You can help me narrow down this list of suspects."

I'm not in the mood to think about the Essay of Doom, but I'm definitely not in the mood for Rio's ranting over the Mad Tagger.

When Rio's obsessed with something, everything—and everyone—else becomes background. You can tell her a million different things, and she'll always find a way to bring the conversation back to her current fixation. She says I do the same with boys, but that's different—or maybe it's not.

"You want to help, right?" She sounds annoyed.

"Of course."

"You're not very convincing right now."

"Rio." I exhale softly, then force a mostly-believable look on my face. "I'm there. Mad Tagger. Whatever you need. Let's catch this criminal."

"Heck yeah!"

"I'll meet you there in five minutes," I tell her.

She grins in a way that should be banned between best friends. One of those "I'm about to snark" grins. "Maybe we'll run into Elijah Burke like the good old days, and you two can finally—"

I hang up on her before she can finish. Clover leaps off the bed as I grab my keys and earbuds. We're out the door before I can decide to fully disown Rio as a friend. I'll wait until after she buys me a Cold Body from Zombie Café.

* * *

"Max, how many times do I have to tell you that French toast is not a dinner dish?"

"It is in this house, Sandra."

The kitchen is filled with the clang of pans, the sizzle of butter in a skillet, and the heady aroma of ripe peaches—one of Dad's favorite recipes.

Dad is at the stove with a red apron cinched around his waist. A gift from Mom, it says "Trophy Husband."

Aunt Sandra, wearing a tragic prairie-rose-print blouse with her burnt-umber hair teased to the heavens, is sitting on a bar stool at the kitchen island. "I hardly see how it's considered a meal," she says, sighing. "It's not very southern either."

"Says the woman who faithfully shows up to the Waffle House every Sunday after the second morning service."

"Hush you. Waffle House is a staple of the south," Aunt Sandra argues. "The Lord has blessed those cooks for their service to the community."

"The Lord has blessed the toilet paper industry with job security, because what that food does to your insides—"

"It's quality dining, Max!"

"Silence your blasphemy, Sandra!" Dad says, barely holding in a snicker.

I watch fondly from the doorway. This is a family tradition—everyone crammed into the kitchen while Dad cooks and Aunt Sandra complains. It's never serious.

"You're lucky the sweet tea is fabulous," Aunt Sandra says before taking a healthy gulp from her glass. A lonely lemon wedge drowns in an amber sea. Condensation rolls down the side of the glass like raindrops on a windowpane. I shudder: sweet tea, an abomination.

Aunt Sandra turns to Mom. "Is this your contribution to today's sacrilegious meal, Abby?"

If there is one thing Aunt Sandra has mastered, it's the art of sarcasm with all the southern venom of a drunk debutante. Mom's from Savannah, which is deeper in Georgia than good old Athens, where Aunt Sandra lives. Mom's accent is a lithe, sweet melody. Aunt

Sandra's accent is as thick as molasses. She's as true-blue southern as that *Golden Girls* character Dad sometimes watches on late-night TV.

"It sure is," Mom replies, happily. "Sorry I burnt the quiche and over-seasoned the deviled eggs, Sandy."

"It's *Sandra*, suga."

"Oh, I know," Mom says with a perfectly timed Disney-princess wink.

Mom's slightly better than Aunt Sandra at sweet bitchiness, probably because Mom's one of seven children. Verbal warfare was a means of survival for her.

Aunt Sandra ignores Mom. "I certainly hope there's pecan pie later." She hasn't met a pie she didn't like. Or devoured in one sitting.

"I could run to Publix for some," I offer.

"The devil is a lie!" Aunt Sandra exclaims, hand to her heaving chest. She's so extra, and it's not just the overuse of eye shadow and mascara. "No true southerner eats store-bought pecan pie, Remy."

I wisely choose not to inform Aunt Sandra that she did *indeed* eat store-bought pie last summer at Dad's birthday party. I'm saving that bombshell for another Christmas when Aunt Sandra deems a poorly fitting reindeer sweater and a twenty-dollar bill are acceptable gifts.

"And, Max, my word, look at my sweet nephew!" Aunt Sandra's chunky gold bracelets clank as she waves a hand at me. "He's barely a hundred pounds sopped in gravy. Heavenly Father! He doesn't need French toast for dinner; he needs a healthy plate of cornbread and country-fried steak and collard greens."

Dad chuckles. "Those are things *you* want—"

"I'm serious. He's gorgeous, but give him a biscuit."

"I'm fine, Aunt Sandra," I say through my teeth.

"Yes, you are," Aunt Sandra confirms, smiling too hard. "You're perfect. I'm just teasing."

I rub anxiously at my curls; heat prickles my neck. I hate this topic. Message received: I'm not built like Brook or toned like Jayden. But I can't change that. I've *tried*. It's this epically loud reminder that my anatomy isn't like my parents'.

I know nothing about my birth parents' genealogy. Maybe my father was weedy. Maybe my mother was tall with a round jaw. Maybe there are three generations of Remy Cameron lookalikes all over Georgia; I'll never know.

My birth mother is dead, a too-true fact I learned from my parents when I was in kindergarten thanks to douchebag-in-training David Waller yelling that my carefully crayon-drawn family portrait was "*Wrong! You can't be* brown *and your parents are* peach!" in the middle of class. But he was incorrect. I'd used *apricot* for my parents and I was damn proud of it. Any self-respecting five-year-old southerner knows peach is for fruit, not skin tones.

David Waller couldn't even color in the lines, so his authority on the matter was nil. Also, Katie colored her parents purple, and that was acceptable.

But I didn't understand. My parents were mine. I was theirs. Of course, we could be different colors and still belong to each other. Right?

My teacher, Mr. Allen, couldn't answer that question. He beamed at me before announcing it was time for recess. Later, he sent me home with a note decorated in gold stars for my parents—REMY IS CURIOUS ABOUT HIS FAMILY TREE.

That's how I found out. Over a dinner of chicken nuggets, apple slices, and reality, my dad told me everything while my mom sat quietly, wringing her napkin and blinking way too much.

I was adopted. My birth mother was dead. My birth father? Who knows?

It's always been me, Remy, the one and only.

There were too many days and nights when I wanted to know more, but I never asked. I was scared. What if all my questions made my parents want me less? What if those answers made me angry? Resentful? Those feelings—the blind inquisitiveness about my heritage—faded eventually. Everything does when you're five-years-old.

I didn't know those other parents. I'm a Cameron. This is my family. But, right now, that familiar crippling sensation chases the sweat down my spine. I'm uncomfortable. I need out.

On my way to the backdoor, I stop by the breakfast table, where Willow sits on her knees in a chair. I peek over her shoulder. She's using erasable markers to draw on Mom's old save-the-date postcards. A superhero, I think? It's part-dog, part-bird with a cape. Willow's imagination is out there.

"Good job, Twinkle Toes." I peck her temple.

Clover chases me out the backdoor.

THE WORLD IS STARTING OVER. That's how it looks from my current view. Dad and Uncle Dawson built this wooden patio four years ago in a summer of sweat and shouting and shared beers with two-too-many close-calls at the emergency room. The patio is slightly raised, enough for my feet to dangle off the edge, but barely stretches into our backyard. A perfect place for barbeques and sitting.

Dad calls it his Home Depot victory. It's a cool place to soak up sun in the spring, so I'm willing to call it whatever Dad wants.

Clover chases an old, drool-soaked tennis ball I toss for her. Tail wagging ecstatically, she brings it back. We love this game, though it never lasts long. But it's a moment of innocence—a boy and his dog, a bond not explained by words. I'm in love with how, sometimes, we don't need words for relationships to exist, just a look, a trust, an action.

Clover quits to lay out in the sun. I can't blame her. I recline on my hands to look at the sky. I love how the sky can look like the sea—blue and endless and hopeful—and how water can look like the sky—quiet and gentle and beautiful. My mind is nothing like either of those things. It's in a tsunami brought on by three earthquakes: the things Aunt Sandra said and Mrs. Scott's expectations and the Essay of Doom.

Who is Remy Cameron? Who, who, who?

How the hell am I supposed to know if I don't know a damn thing about where I come from? About the people who created me? If I knew, would I be someone different? Would I be more like Father X rather than Dad?

"Is this hiding spot from the boring adults exclusive to cool teens or is anyone allowed?"

I look up. There he is standing over me, Uncle Dawson: perfectly straight, pale-blonde hair and acorn-brown eyes squished by his crooked smile. Everything about him is the opposite of Aunt Sandra and Dad; he has sharp features and is tall but thin, a marathon runner's build.

I grin as though the sun lights me from the inside out. "Uncle D!"

"Remy!"

He settles next to me; his longer legs reach into the grass. "C'mere Clover!" Uncle D is one of the few people Clover eagerly waddles to; her head flops into his lap. Uncle D is also someone who doesn't need words. He likes quiet. I do too, in doses.

The afternoon sun flicks gold bars across the yard's yellowing-green grass and against the cedarwood fence. Giant octagons of light brush over the swing set I helped Dad put together on Willow's fourth birthday. A funnel of leaves shakes free from the sugar maple's limbs like a tornado made of fire.

We breathe. We sit in quiet. Uncle D, Clover, and I exist.

"How's school going?"

"Come on, Uncle D." I nudge our shoulders together. "We don't talk about boring crap like that."

"You're right. We don't."

As far as cool points go, Uncle D has earned them all. He skips the usual adult-to-teen topics—school and money and responsibility—to talk about the latest comic-book movie or my new music finds. He was the first adult to give me The Talk, the first adult to make sure I understood what it meant to be safe, to know where to find condoms, to know about the importance of consent.

"Let's talk about boys."

"They suck," I moan.

Uncle D lifts an eyebrow. I shudder. That's right—The Talk also came with an e-mail, an online tutorial about using protection during oral attached.

"I mean, they're the worst."

"Some days."

"Some days," I agree, forcibly ejecting any thoughts of Ian. He's not an option. Ian is just a guy I'm not getting attached to.

"We're not rekindling things with Dimi, then?"

There's that "we" thing adults love to use again. No offense to Uncle D, but when Dimi took my heart into his hands like paper— light, easy to shape, easier to rip apart and discard—there was no *we* to stop the half-hour of shaking under a lukewarm shower. *We* didn't help me get out of bed every morning when all I wanted to do was sleep away the pain. *We* didn't wipe away all those tears, day after day. There was only me.

"Nope," I say. I can feel him studying me. "He's moved on."

"Asshole."

"Uncle D!" I say, partly shocked, but also truly laughing.

"He is."

I don't argue. I used to stand up for Dimi after he broke up with me, because the memories of his affection and attention clouded everything else, because I blamed myself for the breakup. It's funny how having your heartbroken is always your own fault at first.

I redirect our conversation: "How are things with Uncle Gabe?"

Uncle D's reaction is instant. Brown eyes light up like sunlight pouring through a glass of stout. An upward curve pulls at his mouth. The push of his cheeks forms deep crinkles by his eyes. It's the kind of contagious thing that makes my stupid heart roar.

"Good. Things are *really* good."

Our shoulders bump again. I watch the way Uncle D rubs his hands together. His chin is lowered, his mouth twitches. He's holding something in, something big, something important like—

"Oh my god, Uncle D!"

He flinches.

"Are you gonna propo—"

A wild look passes over his face. "Christ almighty, don't let your Aunt Sandra hear you take the Lord's name in vain."

We grin at each other. Uncle D leans forward, legs pulled to his chest, elbows on his knees. He's an awkward grasshopper—like me, but not.

"It's about time, isn't it? Eight years seems long enough, right?"

"Eight *months* is a long time for me, Uncle D."

In Uncle D's eyes, I can see lightning and shadows; love and fear. A million things I thought I knew from being with Dimi, but I don't. Not like Uncle D.

"You're really going to pop the question?" I ask.

"I—" He cuts himself off as if the words are there, but he's scared to set them free too soon. "Yeah."

"Yeah? That's cool."

"You think so?"

"Uncle Gabe is gonna cry."

"I might too."

We exhale together, happy and content. I want to stay here forever.

I was too young to understand the impact of Uncle D's coming out. He was in his mid-twenties; I was transitioning from crayons to markers. I didn't know the doors he was opening or the wars he fought inside himself. He's not like my dad or Aunt Sandra. Uncle D lives in the quiet spaces rather than in the bright and loud center like his siblings. All my life, it's as though Uncle D was in a battle with who he was and who he wasn't.

Then Uncle Gabriel came around. And Uncle D became this Technicolor version of himself. It was like that old movie, *the Wizard of Oz*, where everything suddenly transitions from black-and-white to vibrant and captivating color. Uncle Gabriel is amazing. He's always the first to make a joke, he was always the one to let me climb on his back for a stroll through the park. Because of them, gay wasn't a word I had to incorporate into my vocabulary to understand someone who was different. It just existed, free and normal. I wonder if, for me, being queer will ever mean being free, being anything other than different.

"Hey," whispers Uncle D, nudging my knee, "Another guy will come around."

"No, Uncle D, that's *not* the plan."

"It's not?"

"No other boys. No relationships."

Uncle D rolls his eyes.

"I'm seventeen, and it feels like that's all I am. Boys. Crushes. Dimi." I glare at the grass as the wind bends it. "That's not who I want to be." And then, because my mouth is on a roll and my nerves are free-falling, I say, "I don't know who I am. There's this essay for AP Lit where I'm supposed to figure all this shit out, but—"

Uncle D waits, patient and quiet.

"I have no effing clue." I press my bare feet into the grass, just to feel the prickle against my skin. To absorb the warmth, push back the cold clenching my bones.

Uncle D's hand squeezes my shoulder, then he says, "None of this is easy, Remy."

"Is it ever?"

"Sometimes."

"How do I know who I am if I don't know who I was?" I don't know if that question is for Uncle D or myself, but it's out in the open, sitting between us like Clover.

"Remy." Uncle D's voice is careful, protective. This is Uncle D, who sat outside my middle school for hours when he heard a few students were giving me hell for being different, for being the black kid with blue eyes that liked to wear his pink "Girls Are Awesome" T-shirt once a week.

"One essay doesn't define you," he finally says. "It doesn't."

But what does? I want to ask. Those three words take up so much space in my chest, I don't know how to shove them out. I lower my head.

Uncle D's hand rests on the back of my neck; his thumb rests behind my left ear. It's so familiar. When I came out to him, for the longest time, we sat in silence, and he let me cry. He let me breathe. Then Uncle D grabbed a book from my desk and read to me. I don't remember what the book was about or who wrote it. I only remember

Uncle D's thick accent wrapping around the words. He held me the way Grandpa did. I remember his melodic voice and my shaky breaths.

"Talk to your dad, Remy," he whispers now. "He can—just talk to him." His voice trails off as if to guard a secret, like an answer to my question that he can't give.

The back door swings open, and there's Dad, grinning. "It's game time, boys!"

Uncle D turns to look at my dad. I do too. He's proudly wearing a red sweatshirt with a giant "G" stamped in the middle: University of Georgia, Dad's alma mater. He's one of those diehard UGA fans; he never misses a game of any kind. I swear Dad bleeds black and Bulldog red. It took him a while to accept that I wanted to attend Emory instead of UGA. I think he was hoping I'd carry on the legacy of Cameron men there. But I never planned to. UGA was nowhere on my radar.

I catch Dad's eyes, his expression. There's a little, but noticeable, twitch to his mouth, something that releases softness like a stray pencil mark on a clean sheet of paper. I can't quite put a finger on it until Dad's eyes dance between me and Uncle D.

Dad and I have always been close, same tastes in food, same sense of humor. But my relationship with Uncle D is different. Dad loves me, but Uncle D *gets* me. It's hard to explain. Harder to observe my dad watching us with this small ripple in his kind features, this barely noticeable jolt of jealousy. I don't think Dad knows it's there, not consciously. I wonder if Uncle D sees it too. Dad blinks a few times, then exhales. And it's gone.

"Okay, okay." Uncle D stands, dusting off his jeans. "Let the suffering begin."

Dad blanches, then smirks. "Come on D, say it."

"I'm not saying it."

"Bro, you have to!"

Sighing, Uncle D mumbles, "Gooooo Dawgs."

"There you go. Also, the French toast is done."

Uncle D's smile is renewed. "You should've led with that, Max!" They hook their arms around each other. Uncle D is taller, but Dad's bulkier. Their voices echo in the kitchen as they step inside.

I wait a few seconds. I'm not anxious to watch another football game or listen to Aunt Sandra's choir-worthy rendition of "The Star-Spangled Banner." My phone chirps. It's probably Rio or Lucy. Or it could be Ian messaging me via Facebook.

Nope. I'm determined not to get my hopes up—or any part of my body—about Ian Park.

I punch in my passcode and find a Facebook notification. It's a message from Free Williams. I almost forgot I accepted her friend request. And I still have no clue who she is. We have zero mutual friends; no common interests, and no geographical connection besides Atlanta.

But there's her message: an old, discolored Polaroid photo of a woman cradling an infant. She has deep-brown skin, an afro, a round jaw. She's looking down. In her arms, is a baby with fawn complexion and Dopey ears.

Tiny curls.

Very blue eyes.

Underneath is another message: "Do you remember her?"

CHAPTER THIRTEEN

"THAT'S ENOUGH TENNESSEE WILLIAMS FOR the day," Ms. Amos announces.

A choir of relieved sighs breaks out around the classroom. Paperbacks shut; students shuffle at their desks. I remain slumped, ready to brain myself on my desk. It's not that Tennessee Williams isn't *interesting*; I'm simply not interested.

What I am is squirmy, anxious. I'm a timebomb. I'm thoughts and a blank mind simultaneously. I haven't checked my Facebook in the past hour—not the way I did thirty-six times on Sunday; yes, I counted—but my fingers are twitchy. My phone burns in my pocket.

Do you remember her?

Do you remember her?

Do you freaking *remember her?*

Those four words are all I know. They are my beginning and end. Even now, as I trace a finger across the damaged spine of my book, those four words corrupt my cells, amplify the adrenaline in my blood. I can't stop jiggling my leg or looking around the room as though someone can see my twisted-up organs showing through my clothes.

The universe is screaming, "Remy Cameron, meet your new best friend, Hyperbole."

Two minutes remain until the bell. I want this class to end. I want to shove my earbuds in, crank up anything fast and loud, and force the noise in my head to evaporate.

"Don't forget," Ms. Amos begins, met by the quiet groans of my peers, "your essay presentations must include any type of medium you choose."

Oh, yes. Ms. Amos's last-minute addition to my educational hell. Each essay will be shared with the class in the form of a presentation, with, like, charts or artwork or photos.

"*Medium*? Wasn't that a horrible TV show cancelled before I was born?" jokes Ford. "Can we cancel this essay too?"

Ms. Amos, always prepared for douche-canoes like Ford, crosses her arms. "I'm especially excited about your essay, Mr. Turner. I imagine the number of failed comedians in your family's lineage must be staggering."

The bell finally rings. Ford shoots Ms. Amos a disingenuous grin before high-stepping out the door.

Chloe stops at my desk. "I'm thinking about asking Nancy to help me. She does incredible presentations for clients all the time."

Nancy is one of Jayden's moms. She's a graphic designer. The story is, she got hired to help redesign Tori's, Jayden's other mom, auto garage space. A real romantic comedy ensued with design feuds and accidental coffee dates and a rooftop proposal. I'm a sucker for the way Jayden tells it.

Jayden's moms love Chloe. Chloe loves Jayden's moms. They live in a happy, rainbow-coated world. And Chloe never misses an opportunity to remind everyone of this. It's so unrealistic. Or maybe it doesn't fit the reality shown to any of us outside of TV and movies. I'm not jealous. I'm not. But maybe I am?

Darcy pauses by my desk, giving us a long look before pushing by Chloe with a huff.

"O-kay," says Chloe.

"I'm gonna use music," Zac says, shrugging on his backpack. "I'm putting together a playlist. EDM heaven."

Dear baby Jesus, no one loves electronic dance music as aggressively as Zac Liu. People like that can't be trusted.

"No Chainsmokers," demands Chloe. "We deserve better. *The world* deserves better."

"I'm doing artsy stuff," Sara says. She rubs her cheek. The back of her hand is covered in fading mehndi; the intricate designs curl to the inside of her wrist. "I need to find a boss artist to collaborate with."

"Ian's amazing. You should see his notebook," Chloe says.

"Is he?"

"A-ma-zing. Ask him to help."

"Maybe I will."

Maybe I hope this conversation dies a quick, silent death. I'm carefully avoiding eye contact with everyone. I don't really have an opinion. I haven't seen anything Ian's done except the chalk artwork for Zombie Café. Plus, my input would probably be a bunch of babbling when it comes to Ian. All I think about is that *almost kiss* with him and how nothing remotely close to that has happened since.

Ms. Amos hovers at her desk after everyone leaves. I take my time stuffing my backpack with my tattered paperback, notebook, and highlighter. Briefly, I glance at my phone—no activity, thankfully.

Ms. Amos is watching me. A molecule of panic wiggles down my spine.

"Everything okay, Mr. Cameron?"

"Everything's great," I lie.

Out of all my teachers, Ms. Amos is the most approachable. Well, next to Mr. Riley. She's professional, but her humor and glowing energy removes that untouchable factor a lot of teachers carry.

"Great is such an underwhelming word," Ms. Amos says.

"Fantastic?"

"Weak."

"First-rate?"

"That's dated, don't you think?" She crosses to the front of her desk, head cocked. "I'd accept 'killer,' though."

I snort, then stand, pulling on my backpack.

"Also, remind me not to give you any speaking parts when we do *A Streetcar Named Desire*," she adds. "A thespian, you are not."

To humor her, I gasp noisily, hand to my chest. She's right. In our elementary production of *Winnie-the-Pooh*, I made a very convincing tree.

"It's just the…" I shake my head.

"Are you struggling with the assignment?" Ms. Amos finally asks.

Uh, hello! Respectfully, I don't vocalize that. A quick shrug is my response.

"What about it?"

"Everything?"

"Everything?"

I make a face. "I want it to be perfect. There's so much riding on this essay."

"Is there?"

I almost groan. What is it about adults and turning everything you're trying to tell them into a question?

"I need it to be perfect," I say, hands squeezed at my sides. "But I don't know where to start."

"When I lack a clear view of my writing's endgame, I look to others," Ms. Amos says. "Reading helps. Find another space for your brain to exist for a while."

"Like?"

"For me? Poetry. Do you know Benjamin Alire Sáenz?"

I shake my head. She doesn't look disappointed.

"He's an extraordinary author, but it's his poetry that makes the battles inside of me subside."

Ms. Amos's face holds a richness that only exists in sunsets and the first bite of ripe fruit. I've seen it before. Any opportunity to speak about her heritage—about where she comes from and those who paved the way for her—ignites this supernova from deep inside her. It's beautiful, unfolding across her features and blossoming in the way she talks with passion, pride.

"He creates art with his words," she continues. "I feel a sense of importance, knowing someone like him exists. As if he understands me. In those words, I see that I am who I am for a reason, not by choice."

I take her words in. We are who we are for a reason; it's not a choice. I don't know how to digest it all, so I stay silent.

"Find your art, Mr. Cameron. Your medium." She walks to the other side of her desk and sits. She rearranges papers, grabs a pen. "Life inspires art, but don't forget our art inspires life too. It's an endless circle."

"An infinite loop?"

She raises an eyebrow as if she doesn't comprehend.

"Sorry, my dad works in computers." I point at my temple, "I'm a walking databank of useless tech knowledge and vocab."

"We create things. What we create changes something in someone else, Mr. Cameron. Who you are isn't found in one single space."

I bite my lip.

She cocks her head. "Why is this essay so important?"

"I need to pass this class."

"Not that I should divulge this kind of information, but according to my records, you're doing quite well," Ms. Amos says, smirking— that you-already-know-this smirk.

"Also, I need this essay for…" I pause, chest tight. "…college. I want to go to Emory College of Arts and Science."

"What a lovely place."

"There's an admissions essay…"

She nods knowingly. "Emory is very selective." She sounds eerily like Mrs. Scott. Then she adds, "But you're still a junior, Mr. Cameron. You have time. This essay isn't about you impressing Emory. It's not about being perfect."

I can't tell her the reason I need to be perfect is to impress *her*, not just for a recommendation letter, but because Ms. Amos, with her love for poetry and great authors and the way she lights up about where she comes from and where she's going, has something I admire, something I want for myself. I can't tell her that when I admire and respect someone, I try a million times harder to impress them.

I finally say, "Okay."

I'm an old computer, trying to recycle new information and turn it into a solution. I don't tell her that the other reason I need to ace this essay is because I refuse to be what Mrs. Scott expects me to be.

But who do I expect myself to be?

* * *

THIS IS THE LAST PLACE I should be after school. The bleachers near the large green lawn where the soccer team practices used to be my second home. I'm huddled with my knees close to my chest. My thin, pink waffle sweater barely keeps the bite of mid-October breeze from my skin. The sleeves are pulled over my knuckles. I can feel the bleacher's cool steel through my jeans. The afternoon air tastes of sap from the neighboring pine trees, a burst of allspice, and a hint of tart Granny Smith apples.

My earbuds pump music into my bloodstream. I try not to think about Facebook, about logging onto my messages to reread the one from Free.

Do you remember her?

The photo plays like grainy footage in my brain: those eyes, that curly afro. Part of me feels as if I *should* remember her. She looks almost like me.

Every time I start to type a reply, I wonder if Free sees the three ellipses appear, then disappear. Has she thought about asking me again?

I unlock my screen, check the time. Mom and Willow are having a mommy-daughter Cinnabon date. Lucy's off being Ultra Class President. The last I heard from Rio, it was Mad Tagger this, Mad Tagger that.

I watch the soccer team. A dozen boys run around in tiny shorts, knocking soccer balls into the net—sweat and sticky athletic tops and Gatorade. And then there's Dimi.

I spent exactly ninety-nine-point-too-much percent of my time in these bleachers watching Dimi.

Under the lazy sun slumped against an ageing blue sky, his strong jaw and square shoulders look good. His brown hair sits flat against his head. He's talking to Hugh and Malcolm. They playfully jab each other's shoulders. When Dimi and I were together, I'd lean against the fence and talk to Malcolm between practice drills. He'd tell me about the girls he was into but was too shy to ask out. I was "in" with this crowd.

Not anymore. Most of these guys barely look me in the eye when we pass in the hallways. As if I'm the one who did something wrong. That's the thing, Dimi was my world for months and months. Then I was nothing. An ex-boyfriend.

To some of the jock-assholes: "Dimi's ex-girlfriend." That guy who used to be with Dimitar Antov. I wonder, is that who I am? Am I who I fall in love with?

"Haven't you earned an upgrade from this crowd yet?"

Brook bounds up the bleachers toward me. His bony elbow nudges me. He has this infectious grin—huge and eye-scrunching with rows of perfectly white teeth. It's a nice juxtaposition to the popped collar of his letterman jacket and the humongous headphones hugging his jaw.

"Yeah." I sigh. "No. I dunno."

"Come on, little dude." Brook always calls me that. He's only a year older than me and a few inches taller. But I never complain. Secretly, I think it fits.

"Maybe this is just my thinking spot?"

Brook shoots me a doubtful look. "Little dude," he starts, shaking his head, "Even Silver is too fly for these losers."

It's true. Silver tries to hide in the shadows of the trees to smoke. None of the coaches ever see him, and that's not a compliment to his covert skills; it's just their obliviousness to anything not green, black, or white.

Silver's the quietly observant type. He's too cool for anyone, me included. The students have a running bet that he'll be that guy who drops out, becomes a famous actor, and destroys all evidence he attended Maplewood High. Good for him.

Brook nudges me again. "So, what's up with you?"

"What's up with *me*?" I try—and fail—to ignore the unearthly high-pitch of my voice on that last word.

"This isn't you." He waves a hand around my face. "Where's the super-social, livewire I've seen the past two years? He's missing."

"Have you filed a report with Lieutenant Parker yet?"

"Nope."

"You should." I shove a hand into my untamed curls. "But if you're gonna turn me into one of those social media Missing Persons posts, please only use photos from the fourth-grade Christmas pageant."

"Why?"

"Because I was the lead elf and looked damn good in candy-cane socks and green Converse!"

Brook's laugh booms, scaring a few birds. Mine is quieter, but the unraveling knots in the pit of my stomach feel good—nauseating, but good.

"There he is."

I try to duck away when Brook goes to scrub my curls, but he wrestles me, and my halfhearted fight dies.

The unspoken trust between Brook and I started long before Lucy and his extreme make-out sessions, before he invaded our lunch table with his husky voice and video game obsessions. Circa freshman year, we didn't know each other, but that first moment of eye contact, the head-nod in the hallway said it all. It's the same kindred connection I have with Janelle Peterson and the same one Brook shares with Charles Barnett.

That connection is how the four of us were the first to find Imani Donaldson, a freshman, the Monday after her brother was shot and killed in a misunderstanding at a club downtown the second week of school. We were the only five black students at Maplewood, huddled in a corner, comforting one of our own. The silent "we're in this together" exists like plasma in our blood. When I came out, Brook didn't blink an eye. He saw me in the hallways, shrunken and nervous, and walked right up to me for a fist bump and a "you've got this" that was said with his eyes before he walked on.

"What's the story, little dude?"

Before I can answer—and I still don't have anything acceptable to say that won't sound as though I'm utterly *lost* right now—he adds, "And this is me asking. Lucy didn't put me up to anything."

"That makes it sound like she did."

"She didn't."

I believe him. *Unspoken trust.* "Nothing big." Everything feels big right now. My cold fingers curl tightly around my phone. The strains of some indie pop song beats through my earbuds. I want to curl into the melody, let the lyrics ink across my skin—any means of escape.

I angle my body in Brook's direction. "Who's your favorite music artist?"

He gives me a long look before he replies, "Childish Gambino," as if my out-of-nowhere question doesn't faze him. That's the thing about Brook—he's so easy-going. He's not overly-curious. He's just walking the tracks of life, never worried about the train slamming into him.

"Janelle Monae is dope too," he says, smiling. "But my favorite is Sugarland."

I blink at him a few times. "What in the actual eff? *Sugarland*?" There goes my voice again, all screechy and abnormal.

"Sugarland."

"You're kidding."

"What?" Brook isn't the least bit self-conscious about this confession.

"Nothing."

"You don't like them?"

"I don't *know* them." I mean, I do. We live in Georgia. During the summer, there's this seriously incredible laser show at Stone Mountain Park, a theme park set around a rock that has three Confederate soldiers carved into its peak. The lasers illustrate historical events and cartoony stories and patriotic themes across the rock's surface while people sit on a giant lawn to watch. They always play randomly popular country songs during the performance. So, I know a few country musicians, but not really.

I don't like to throw around stereotypes, to box anyone into a package not meant for them but Brook's never come off as someone who'd call country music his jam.

"Oh, little dude," Brook's pulling out his phone, opening YouTube after he's keyed in the passcode, "You haven't lived until you've heard 'Stay' live."

Full disclosure: Brook's right. I can't quite get my mouth to tell him, but the strum of an acoustic guitar accompanied by a raspy voice wrapping around broken emotion wrecks me. Maybe my shaky inhale after the song ends tells him. Maybe I'm thinking about Dimi.

"This is the stuff my pops raised me on," Brook tells me. "Willie and Loretta Lynn. Grassroots music. It wasn't a good day in our house if you couldn't bob your head to Garth Brooks." His expression is flooded with honesty and joy. As if someone took a memory of his, unfolded it, pressed out all the wrinkles, and let him hold it again.

"Now my G'ma…" He reclines onto the seats behind us. "…she played nothing but gospel music. Every day. I didn't miss a Sunday of Mississippi Mass Choir or Shirley Caesar. On my pop's birthday, she plays Aretha Franklin's version of 'Amazing Grace,' and we just sit together. We hold hands and listen."

Lucy told me Brook's dad died young from heart disease. That's the reason he's so into sports. He eats healthier than any teenager I know and savors every second of life. His dad's death is also why Brook does everything his mom asks him to. He doesn't want to disappoint her. To leave her empty-handed. The weight a child carries to impress a parent is bigger than anyone acknowledges.

"Country music and gospel?" I ask.

"And hip-hop."

"That's all over the place."

Brook shrugs, but it's carefree. "I don't let my music tastes define me."

"Music doesn't define us," I echo, my voice small but dying to be confident.

Brook's legs stretch out to the bleachers below. He's an endless road of limbs and smiles. "You like that one band—"

"POP ETC," I confirm.

"Yeah, them." He makes a weird face, then says, "But that's not all you are, right?"

"Nope."

"I mean, I've heard the stuff you listen to and, good for you, but that's not my thing. So what? It's part of what makes you Remy, but not all of it."

"Because music doesn't define us."

"Exactly!" He claps, excitedly. "It's a fraction of who we are, right now. It'll change."

He's right again. I went through a minor—underlined and bolded—showtunes phase. It lasted a summer.

"These things come and go. People come and go." He's motioning toward the field, toward Dimi. "They don't make up who we are."

"Do you know who you're meant to be?" I ask.

"What do you mean?"

"I—" Everything halts in my voice. The brakes slam on my thoughts.

I can't seem to explain it to him, to ask the questions I want to ask, because Brook, the country-loving, gospel-jamming, happy-as-hell guy always seems to know who he is, who he's meant to be. Lucy, as uncertain as she is about the SATs, is confident in everything else about herself. Nothing rattles Rio from being Rio.

"Never mind," I whisper.

Autumn wind whistles between us. The soccer team huddles amid laughter and noise and water bottles. Dimi is in the center. All I see is the guy who was my first love, who broke my heart. The guy who is now a *was* and no longer a *is*.

Brook stands. "I've gotta run. Can't miss the bus or Ma will kick my ass."

During the day, Brook's mom works at a bank. She spends her evenings picking up shifts at a Waffle House across town. He catches the bus there every day he's not working at the movie theatre. Brook's mom has one goal: Keep him at Maplewood so he can earn an athletic scholarship. She has a great relationship with Coach Park. Everyone's confident Brook, all-star swimmer three years now, is headed to a good swim program and possibly the Olympics. I can't wait to cheer him on.

At the bottom of the bleachers, he turns, then says, "A little bird says you haven't called him yet?"

"A little bird?"

"Okay," he chuckles, "Ian's more like a pelican."

Every muscle in my face reacts to the sound of Ian's name.

"He's kind of weird," I say.

"A good weird."

"A good weird." I agree, and when did this blushing thing become such a problem? Also, that last crack in my voice? Uncalled for.

"He was totally casual when he said it," Brook says, his tone betraying him.

"Totally casual?"

"Mostly." Then Brook gets serious, which usually frightens underclassmen, but I've seen this dude cry during Pixar movies. I'm immune. He says, "As his best friend, I'm authorized to harass you about these things."

"What things?"

"You know, *things*."

"Our friendship?"

"Yes, that." Brook sighs loudly with his hands shoved into his jacket pockets. "But, also, because I've been his best friend for five years, so I know other things."

I raise an eyebrow. *Other things* is a loose term, and I'm not about to out Ian if his best friend isn't going to be clear.

Brook drags a hand down his face. He hesitates. "My weird-but-hilarious best friend has a boner for you. I'm politely—but in an I-will-kick-your-ass-if-you-play-him way—asking you to consider calling or texting him. Sometime soonish."

I choke on my spit. Did Brook just respectfully threaten bodily harm? And why is my heart jumping like a kid ten seconds from overdosing on sugar in one of those bouncy houses?

"I, uh—" No, no, no. I'm not having this conversation. Remy Cameron is not dating this year.

But Brook's foot taps on the grass, so I say, "Okay."

"Okay? Seriously?"

"I'll text."

"Wow. Didn't think that would work."

My jaw drops, eyes widening. "You did just threaten to crush me like a Coke can."

"I'd never do it," Brook admits. "Lucy is savage when it comes to you."

We share an amused look. It's true. But out of all the guys Lucy's dated, which isn't many, I like Brook best. I think he feels the same about me. He starts toward the large oak tree where the bus stops but pauses. "This is all off the record, little dude."

"Of course."

"He's a weirdo, but in a good way, I promise."

It doesn't take much effort for me to believe Brook. Unspoken trust. But I give him a nod for assurance, and then he's gone. And I'm left on the bleachers, reconsidering my whole "Thou shall not date this year" philosophy.

All because of Ian Park.

CHAPTER
FOURTEEN

Message from Remy Cameron
    Is that me?
    Sent Oct 29 10:10 a.m.

    Message from Free Williams
    Yes. And your mother. Do you remember her?
    Sent Oct 29 10:41 a.m.

    Message from Remy Cameron
    She looks like you. That means you're...
    Sent Oct 29 10:44 a.m.

* * *

Rio's bedroom is filled with the sounds of noisy indie rock. But I don't hate it. I also don't know what that says about me nowadays.

    "Who is this again?"

    "Why? Do you like them?" replies Rio without looking at me.

    "Maybe."

    "Shocking, considering your music taste is the equivalent of Clover's daily dump."

    I smirk. "Why am I your best friend again?"

"Because the Witness Protection Program couldn't afford to hire you a better one," she says without missing a beat. "Also, your life would be pathetic without me."

"Don't you mean my life would *suck* without you?"

"Don't go quoting Kelly Clarkson in this sacred space, Romeo," Rio says sternly, but with this subtle fondness. "I'm not above tossing your scrawny ass out my bedroom window."

"Promises, promises."

Rio doesn't respond. She's studying the wall closest to the window while I begin examining the ceiling of K-pop horror above me. Preteen Rio was so much fluffier than this current Mad Tagger-obsessed incarnation.

"Any new clues?" I ask.

Again, Rio's silent. I expect that much. She's in front of her SUSPECT WALL—capitalized, because Rio's dramatic like that. Most of the wall is covered by a giant map of Maplewood. Red X's signify where the Mad Tagger has left their calling card. Polaroid photos of all their art are pinned to the map. Cutout yearbook snaps showcasing all the prime suspects and lists of evidence dangle from red pushpins.

Ford Turner. Lexi Goodwin. Malcolm Stone. Hiro Itō. Andrew Cowen. Wait…

"Is that *Ian*?" My voice is strangled.

"Yeah."

"Why?"

"Why not?" She keeps her back to me. "He's an art geek. He has a car, access to the school after hours via his dad. None of us hang out with him outside of lunch. We don't know much about him—"

"He's Brook's best friend," I counter.

"Does that give him a pass? Andrew Cowen is Brook's friend, too, but he's a suspect."

"So? If they're both connected to Brook, why isn't he on the list?"

Rio makes an annoyed noise. "Brook Henry is the living definition of a stuffed teddy bear. There's no way he'd do it."

"Cute and cuddly doesn't eliminate potential criminal status," I argue. My heart is pulsing strongly, like a warning. I need to shut up.

"Do you have any reasons why Ian's innocent other than the Brook connection?"

Yes, waits on my tongue. That almost-kiss vibrates against my mouth. The ghost of his hand in mine chills my skin. "No," I whisper.

"Then he stays," says Rio, firmly.

"But…" I can't finish. I can't tell Rio, my best friend, about Ian. About Ian and me. Not that there's an *Ian and me*, but still. Besides, Ian's just a face in a bizarre line-up that also includes Principal Moon, Mr. Riley, and Chloe's dad. The whole wall is a love letter to old-school murder mysteries, ransom-note-style.

Music talks for us. It's a happy, clappy song, so I can't complain. I should be at home studying or working on the Essay of Doom. But why? Weekends are for being anything other than yourself. Weekends are for irresponsibility and treating the world like that bowl of uncooked cookie dough you're not supposed to eat, but you do.

"Sara came by another GSA meeting," I mention to escape the tension of our previous discussion. Rio hums, scrutinizing a photo with a pen pressed to her pale pink lips. It's obviously an invitation for me to keep talking. "Another failed attempt to get us on the homecoming bandwagon."

"Uh huh."

"She doesn't get it."

"Uh huh."

"It's just… strange."

What I don't tell Rio is how, after the meeting, Sara lingered in the back of the classroom, staring at all the other students. Her rehearsed, pyrotechnic-expression remained, but there was a hollowness in her eyes. She didn't say anything to anyone.

Sara is a homecoming-princess-in-the-making. Quiet isn't her style. That twitch of her mouth and her searching eyes replay in my mind, as if a fraction of her wanted to be there, to belong to this *thing* she hasn't figured out how to be part of. It's been haunting me for a few days, especially since *I* didn't say anything to *her* about it. I should've.

"Mr. Riley is talking about doing a group event for the club."

"Uh huh."

"Something for Halloween."

"Uh huh."

"I thought maybe bowling?"

"Uh huh."

Ignoring her robotic responses comes naturally. When Rio's in a headspace, I don't dare enter. My feet are in the air, and I stare at my pink-and-yellow polka dot socks.

"Would you like to go?" I don't wait for her to answer. "We could dress up, eat pizza, go bowling—"

"You'll fall and bust your ass. I'll happily record and post it on Twitter."

We're not looking at each other, but I can tell her smile is as wide as mine. It's that third-grade-best-friends feeling. These smiles are heart-shaped mementos pinned to the scrapbook of my brain.

"Sara's dropping mad hints about homecoming." The wall Rio's bed is pushed against is decorated in those cheap glow-in-the-dark stars and planets, a parting gift from Jo-Ann Fabric. I haven't decided if I like them or not. "I think she wants me to join the committee."

"You're anti-committee."

"Well, duh."

"Then there's nothing to discuss," says Rio. "Unless…"

I hate that giddiness in her tone.

"Remy Cameron, you want to go to the dance!"

I clutch a pillow over my face and scream.

Rio softens the music to say, "I'll totally be your D.D."

Designated Date. Rio's nailed this role flawlessly before—and after—I came out. For every school dance, weekend house party, or group movie date where everyone else was straight and I was— fashionably and miserably—single. She even owns a mandatory dress for such occasions. It's bluer than the afternoon sky with white skull silhouettes stamped across the fabric and a slight ruffle to the hem. Rio is a mythological god in that dress.

I grin at my socks. "Nah, I'm good."

"You're sure?"

"Positive."

"Good." Her focus hasn't left the wall. "We have a pact about this, remember?"

I do. I sit up so my elbows support me. "Okay. What's the deal?" I watch her pace in front of the wall. Her mouth is scrunched, and she looks ready to either punch something or yell, maybe both. "Give me the tea."

"There was another incident," says Rio, not commenting on my casual usage of gay lingo. That's not like her. "Wednesday. The library doors were tagged with 'This way to freedom or the best nap you've never had.' Kind of lazy."

"Extremely lazy." It's half as bad as that Mad Tagger imitator outside of Maplewood Middle. Willow could've come up with a better message. "When did it happen?"

"After school. Soccer coach saw it when practice was over."

Wednesday. The same day I just happened to be sitting in the bleachers, watching the team—and Dimi. The same day Silver was hiding—badly—by the trees. The same day Brook stopped to talk.

"That's, uh, interesting."

I'm trying hard not to put clues together. Not to think about Brook leaving to catch the Marta before practice ended or Silver finishing his cigarette, then following the fencing all the way to the school's backdoors.

Brook can't be the Mad Tagger. He *can't*. Rio's right: he's squeaky-clean and borderline perfect and the soft embodiment of school spirit. He's got this big future ahead of him—all these expectations. Plus, Lucy would kill him. Not hypothetically, but full-on, top story on the evening news, Lifetime docuseries on how she did it, kill him. Rio and I would provide the alibi. I like Brook; he's über-cool, but *this is Lucy*. She let me cry on her bedroom floor in yoga pants with a pint of Ben & Jerry's after the whole Dimi-broke-me thing.

"Andrew's annual Halloween party is this weekend," I say.

"Are you going?"

"Nope." I sigh at the ceiling, not out of disappointment, though. I'm looking forward to wreaking havoc on Ballard Hills with Willow. "Are you?"

"Nope." Rio sighs too. "I'm actively boycotting that massive pile of social diarrhea."

"Why?"

"Just because I'm popular-by-association thanks to the Junior Class President and the leader of the New Americana Gay-Straight Alliance..." I groan loudly, but only at the Halsey reference. "...that doesn't mean I actually enjoy going to all the patriarchal functions intended to get the dude-bros at our school drunk and laid."

When she looks over her shoulder at me, I mouth "Wow" with wide eyes.

"I have other interests," she says. "I have integrity." The *Mean Girls* poster hung over Rio's desk politely disagrees. "Anyway, that's not why you're here." Everything about Rio's posture is accusing—the hands on her hips, squinted eyes, puckered lips.

I fake astonishment for six-point-two seconds, but I know I can't get away with this kind of bad acting when it comes to Rio Maguire, junior detective. Maybe it's because, as journalists, her parents are always looking for an angle. Maybe she's just super-intuitive. Or maybe a decade of friendship has made my poker face weak.

"I..." The words don't come.

I think I have an older sister. And, by the way, she found me on Facebook and I'm generally losing my shit every time she messages me.

"My essay for AP Lit is killing me."

Yeah, I chickened out. All those thoughts about Free that pinwheel in my head never make it to my throat. I just can't tell Rio. I can't admit that I've repeatedly searched Free's Facebook feed and stalked her Instagram. I've seen a dozen different photos of that same woman— my mother, but a little older, frailer, with dead eyes and less volume to her smile. Free has the same eyes, the nose, the wide grin, so many characteristics that are just like... Me.

"The Essay of Doom?"

"That's the one!"

"What're you struggling with?"

That I keep thinking about bringing up Free to my parents. But every time I get close, my jaw locks up.

I can't just ask, "Hey, Mom and Dad, did you know I have a sister? Did you know she existed? By the way, it's cool if you knew, but what the fuck?"

Rio's staring at me, head cocked.

I swallow, feel the saliva trying to maneuver around the gigantic lump in my throat. "All of it?"

"All of it?" Rio repeats.

I tug out my phone. On my Cloud, I have last night's draft saved. I read it out loud to her:

> "I have tried to write this essay five different times and have come to the same conclusion after each failure: I'm an enigma.
>
> I'm a 500-piece puzzle with only 472 pieces and the picture on the cover of the box is too faded to recognize.
>
> I'm a book with pages from other books and chapters that start but never finish, a plot too chaotic to absorb.
>
> I'm Remy Cameron.
>
> Unfortunately, I have no idea what that means anymore."

"It's a start," says Rio, pulling her hair into a ponytail. "And you do know yourself."

"I do?"

"Duh!" She smirks, walking right up to the bed. "You constantly walk around like you own every little thing about you. You're so damn confident it's annoying."

"I'm not." My protest is as halfhearted as her ponytail.

"Yeah, you are. You've been that way since you came out."

I bite my thumbnail. Here's the thing: Just because I came out at fourteen doesn't mean I'm one-hundred-percent secure in myself all the time. Coming out doesn't equal indisputable confidence. It means that, for those precious seconds it takes to identify yourself to someone else, you're brave. It doesn't last.

"I'm just borrowing my ego from you," I say.

"Plagiarizing is more like it."

Our laughs are in synch. Mine is a little watery, but Rio doesn't make any noise about it. She pokes my nose, and I swat her away.

"It's not that serious, Remy."

"But it is!"

"To who?"

"Emory. Mrs. Scott. My parents."

"I doubt your sweet-as-apple-pie parents give a flying eff about a damn essay," says Rio.

"I disagree."

"Obviously." Rio shakes her head. "At least your parents are around to talk about these things." A thin layer of hurt blooms in Rio's voice.

"Yours are right downstairs, you know," I say, lighthearted. I can hear them playing music in the kitchen—Duran Duran, of course.

"Yeah. Today."

"But—"

"Holy mother of Buffy Summers." She groans, hands thrown in the air. "Do some research. There are, like, hundreds of ancestry websites nowadays. Figure. It. Out."

I whisper, "It's hard. I'm adopted."

"No way," deadpans Rio. "Is that why your parents are white?"

I chuck a pillow at her head, giggling. My aim is terrible, and it thuds against the wall before sliding down to the carpet. Rio ignores it.

"Your parents have to know *something* about your dead mom, right?"

A flash of cold runs from my hairline to the tips of my toes. Talking to my parents about my birth mother again isn't a bridge I planned to cross. It's a journey I've been avoiding for years, simply taking the long way to figure out who I am. Maybe it's unavoidable? It's that ten car wreck right in front of you with no detour to get to your final destination.

"I-I can ask," I stutter.

Rio turns back to the suspect wall. "Good. I need to focus a little less on Remy the Unknown and more on this Mad Tagger case."

I fall back on the bed, feet in the air, arms spread out. This is why AP Lit sucks. Average literature students wouldn't be forced to question their existence. Normal lit students talk about Shakespeare and the absurdity of *the Catcher in the Rye*. I'd kill for Holden Caufield-levels of angst. My current emo-shit-storm is the stuff freshman year of college is made of.

I clutch my phone for a second before pulling up the Facebook messenger app. My hands shaking, I take three tries to login. Free hasn't replied to my last message. Maybe she's busy. Or maybe she's given me enough clues to put it all together. She expects me to know she's my sister.

I jab out a message:

Message from Remy Cameron
Can we meet?
Sent Oct 29 2:43 p.m.

Tiny tears sting my eyes. My breathing is shallow and quick.
I can do this, I can do this, I can do this.
I hit send.

I don't have to linger in the black hole of my unknown existence for long. I don't have to wait for the three ellipses to indicate Free's writing back. My phone's already vibrating: an incoming call. It's not Free, though. That doesn't mean the large knot in my stomach loosens. It tightens, but for a new reason, a better reason.

An Ian kind of reason.

CHAPTER
FIFTEEN

IT'S FRIDAY NIGHT. IT'S HALLOWEEN. And Mom is watching me as if I ate the last of her peanut-butter-swirl brownies. That last part might've happened. But that's not why she's staring at me.

"You're plotting something, Remy Cameron."

"I'm not."

"Oh yes, you are."

"I'm not. You have no evidence."

"You have that look. You know the one."

I don't. I mean, I don't think I do? Guilty is my least favorite expression. It's impossible to look Mom in the eyes, mostly because she's wearing this awful platinum blonde wig to complement her costume, which is orange pants and a turquoise top with fringe—lots of fringe.

"It's Christina Aguilera, circa 'Genie in a Bottle' phase," she announced earlier.

I don't really get it. Then again, I haven't researched that part of Christina Aguilera's history on YouTube either. Still, I'm determined not to look her in the eyes.

I sit on the sofa hugging a throw pillow while Mom fills three glass bowls with bite-sized candies. The kids of Ballard Hills are going to hold her for ransom unless Dad hands over full-size bars. Our community isn't notorious for late-night criminal activity—Mad Tagger aside—but Halloween is a pretty serious thing. It's overloaded with ravenous teens searching for anything high in sugar content.

Squinting, Mom walks up to me. "I smell body spray and deception."

"Mom!"

It's complete bullshit—the first part, at least. I'm not one of those guys who rocks body fragrances meant to attract your crush and small woodland creatures the way all those commercials advertise. Aromatherapy body washes? Definitely. Today's scent: orange zest and ginger with a mild hint of deception.

Mom's eyebrows lower. "What's your endgame here, Remy?"

"Twix and pixie sticks?"

"What else?"

"Twizzlers, but only the original kind," I say with a little more confidence.

Mom sizes me up. Her bad cop routine is rather intense; immensely better than Dad's. "A likely story," she says, drawing back. "I'm watching you."

"I'm watching you too!" Willow yells, running into the living room fully-dressed.

Our trick-or-treating tradition started three Halloweens ago. Mom came down with the flu and couldn't march us around the neighborhood. Dad offered to replace her. He was wearing a foam banana costume and... no. On the verge of adulthood, at the ripe age of fourteen, I threatened to boycott every major holiday for the foreseeable future if I didn't get to fly solo with Willow. Famous last words. It's been my duty—and privilege since Willow's so cool—ever since. The two Cameron kids braving the wicked streets of Ballard Hills alone.

But this year—

The doorbell chimes, along with the Wicked Witch of the West-cackle Dad installed for the occasion. Yep, we're overflowing with all kinds of lame traditions in this neighborhood.

"Mine!"

I leap from the sofa, disposing of the throw pillow. I hit a perfectly timed high jump over poor Clover on the way. It's hard to ignore Mom's "The aroma of a trap is all over you, Remy Cameron!" as I reach for the doorknob.

Ian Park is standing on my front stoop, carefully patting his severely spiked and gelled hair as though it's out of place. It's dyed dark green, which really brings out the moss and amber in his eyes. He's wearing a dark suit with a pale-yellow shirt. The collar's popped and a skinny tie hangs loosely. I have no idea who he's supposed to be, but he's freaking adorable.

"Hey."

"Whoa," says Ian, half-laughing. "Um, tiger?"

Absently, I touch my face. I forgot.

Mom helped with the face paint, only giggling every five minutes. I'm wearing an orange-and-black tiger-striped hoodie and ripped, dark, skinny jeans. Mom put together a headband with faux-fur tiger ears, but I nixed that.

"I'm Hobbes."

"Who?"

I regret every life decision I've made in the past forty-eight hours. Of course, he doesn't know who Hobbes is. *I* shouldn't know who Hobbes is. Clearing my throat, I say, "Hobbes, as in *Calvin and Hobbes*, the comic strip."

He blinks at me.

"Willow has a mild obsession with the Sunday comics. Halloween is our thing, and since last year…" My voice trails off in a painful squeak.

Ian's hand is carefully hiding his amused smirk. "What about last year?"

"Nothing."

"Oh, come on."

"It's nothing."

"Bet I can find it on Facebook if I—"

"We went as Franklin and Sally from the *Peanuts* comic strip!"

That's all it takes. Ian cracks up, and I wither under intense embarrassment. This night really was a trap, a trap for one Remy Cameron.

"That's so perfect," he says.

"Yeah. Well," I mumble, shoving down the "and so are you" that's raging up my throat. "Anyway, *who* are you supposed to be?"

Ian squares his shoulders; his chin is smugly cocked. It's kind of hot. I'm so screwed.

"Spike Spiegel," he replies.

"I'm sorry, a what?"

His shoulders deflate. This time, I'm the one holding in a chuckle. Ian mutters, "The main character from *Cowboy Bebop*?"

"Is that porn?"

"No!" Ian's face wrinkles. "Spike Spiegel!"

"Never heard of him."

"It's from an anime," he tries to explain. "Spike is this cool-but-uncool bounty hunter. Super cocky. People love to hate him."

"Okay."

"Seriously, you've never heard of him?"

I shrug. "Is this one of those cosplay things? Practicing for Dragon Con next year?"

"Exactly, Tigger."

"I'm not—" I stop, mid-breath, when a playful smile inches across Ian's mouth. Touché. Something suspiciously tingly crawls down my chest, right into my organs, and it's going to take *years* for me to forget that sensation. Ian licks his lips and that feeling sinks lower. These jeans can only hide so much.

"That doesn't sound like trick-or-treaters at the door, honey!" Mom singsongs.

My plan—because this is not a *scheme* and I have nothing to hide, thanks Mom—did not include introducing Ian to my parents. I love them. I love Willow. I've had plenty of friends over before. Even Dimi's been here. All those visits have included old photos of chubby-baby Remy and video documentaries of past birthdays and one too many reminders of the time I upchucked a colorful stream of melted cotton candy after riding a mini-rollercoaster at Six Flags Over Georgia. But this feels different. I can't figure out how, but maybe Ian's different from Lucy or Rio, different from Dimi, which, he can't be, right?

Ian's not even in the Boyfriend category. Or Casual Hook-Up category.

"Is that a friend of yours?"

"Uh, yeah?"

I can hear Mom approaching, Willow too. This is happening.

Like an adult, I suck it up. I open the door farther and step back, my best invitation for Ian to enter the Cameron House of Baby Photo Embarrassment.

Ian removes his shoes before crossing the threshold. I stare, eyebrows lifted.

"It's a habit. We take our shoes off at my house," he says.

"Oh. Cool," I say.

He steps inside. We linger, standing in a void where our eyes meet and our breaths synch, and I almost feel as though every one of our cells is moving to the same rhythm. I almost think this might be more than a crush.

"Hello, there."

Our quiet moment is interrupted by Mom and Dad and Willow, who giggles from behind my legs.

I introduce Ian to my parents. They shake hands. Ian's voice is clear but soft, as if his nerves are choking his larynx. Mom is chatty; Dad is corny. I'm mortified.

"And you must be Calvin, right?" Ian asks, peering around my legs at Willow.

Ian calling her Calvin draws Willow out from behind me. With a toothless grin and gleeful voice, she goes on and on about Ian's hair. I'm more than a little proud of Willow's costume: red-and-black-striped T-shirt, black jeans, hair just as spikey and gelled as Ian's.

Mom mentions something about photos and I immediately intervene. "Right, so we're just gonna go…" I motion toward the door.

Dad nods his approval and slings an arm around Mom's shoulders to stop her protests. But Mom has this look in her eye. Ian and I are a little close. Our hands dangle in close proximity. It's the perfect set-up for bad-motherly thoughts, as if she's planning our wedding.

It's definitely time to leave. I mumble, "Who's ready for candy and fresh air?"

Willow runs to retrieve her ghost-painted candy bucket from the kitchen. Ian grabs his shoes, but not before Clover vigorously sniffs them. I sincerely hope she's not plotting where to mark her next territory.

I escort Willow and Ian and my inch of dignity out the front door.

BALLARD HILLS IS LIT ORANGE by streetlights and gray-blue by the almost moonless sky. We cover most of the neighborhood—and a few adjacent ones—in under two hours. It's a leisurely stroll, because Willow has short legs and I'm in no rush to lose Ian's company.

The streets aren't super-crowded. Sporadic groups of pre-teens are followed by bored parents or older siblings. The occasional duo of teens smuggle eggs and toilet paper under their hoodies.

Everyone is really into Halloween around here. Pumpkins and cotton-ball ghosts are everywhere. But no one's lawn is as decorated as Mr. Ivanov's. Willow's bucket is stuffed to the brim with candy. I carry it for her, pouring the excess into one of those reusable Publix grocery totes Mom packed in case of a candy emergency.

Willow's a smash with the adults. Old-school costumes easily beat out all the princesses and *Transformers* and Disney knockoffs. Everyone slides her an extra piece of candy while raving over how in-character she is. Of course, she is. Willow wouldn't have it any other way.

I get a ton of "And look at you, the perfect companion!" It cracks Ian up every single time. I'm not earning any extra cool points parading around as a tiger with my younger sister, but it's not so bad. Willow's happy; that's enough.

But there's also the occasional exchange with a nosy adult: "Oh, are you her babysitter?"

"No."

"Tutor?"

"She's *seven*."

"Kids start young these days! My nephew Jake is studying French and—"

"I'm her *brother*."

That always triggers a brief odd look before they put on a tight smile and counterfeit cheery eyes. They pass over handfuls of candy, more than they gave the last trick-or-treater, as if that's an apology or an easy way out of their closed-minded observations. Whatever. It's all for my sister.

"We got so much!" screeches Willow.

We're clearing Hopper Street, headed home. I'm the navigator. Ian's humming '80s songs. Between us, Willow marches, wide-eyed, already dreaming of the sugar overdose she's about to experience after Mom investigates every piece of candy.

I used to hate the endless wait for Mom or Dad to inspect the candy. I mean, I get it now. People are messed up. But it was still hell on a seven-year-old dying for a mini-Reese's cup and a pound of M&M's.

"You killed it tonight, Willow," I tell her.

She's shaking her hips to whatever upbeat song Ian's singing. He's so damn off-key, but I can't help snapping my fingers to the beat.

"Okay, favorite candy?" Ian asks.

"Gummy worms!" Willow shouts, without hesitation.

I laugh. The last time I gave her a bag, she ended up with rainbow teeth and tongue. Mom did not approve.

"Gross, Twinkle Toes." I use my free hand to pat her softening hair. "Those come from the dirt!"

"And I love them!"

I look over at Ian: grin-scrunched eyes, fluffy green hair, and skin bronzed by orangey light. My stomach flips.

"What's yours?" he asks.

We never break eye contact.

"Reese's peanut butter cups."

"The minis?"

I make a face and his cackle echoes through the entire neighborhood. "Full-size. Like me."

This time, he makes a face—one of those "save the bullshit" faces.

"You?" I ask out of politeness, out of a sudden need.

"Candy corn."

"Too sweet."

Ian slows down; Willow mirrors him. "Too sweet?" He tips his head back and beams at the crescent moon. "Coming from the guy who takes his little sister trick-or-treating instead of partying with kids his own age?"

I'm not close enough to punch his shoulder but I telegraph it with fiercely squinted eyes.

"I think that's pretty sweet," says Ian. "Very sweet."

I bite my thumbnail. "Pretty corny, Ian."

"Candy-corn-corny?"

I choke-snort and cover my face. Ian freaking Park.

"Come on Spike Spielberg."

"Spike *Spiegel*," Ian corrects me.

"Whatever you say, handsome."

And... wait. Did that just come flying out of my mouth?

I blink so hard, everything in front of me turns red, yellow, and green. Then I chance a look at Ian. My moment of regret for having zero chill dies at the sight of Ian quietly observing Willow. She's stopped in front of Mr. Ivanov's house.

"Hey," Ian says, hesitantly. "Can I hold your hand?"

The neighborhood is so noiseless. People are turning off their front-porch lights. One-by-one, Ballard Hills' residents are saying goodnight to October.

Willow reaches up for Ian's hand. She's seven levels friendlier than I am when it comes to strangers, but she's not big on physical contact. Willow doesn't latch on to new people. I've always appreciated that, even if it meant she never connected with Dimi. Maybe Willow saw something I didn't. Maybe younger siblings know a trash fire when it's right in front of them.

But this just happens. Willow latches on. Ian swings their hands back and forth. I lead the way, wearing a dopey smile and overdosing on something way better than Reese's.

"So."

"So?"

"Yeah."

"Cool."

Ian laughs breathily. His eyes are soft, that midway between green and brown. "I think we're capable of more than one-syllable words."

"Are we?" I tease.

"Yes, we are." His head tips back for another laugh. Obviously, we haven't made much progress.

We stand in the foyer of my house. Clover's sniffing around our feet. Ian's wearing two different socks—one blue, one yellow. His shoes are lined up neatly by the door. I can't stand still; my Vans keep squeaking on the hardwood floor. The noise is probably pissing Mom off. She's an earshot away, in the living room, with Willow tucked into her side. They're watching the last of *The Nightmare Before Christmas*. Up next is *Hocus Pocus*. It's a Mom-Willow tradition.

Ian's phone buzzes for the sixth time. He doesn't check it, but he tells me, "It's Brook. Seems like Andrew's Halloween thingy is the place to be."

Oh, yeah. Andrew's annual Halloween bash. I forgot.

"Should you be there?" I ask, biting my lip.

He shrugs, leaning against the door. "Not really."

"Not really?"

Ian shrugs again. This whole nonchalant thing isn't very convincing—not on him, at least.

"I had fun."

"You did?"

Ian motions toward the living room. "With Willow. Not you. You're kind of boring."

"I pride myself on my boringness. It's a trademark."

"Is it?"

This time, I shrug. It's amazing how many competent conversations I have using only shrugs and blushes and gross smiles. "Do you want to go? To Andrew's?" I ask.

"Do *you*?"

My shoulders start to lift, but I squeeze my muscles so tight my spine aches. I can feel Clover at my ankles; her wagging tail hits my calves. "I don't think so," I finally say. "Wasn't on my to-do list for tonight."

That draws up the corners of his mouth. "What was?" he whispers.

And there it is: the Infamous Remy Cameron Blush, conquering my cheeks and nose and neck like a boss.

I don't answer his question. He doesn't seem to mind. We opt to go with a staring contest, one that I'm certain he's going to win because looking at this boy is like staring into the heart of a star.

Then Mom yells, "Go to the party! It's a Friday night and I'm having a *No Boys Allowed* night with my daughter."

I've officially entered the Hellmouth.

Serious credit to Ian: He manages to slap a hand over his mouth before any noises escape.

"But Mommy," Willow says, "Remy's not a boy. He's my brother."

"Thanks, Willow."

Mom whispers something, giggling. Then Willow shouts, "Yuck! No boys allowed! Leave, Remy!"

Perfect. Mom probably mentioned something to Willow about Ian. And kissing. Fifty cool points deducted from the House of Abby Cameron.

"Come join us, Clover!" Mom calls, still half-laughing.

Clover scampers to the living room. I can imagine Mom and Willow sitting on the floor with candy spread around them like a teeth-rotting castle.

"And Remy," calls Mom, a warning in her tone.

"I know, I know. No alcohol. No drugs." She's given the same speech since I was fourteen.

"That." There's fondness in her voice. "But, also, if you're not home by curfew, I make no guarantees I won't demolish your bounty of Reese's from tonight."

I shut my eyes and inhale deeply. This is torture. But I know she's not lying. Mom and I share a peanut butter addiction. When I open my eyes, Ian's still leaning against the door, still staring at me.

"So."

"So?"

Back to square one. Both of us hesitant and twitchy and nervous.

"Party?" Ian offers. He's already slipped back into his shoes.

I want to think of something great to say, something funny, a way to tell him I'd give anything to keep this night going. But I don't have to. Ian's hand is extended toward mine. With a choked voice, he asks, "Can I hold your hand?"

I guess that's the Universe's stamp of approval.

CHAPTER SIXTEEN

THE COWEN'S HOUSE IS THREE neighborhoods over from mine. There are distinct differences between Ballard Hills and this gated community. Here are newly-built brick houses with long driveways. Everything is brown and gray and modern. Every car is a sleek, new model; every hedge is trimmed by the gods' hands. Inside is furniture meant for looking, not touching.

Andrew's kitchen is a fifty-car pile-up, also known as half-drunk high schoolers on a Friday night. I'm in the middle of it. It's not so bad; I'm shoulder-to-shoulder with Lucy. The tips of her hair are dyed dark green like Ian's. She's dressed as a character from the only anime I'll ever recognize: *Sailor Moon*. She's Sailor Pluto.

Even in the overcrowded kitchen, where people shout and laugh, I can hear the music. It's so loud, it vibrates under my feet: techno, hip-hop, corny pop, then EDM. I assume the DJ is one of the Liu twins.

"This is wild," I yell to Lucy.

She sips a room-temperature beer she's been nursing for twenty minutes. Everyone has a red plastic cup filled with something foamy or colorful. Carly Johansson spills into the room, giggling. She has a thing for Fireball Whisky. I have a thing for not dying, so I typically avoid her. I've stuck to off-brand lemon-lime soda since arriving.

Fun fact: I'm cool with being the sober one at these things. Like, what's the big deal with getting hammered? I'm just as sociable clear-headed as all the other people chugging beers and sneaking shots from the Cowen's bourbon collection.

"This is gross." Lucy makes a face.

"You can stop."

"I could." Lucy swallows more of her drink. "But then I'd be like you."

"A beast at Scrabble?"

"An oversized kid dressed as Tigger."

"Hobbes."

"Who?"

I shake my head. "Never mind. Keep drinking."

"Oh, I plan to." Lucy salutes me with her plastic cup. I respond with an equally cheery middle-finger. Why am I here again?

Ian. I've been spectacular at ignoring the fact that Brook snatched him away the moment we crossed the Cowen's threshold. That's only because Brook is dressed as Barack Obama: spray-painted gray hair and freshly-pressed suit and sunglasses. Also, it's not as if Ian doesn't have his own set of friends—mainly Brook's swim buddies—to hang around.

It doesn't bother me one bit. I haven't spent the past five minutes daydreaming about messing up Ian's over-styled green hair with my fingers, kissing his chapped lips, learning the words to all of Ian's favorite '80s songs just to impress him. That's stalker-level creepiness.

I'm cool with my current activity: People-watching. A semi-circle of sophomores is passing around something that definitely isn't a cigarette. They inhale, choke, giggle, then pass. Girls gossip by the fridge. A freshman yells about a frantic game of Beirut in the basement. Something inappropriate is happening near the pantry. Something very inappropriate is probably happening in the Cowen's master bedroom.

Joslyn, Andrew's older sister, is in charge. She's done a decent job of frightening kids off the front lawn to keep the cops away. But her main concern is this muscle-head with a mohawk, dressed in an Atlanta Falcons jersey, sipping a Corona.

"I heard he used to go to our school," Lucy tells me. "Seven years ago."

"Seven?"

Lucy nods and hiccups, then adjusts the hem of her garnet-colored skirt. Joslyn is a freshman at Georgia Tech, *the college of Jules Littleton,* so my expectations were fairly-low.

I entertain myself with all the sick costumes. Chloe is Dorothy Gale from *the Wizard of Oz,* except she's wearing this cool, blue gingham button-down instead of a dress. Her dark-cherry Doc Martens are brushed with a layer of glitter.

Next to her, Jayden's Glinda the Good Witch—fuchsia hair and a lopsided glitter crown. His bubblegum-pink T-shirt reads: "Fairytale Nightmare." He manages to pull it off in this chic-masculine way, not that he's out of place in this group. A girl dressed as Legolas from *The Lord of the Rings* is two feet from him. A line of college-aged guys wears flirty nurse costumes with skirts far too short against their hairy legs. None of the soon-to-be-frat bros here would give Jayden any trouble about his outfit. All the jocks at Maplewood love him. Once, I overheard a few of the football players after practice:

"Jayden's a beast."

"I mean, yeah, he's a cheerleader and wears really out-there clothes sometimes, but it's all for fun. Dude's not serious about it."

"Plus, he's into girls!"

"Dudes *and* girls, bro. That's what bisexual means."

"I know what bisexual means! Anyway, he's still a legend. He's not dainty and shit. And he can belch the alphabet when the occasion calls for it."

For the record: There's never an occasion for that. Ever. Period.

"I'm surprised you came," Lucy says over the rapid-fire beat of a hip-hop song.

I give her a halfhearted shrug. "I can be social."

"Yes, you can. But you don't party."

"I party. I party so freakin' hard, Lucia."

"You do not."

"I do too!"

"What are you, Willow's age? 'I do too'? You sound whiny."

"And you sound jealous that I'm having more fun than you and I'm *sober*."

Lucy snorts, then takes a long swallow of her tepid beer.

It's a fact: Overcrowded parties like this aren't exactly my scene. I mean, I've been to a few, mostly because of Lucy. It took a while for me to shed my freshman skin and become comfortable around alcohol and loud music and people dry-humping in public. I'm more of a small-group-cramming-into-a-booth-at-IHOP guy. But I'd rather be here than spending Halloween night at one of Darcy Jamison's Holy Teen Night events. Not that she'd *invite me*.

"You coming tonight has nothing to do with my boyfriend's best friend, right?" Lucy asks with a smirk that should not be worn by anyone's best friend.

"Nothing at all."

"I saw you walk in with him."

"Total coincidence." Jesus, even my lie falls flat.

"You two looked cozy."

"The weather's nice tonight."

"What?"

I pointedly look away from her suspicious glare. From the kitchen, there's a clear view into the Cowen's living room. In the middle of a lush gold sofa is Silver. He's dressed as the Mad Hatter—not the sadistic Tim Burton adaptation, the pure Disney version. Sorority girls try to flirt with him. Quiet and curled in on himself, he ignores them. He's so out of place—like me, but more noticeable. Part of me wants to walk over to him. Maybe talk. The problem is Silver's only ever spoken six times to me. Four of those were "door" when he was trying to sneak away for his daily smoke break, and I just happened to be in the way.

Lucy clears her throat. I guess our conversation isn't over.

"I needed to get out," I finally say.

"It had nothing to do with Ian Park?"

By the fridge, something drops and shatters. Andrew barges in, parting the sea of seniors blocking the keg. He shouts, "Mom's teacups!" clearly having a mini-heart attack.

I turn to Lucy. "Just a lot on my mind. Didn't want to stay at home and turn emo."

"Remy Cameron, Emo Kid? I've seen that version."

"It's not pretty."

She almost chokes on beer. "It's not."

Something in Lucy's glazed eyes tells me she understands. I don't have to explain the way, sometimes, it feels as if the walls are closing in, and the air is so damn thin. She gets what it means to be a high school junior trying to survive the semester.

"I still think you're deflecting," she says, tipping her nearly empty cup to her lips.

"I'm not."

"I call bullshit."

"I'm calling your mother and informing her your vocabulary has been reduced from the PSAT drill words you've been working on every weekend to basic, Adult Swim lingo."

I give Lucy extra credit. She's able to side-eye me, sip beer, and flip me off all at once.

"I need some fresh air," she says.

Ah, yeah. "Fresh air" is code for "cigarette break."

Lucy doesn't invite me to join. She never does. Secondhand smoke and I aren't friends. She downs the remains of her beer, then carelessly places the cup on the counter behind us. Something wistful passes over her eyes, as if for a millisecond she wants me to come along, as if she doesn't want to be alone. But it disappears.

"See you soon?"

I nod at her. She vanishes into a crowd of people exiting the back door.

Alex or Zac plays more EDM tracks. Fantastic. All this party needs is a drunken round of Twister and some kid vomiting in the bushes, and we'll have reached Netflix-levels of teen parody.

A guy wearing a child's size Gryffindor T-shirt and scarf bumps into me. Pink liquid spills from his cup onto my shoe. Un-freaking-believable.

I glare at him. I don't recognize him from my year or even Maplewood's halls. His lips are puckered. A galaxy of freckles is spread across his face. His hair is on fire—whether dye or naturally, I can't tell.

"Who're you supposed to be?" he asks.

"Hobbes."

"Excuse me?"

"Hobbes, the tiger?"

"Jesus Christ Superstar, what is that?"

"I'm Tigger," I say, deadpan, and he snaps his fingers excitedly.

"*Winnie-the-Pooh* is my Patronus, my dude!"

"I bet," I sigh, then scoot around him before I lose more braincells talking to this guy.

My options for a new conversation partner are limited. I know a lot of people at the party by face, but not on a real level. I have my circle of friends. And then there are all the Maplewood students who nod and wave at me during school: the ones that know me as Remy, the Gay One, Lucy's Best Friend, The GSA Club President, Rio's Sidekick, and, my favorite, the Openly Gay One Who Used to Get It On with Dimi, the Hot Soccer Player. All these labels make me think about the Essay of Doom, and that kills my buzz. My sober buzz.

I look around for anyone other than Lucy. Jayden and Chloe are cuddling in a corner. Zac is... dancing? Or having a stroke. It's hard to tell. And there's Sara, who strolled in an hour ago dressed as Storm from X-Men, in thunderbolt earrings and an iridescent silver hijab. Sara and I talking at a party? That's not happening unless Lucy's involved.

The house is so congested. It's as if all of Dunwoody decided to simultaneously descend on the Cowen's. In the heart of it all, Brook is leading a conga line. I spot Ian, shimmying with the other swim team guys.

Our eyes meet. Something in his expression relaxes, as though it's just for me. I'm probably imagining that. But a tingle races from my arms to my toes. I watch his dimple, then his eyes. I watch until the conga line disappears into the kitchen. And then I exhale.

"Well, this situation just got real gay."

It's Sara, next to me. A row of gleaming gold bracelets jingles as she drinks from a red plastic cup. She's wearing opaque contacts, and it's kind of scary, but truly epic too.

"Every good situation is gay. Real gay," I say.

"True that."

We laugh, low and to ourselves, then Sara freezes. I do too. As if she's just realized what came out of her mouth. I pretend it didn't happen. For her sake, not mine.

"I need more gin," she mumbles.

"I need to pee."

We don't exchange goodbyes. Hell, we don't look each other in the eye. Sara shoves her way to the kitchen, and I trip on my shaky feet trying to locate a bathroom—or a time machine to erase the last thirty seconds.

THE LINE TO USE ONE of the upstairs bathrooms is much shorter than the one downstairs. It's a small victory. But it means I'm forced to stand between two girls, who alternate between texting and making out, and a sophomore soccer player. Kip? Keaton? I can't remember. He obviously recognizes me, judging by the way he won't make eye contact for more than five seconds without flinching. The curse of Dimi's ex-boyfriend strikes again. Luckily, I have my phone out, watching old *Steven Universe* episodes on YouTube.

I think about texting Rio. She wouldn't approve of me attending Andrew's party. Also, she's enjoying her own Halloween tradition—laughing her ass off at campy '80s horror movies. I'm chickenshit when it comes to Michael Meyers and Jason Voorhees. But Rio? She's a brave little toaster.

"Quick. Pretend you were holding my spot in line."

I startle, nearly dropping my phone. To my right is this guy, grinning lazily, his shoulder pressed to mine.

"What?"

"I can't stand all the way in the back. My bladder will malfunction."

A quick look over my shoulder tells me the line is much longer than it was five minutes ago. It stretches down the hall, onto the stairway.

I glance back at the guy. Thick, wavy hair is pulled off his face by a hair-tie. It's the same color as his eyes—maple brown. He has a square jaw with a rose-hue to his cheeks and the bridge of his nose. He's taller than me, older than me too, I think. Cute.

Correction: This guy's hot.

Functional words float in the ether rather than out of my mouth. "Uh…"

"It's cool."

"It is?"

"We'll just do the buddy system," he says as we inch forward. His cologne smells like cedarwood. His breath smells like beer and lime.

"Like, go in together?"

"Promise I won't look at yours unless you want me to."

I sputter. He pats my back, then his hand lingers between my shoulder blades. I don't know how to react. His palm is hot, and his eyes have that glassiness that comes from drinking too much.

"We can't—"

He cuts me off. "Whoa, nice eyes." He leans closer. I draw back, right into the wall. He chuckles, then says, "I mean—dude, *nice eyes.*"

He says it in this straightforward way. His lips curve up enough to show his white teeth; his eyes run over me. Definitely not straight.

"They're so blue," he continues. "I've never seen that on, like, a…"

"A black guy?" I say, because I can tell he's struggling. It pisses me off when people act as if black is *offensive.* That's what I am. Say it.

"Yeah, a black guy." His eyes continue to roam over me.

I don't know how to respond to that. His hand is still on my spine; his deliberate fingers map out each knob. I'm sweaty and uncomfortable.

"You're cute."

"Thanks?"

He laughs, head tipped back, neck flushed. Three moles form a zigzag pattern against his skin. He catches me staring, then winks.

Now I'm blushing.

"I'm Liam, by the way." He extends the hand that was once on my back. I shake it, but only briefly. Then I wipe the sweat from his palm on my jeans. That doesn't seem to bother him.

"Remy."

"Seriously? Dude!" His eyes are lit like his lopsided smile. "Remy as in Rembrandt? You mean like that rat from *Ratatouille*?"

I make a face. Major confession: I hated it when kids teased me about my name. No offense Pixar, but I don't want to be compared to a rat. No one does, no matter how funny that movie was.

I sigh. "Something like that."

"That's adorable." He's back to leaning in my direction. "Like you." He licks his lips, then his teeth catch the bottom one. "I've never been with a guy with eyes blue as yours. It's hot. Like, a black guy as cute as you with blue eyes? That'd be nice."

We've stopped moving. Well, I have. The heels of my shoes and the wings of my shoulders are against the wall. Liam is in my breathing space.

Soccer Ally of Dimi clears his throat rudely. "Get a room."

Liam ignores him. His fingertips skim my hip.

"I've never even been with a black guy," he whispers. "I've wanted to. And you're so damn cute."

I flinch. My fingers curl into a fist, but I don't swing. I think about it over and over. But he's taller, probably quicker. The last thing I need is Lieutenant Parker crashing Andrew's party to arrest me, self-defense or not. The last thing I need is to be plastered across the news as the angry black kid who decked a more-than-deserving white male.

"Interested?"

"Nope."

Liam frowns. "Why not?"

I shake my head. Every breath entering and exiting my lungs feels as if it's made of fire. Frustrated tears prickle my eyes. This isn't happening.

"I'm not—"

"Interested," Brook finishes, appearing out of nowhere. His body fits between mine and Liam's. He's the same height as Liam but bigger, with square shoulders and tension running through his forearms. "Maybe you should leave it at that."

Liam stumbles back, hands raised. He'd look like the perfect victim to anyone watching us now.

"We were just flirting."

"Were you?" Brook's jaw tightens.

Liam tries to look past Brook toward me. I shrink, struggling to steady my nervous breaths.

"It was nothing." Liam shakes his head; his face is scrunched. "No biggie, bro."

Brook steps toward Liam. I want to reach out just in case he decides to clock Liam. Lucy would lose her mind. And Brook could lose a potential scholarship.

"I'd like to believe my ma is a little more selective with her sperm donors," Brook says with this tight smile, "so we're definitely not bros. Not even close."

Liam *pffts*. "Yeah, whatever. Was just trying to get my dick sucked." Then Liam storms off, flipping us both the middle finger.

I'm frozen, slumped against the wall like a puppet without a ventriloquist.

"Hey." It takes me a second to realize Brook's helping me stand straight, ruffling my curls. Now his smile is kind, as though he hadn't been three seconds from ripping Liam's face off. "He's gone."

"He's gone," I repeat, throat dry.

Brook's eyes trace my face, as if he's waiting for me to snap back to myself, as if he *hopes* I do.

It takes a minute. Then I greet Brook with a shaky laugh. "That was wild," I say, instead of "I can't believe that dick." Rather than, "He only wanted me because I'm black. Because I have blue eyes. Because I was a fetish." I don't say any of that.

"Sorry that went down," Brook says, rubbing the back of his neck.

I blink at him, confused. Does Brook think this is *his* fault? That I was picked out of a house-filled with people because I'm black? Because Liam has a boner for things he's never had? Because some people fetishize race and are complete assholes?

"Don't apologize," I say, almost angrily.

He frowns and doesn't say anything else, as if we both comprehend. This is how it is. This is what it means to be black at Maplewood.

"Anyway, I'm here 'cause there's a certain someone waiting at the bottom of the steps for you," Brook says. "He's ready to leave. I guess you are too?"

When I nod, Brook exhales a happy sigh. "Good. My best friend is too spineless to say he wants to walk you home. Weird guy."

"A good weird," I say with way too much enthusiasm.

Brook says, "The best kind of weird."

He pulls me under the wing of his arm, then waits a moment as if I'll react negatively to someone touching me after what just happened. I almost do. Then my shoulders relax, and Brooks hauls me closer. He leads me toward the staircase while rambling about all his weekend date plans with Lucy.

I'm confident Brook won't tell Ian about any of this—unspoken trust at its finest.

CHAPTER SEVENTEEN

"WE'RE ALMOST THERE."

"Almost where?"

"Somewhere."

We're back to this again. Somewhere, somewhere, somewhere. To be honest, I love following Ian to Somewhere. Anywhere, really. He guides me with a shy expression and his hand wrapped around mine. Our fingers have found this natural home, interlocked, so our fingertips learn the surface of each other's knuckles. Mine are a little rough; his are inexplicably soft. It all works.

We're not too far from Ballard Hills; we're close to Maplewood Middle School, but not. Near the spot where we first reconnected, while I was walking Clover and he was running and we were both lost-and-found. Yet, this feels like being in a completely different world. Trees tower over us. The sidewalk is covered in pine needles— autumn's love letter to humanity, a mint-green pathway to Somewhere.

I don't ask Ian about where we're going. Instead, I ask about California, about his halmeoni. He sheds his inhibition as if it's an extra layer of clothing in the summer. Ian misses the beach, but not the water. Ian loves the sunsets but hates the coconut scent of suntan lotion. Ian's grandmother is Korean-Mexican. He inherited her love for spicy foods. Most Sundays, she cooks his favorite meal: buldak with nuringji—deep fried, bite-size barbequed chicken coated in a chili sauce, served with a thin crust of slightly brown, crunchy rice found at the bottom of the pot.

I tell him about my Dad's French toast obsession and about Mom's passion for pop culture. I don't tell him about Dimi, and he never mentions any of his exes, and that works too. We exist in a space outside of reality and inside of our racing hearts. I don't think I'll ever leave.

Somewhere ends up being a clearing just behind the trees. It's a place I've never been, or maybe I have, but never paid attention. Nothing hides the sky. It's a navy canvas, marred only by stars flicked against its surface like white paint splatters. There's not a single cloud.

"Somewhere." Ian presents it as though it's a gift, with his free hand stretched outward. And it is, wrapped with a lovely crescent-moon-bow smack in the middle of it.

Ivory light swims through my vision. My heart floats on a bed of unexpected emotions—happiness, nerves, and anticipation. For what? I have no idea. I don't think I want to know.

"What do you see?" he asks, quietly.

"Everything."

"Yeah." His fingers tighten around mine. "Me too."

It's the most calming thing—standing in our silence, breathing in the unsaid words, exhaling the smiles they produce. This is exactly what I needed to get my mind off Liam, to take me away from how that made me feel: like a prize. Even in the queer community, race plays a factor. It's the deciding piece in whether you're desired or rejected, a swipe left or right. For some, it's this holy grail, a checkmark on their bucket list. I didn't want to be anyone's checkmark. I didn't want anyone to want me because of my race. I wasn't a prize.

The night air smells like heat and sugary sap. All the insects are humming their nightly opus. When I turn to look at Ian, he's watching me.

He says, "There's one rule to Somewhere: You can't leave alone."

"What?"

"There's one rule. You can't leave alone."

"I'm still here."

"But you went away for a moment."

I did, for a moment too long. But my fingers tighten around his. Without question, I know he can feel my heartbeat through my palm. I'm not ashamed of how fast it thumps—because of Ian freaking Park.

His eyes, hazel and blinking repeatedly, move across my eyebrows and cheeks and jaw. But he's not coveting me the way Liam did. He's only observing, learning my face as if he might forget it. Funny thing is, I know he won't.

But I need to remind him. "Can I—" The words fizzle in my throat like carbonation. Then, my courage hardens like fired clay. "Can I kiss you?"

My request hangs between us. This is a moment too, except it doesn't last long.

Ian licks his lips. "Yes."

"Okay." I try not to sound surprised.

He trips getting closer. And I laugh, briefly. Then I kiss him. Our lips are gentle but sure. Our noses are awkward; then his hand touches my cheek, and I find a rhythm. I bury every nerve not attached to my heart into the kiss. Ian kisses back as if he's falling from orbit and I'll be the one to catch him. With my fingertips cupping his chin and my eyes shut, I catch him.

We pull apart on a hiccup—from me—and a shudder—from him. "Wow."

I blush. Or my cheeks try to, but there's a lot of blood flowing south of my navel. "Have you ever—Was I the first boy you kissed?"

He nods, eyes lowered.

"Wow."

"Don't get an ego."

"Too late." I snort, and his eyes lift, crinkled by his upturned mouth. "It was good, right?"

"Six out of ten."

"Six?!"

This time, he chuckles. Gently, he says, "But I have nothing to compare it to. A second kiss might raise my score."

Instead of pointing out the flaws in his math, I step on his toes and kiss him again. And a third time. A fourth time just to secure my superiority over any future kisses. Not that I want him to have anyone else to compare this to. I want to be the only one in his Somewhere.

It's after midnight. October kissed Georgia goodbye in a whisper of jack-o'-lanterns being blown out and a shout of teenagers high on sugar and an explosion of toilet paper across tree branches and houses.

I'm half-curled on the sofa with Mom. Between us, Willow's asleep. Her little lips are parted; whistling breaths escape. Clover's nearby, shamelessly snoring. Exhaustion weighs on me, but I'm still wired by Ian's kisses and by the way he held my hand all the way back to my doorstep.

We sit in the dark. The blue of the television glows on our faces. *It's the Great Pumpkin, Charlie Brown* plays on a loop, a Mom-and-me tradition. All the characters are dancing manically to the "Linus and Lucy" theme.

"Late night, Remy."

These are the first words she's said since I tiptoed inside, three minutes past curfew. To be fair, I wasn't late. Time doesn't exist during kisses on the front step, at least, not during Ian's kisses.

I clear my throat. "Not too late."

"I've seen worse." I can hear the snark in her voice. Dimi was a terrible influence. If I was making out with him—or other things—I was usually grounded for coming home too late *because of him.*

"Sorry."

"Don't be. You're young." Her hand is on my head; my curls twine around her fingers. "Ian seems nice."

I squeeze my eyes shut. "Yeah. I guess."

"Uh huh."

She's waiting for more. I'm afraid to give it to her, not because my mom isn't great with me being gay or dating, but because I haven't pieced together what information is worth releasing and what I need to keep close to my chest, just in case Ian's nothing more than a friend. Friends that kiss but don't date exist, right?

"He likes you."

"Okay, let's not assume things, Mom."

"It's not an assumption." When my eyes open, she's smirking— that I Know Things smirk trademarked by most moms. Then, in a serious tone, she says, "Be careful. Not with just your heart; use protection."

I resist screaming out of respect for Willow. But it burbles in my throat, lava-hot. "*Mom,*" I hiss to alleviate some of the pressure.

"I'm not ready to be a grandmother." The urgency has faded, replaced by humor. "I haven't even gone through my Britney Spears phase yet."

"Which one? Catholic schoolgirl? Snake girl? Shaved head? Barefoot at a gas station?"

"Oh, honey," Mom's mouth curves upward, "All the Britney phases are important."

In the dark, the television screen's bluish glow brushes over Mom's crow's feet, across those miniature wrinkles around her mouth. Her strawberry-blonde hair is beginning to lose some of its luster. She's not *old*, but age is catching her.

Her fingers shift in my curls. "I want to be that cool grandmother who still wears sports bras and track pants."

I groan. "That won't be happening," I say. "I'm gay, remember?"

Mom blows a raspberry that shakes Clover awake. It's almost the same reaction she had when I came out. I was thirteen and decided to do it the summer before freshman year, before the Age of Remy, the Gay One. She and Dad were right here, on the sofa. I told them in the most unique way I could think of: strolling into the living room, ruining a perfectly nice button-down shirt by ripping it open like Clark Kent changing into Superman to reveal a T-shirt that said "PROUD" with a rainbow over the letters. I thought I was badass.

Dad blinked at me for a minute, head cocked. He was confused. But Mom—she blew a raspberry, pulled me down between them, and turned on coverage of NYC Pride. We watched, the three of us, all the rainbow flags and floats filled with dancing people and joy, pure joy.

"Okay, so what's the big deal?" Mom said. Then she laughed, wetly, with my head tucked under her chin. "*We're* the proud ones, Remy. Thank you for being yourself."

Dad patted my curls and whispered, "Love you, kiddo."

That was it. Honestly, it was incredible. I cried afterward, locked in my bedroom, with power-pop on full blast. But I wasn't sad. I was so damn happy. Yes, it took Dad some time to adjust to me talking about boys *like that*. No, Mom didn't join the local chapter of PFLAG. They both struggled in the beginning with Dimi. It was frustrating, but I recognized something important: My parents aren't perfect.

"Being gay doesn't mean you can't have children, Remy," Mom reminds me. Her lips are pursed; her intense eyes watch me. I sense a speech coming. "When doctors said I couldn't have children naturally,

I didn't mourn the loss. Your father didn't either. We knew what we wanted. Adoption was the best thing ever."

I blink at her. Everything around us softens: Clover's snores, Willow's exhales, the television.

"Adopting you was the best thing," she pauses. A grin overtakes her face. "Adopting you *is* the best thing that happened to us. You know that, right?"

"Yeah."

"The best thing, Remy."

Our smiles are the same size, shape, everything. Is that possible? I'm not their blood, but so much of who I am—internally and externally—is my parents.

"What about Willow?"

Mom snorts, glancing at Willow. "She's okay."

I don't bother to restrain my giggle. Willow shifts, curling into me. Mom washed her hair, and I tuck a still-damp lock of it behind her ear.

"You'll make a great dad someday, Remy."

"Yeah?"

"The best," she says, toying with my curls. "You'll change some-one's world."

"Like you did for mine?"

"No," whispers Mom. I think she might cry. "Like you did for ours."

We fall quiet. My mind doesn't. It buzzes and roars with new thoughts: a birth mother, a sister, a possible birth father, people who might change my entire world. I'm not sure I want that.

CHAPTER EIGHTEEN

Message from Free Williams
  Saturday. Aurora Coffee. Little 5. Meet me @ 10 a.m.
  Sent Oct 31 9:19 p.m.

* * *

Meeting the sister you didn't know you had is the SAT of familial situations. You can prepare all you want with cram sessions studying her Instagram, her Facebook. You can research her zodiac sign to anticipate her personality traits—I didn't do that but I think Rio would have.

I should've invited Rio. No. This is awkward enough. Texting Rio "Hey, do you wanna spend Saturday morning meeting my birth sister? BTW, I have a birth sister... crazy, right?!" isn't the way I want this to go down. It's not the way I want any of my friends to find out about Free. Do I want my friends to know about Free? I still haven't decided.

Aurora Coffee is a chill, old-school-meets-now coffee shop. It's in Little Five Points, a two-and-a-half-mile strip of shops gathered in Midtown. Little Five is a black hole of hipsters and city-dwellers and bohemians. It's also where suburban moms go to find vintage clothes in their horrible attempts to appear cool.

The vibe of Aurora isn't Zombie Café, but I still like it. An entire wall of posters advertising indie bands and comedy shows and drag performances is to my left. A creepy mural of snowy mountains and phoenixes with TVs for faces line the opposite wall. Burnt-orange plastic chairs and wooden tables clutter the space between the door and bar.

Every customer has a neatly-kept beard or tattoos or flip-flops. I stick out, at a table near the front. Maybe it's my curls. Maybe it's the ultra-blue Vans with no socks. Maybe it's my nerves vibrating. My leg won't quit shaking. I've only had three sips of my iced coffee. I'm too busy checking my phone and tracing a finger over all the names carved into the tabletop and watching the glass doors. I'm early.

I keep typing and deleting a text to Ian. I hope he's asleep. I hope he doesn't see those three ellipses appearing and disappearing. What do I say?

Thanks for spending your evening with me and my little sister. BTW, you're an amazing kisser!

There's nothing wrong with that. As truthful as it is, it's not enough. It's missing something, like me. All my life, I've been missing something.

"Wow. You really look like *him*."

My eyes raise.

Free Williams has been misrepresented by her Instagram photos. She's *stunning*. A cloud of loosely-flared curls as dark as her thick veil of eyelashes frames her face like a lion's mane. Her dark brown eyes are wide, very expressive. Her skin is like the edge of autumn—rich-bronze.

She flops down across from me, dropping a hefty bookbag in the chair next to her.

I can't take my eyes off her. We don't look *exactly* the same. But we have similar noses and cheekbones. Her mouth curves a little at the corners the way mine does when I'm about to smile.

My voice cracks. "Him?"

"Your father."

I flinch hard. Some of my coffee spills. Free arches an eyebrow as I try to clean up my mess with napkins. "Sorry."

"Don't be," she says, leaning back. "I guess that's new for you? Someone mentioning your real dad?"

"I have a real dad," I hiss. That's new, too, the frustration. "Sorry. It's just, I have—"

"Parents? A family?" That curvy smile returns. "Yeah, I've seen pictures. Your... that guy who knocked up our mother was quite the self-absorbed jerk, anyway."

"I don't know anything about him." *About you*, rests on my tongue.

"You wouldn't want to know him."

That stings. It also ignites this curious flame in my ribcage. What's he like? Are parts of me like him? Do we share more than physical features and a connection with a dead woman? I force myself to chug the rest of my coffee, struggling to breathe.

"That was a truly shitty thing to say," Free comments. "My bad."

"It's okay," I say, though it's not. I'm caught in this warped reality where I have a sister and an unpopular father and a dead mother. It's as if I'm six years old again, accepting the reality that I'm a Cameron legally, but not by birth. My hands shake under the table.

"Let's try again. I'm Free." She wiggles her fingers in a casual wave. This girl is all chilled energy. She's jazz in the summer; a cup of hot cider in December. "Free Williams. I'm your—"

"Sister," I say, quietly; not ashamed, just quiet.

"Half-sister," she corrects.

"Oh."

"Different dads, obviously." Free pushes curls away from her cheeks. "Our mom and my dad dated in high school. It didn't work after she got pregnant with me. She didn't love him. He didn't love her. No biggie."

She says it as if it doesn't hurt, as if it truly is no biggie. I can't imagine Mom and Dad "not working." Then again, I didn't imagine having a half-sister, but here I am.

"So, Remy." She says my name with a curl to her lips; not teasing, just amused.

"Remy Cameron." My voice still squeaks. "Rembrandt."

"I still can't believe she named you that." Her laugh is fond, like a lost memory returning.

"It's not the best name to avoid being teased about." A giggle squeezes through my tight throat.

"Who're you telling? Try growing up Frida!"

"Frida?"

"Like the—"

"The painter," I interrupt, then my face heats when she smirks.

"Mom had a thing for the arts. She loved painters." Morning light tickles through the door and grazes her heart-shaped face. Something tender but haunted moves in her eyes. "That's all she ever wanted: to be an artist. To have one finished piece hung in a museum or art gallery."

"Really?"

"It never happened, though. Too many distractions."

"Distractions?"

"Yep. Being a single mother. Raising a wild child like myself. Work. That... *man*." The last word comes out sharp. A slow-build of venom pollutes my blood. I hope I'm nothing like... *that man*. Nothing at all.

"She'd say, 'Frida Williams, be somebody. Make the world remember you.' And I'd look her dead in the eye and tell her I already was somebody. I was *her somebody*." Free's fingers toy with the collar of her sweatshirt. It's been cut to shreds, then put back together with safety pins. The Agnes Scott emblem is mangled but familiar.

"What happened?" I ask, too quick, too urgent.

I want to swallow the words. Seventeen years of life, life without birth parents or a half-sister, invade my core and infect my cells and curiosity stands atop Mount Who Are You, glaring victoriously at me.

Free's expression is lighthearted, but her eyes darken. Maybe she's caught in this time warp too. Maybe we're both not ready to walk into this new world.

"What do you want to know?"

"Um." I look down at the scarred tabletop.

"What happened to her? What happened between her and your... Is sperm donor too harsh?"

I shrug. "Seems accurate."

Her raspy laugh invades my ears again. I kind of like it.

"Why she gave you up?"

"Uh…"

"How'd I find you?" Free's eyebrow is arched high, as if she knows that's my number one question.

My neck is hot. My ears burn. Every muscle in my throat constricts, preventing the raging yes from escaping my mouth. Finally, I whisper, "All of it."

"All of it? Hmm." She cups her chin in one hand. Free has more rings than fingers. She says, carefully, "Okay."

"Okay," I repeat, uncertain.

"But first, coffee."

THERE'S SOMETHING INTENSELY BIZARRE ABOUT listening to someone tell the history of a family that didn't exist a month ago. It's an out-of-body experience. Everything is muted except their voice. I'm breathing, but I'm not. My iced coffee is watered down, but I keep drinking, because my throat is too dry to talk.

The only thing that exists is Free's voice and eyes and curls. She tells me about Ruby, our mother: her eyes, her voice, her art. Free talks about where she was born, where they lived.

"Decatur, where it's greater, baby!" Free says with that infectious laughter, with an easiness, as if she's not exposing her bare bones to her newly-discovered brother. *Half-brother.*

Free talks with her hands. Everything is dramatic, overwhelming as Times Square. She fills in the gaps about what happened before I was born. Where Ruby worked: line cook during the day, art gallery custodian in the evening. How Free stayed with a different neighbor every night. All the Christmases they spent at Waffle House, then the movies. Ruby was an only child. Her parents—my unknown grandparents—are dead.

"Were you lonely?" I ask, shyly. I haven't found her line between curious and nosy.

"Boy, I was popular!" She slurps down iced coffee. She takes it with vanilla and cream, almost like mine. "I was always over at a friend's house, playing superheroes and climbing trees. You couldn't keep me out the pool in the summers."

I think about how Willow loves to swim, too. And then this fuzzy guilt plops on my chest. Should I be thinking about Willow? Is that wrong? To have all these fond, high-definition memories of my adopted sister and relate them to pale, faded memories borrowed from my birth sister? I don't know.

"Was she happy?"

Free's eyes finally leave mine. "Sometimes. When she was painting, she was in the clouds. When we did meaningless things, like run barefoot in the grass. Most days, whenever she didn't…"

Her words trail off, and I don't question the rest. I know I shouldn't. Not yet. Not until Free is ready to tell the story.

"She loved too easily," says Free. Lips pursed, she stirs ice around her cup with the straw. "Way too easy. I suppose that's how your—"

I clear my throat.

"*That man*," she says with a bite to her voice, "had such a lasting impact on her."

It's me who's quiet, this time. I'm not ready to talk about him. Not yet. "Who was her favorite painter?"

"Vermeer. Hals. Ruysch." Free rolls her eyes. "That woman loved her Dutch Golden Age."

"Favorite movie?"

"She loved old-school stuff. *Imitation of Life*."

"Never seen it."

Free's neon-bright laughter has darkened. "The irony of that movie and her life."

"Did she like music?"

"Jazz," she says. Her eyes are crinkled, amused. "And anything by a singer-songwriter."

I sense Dad would appreciate that. Maybe Dad and Ruby would've been friends. Maybe I shouldn't think that way.

"What—" My throat closes around the rest of the words. Behind my eyes, this throbbing sting begins. *I'm not ready, I'm not ready, I'm not ready…* "Why did she—"

Free lowers her cup. Her hand is warm, strong, as it wraps around mine. My hand is trembling. That little spark of brightness returns to her eyes. She squeezes my hand.

"That man and our mother dated for a few months. Then she found out she was pregnant with you. It wasn't a fairytale love, but she seemed happy." Free holds my gaze. "She loved him. Hardcore.

But he wasn't in love with her. He loved the thought of being loved, but not returning it." That sounds familiar, like a page in a book I've read cover-to-cover.

"Six months into her pregnancy, he bailed. She crumpled like wet paper."

I suck in a breath, though my lungs hurt, though every part of me is numb except that sensation behind my eyes and the skin her hand touches.

"My dad always said, 'Ruby loved the sauce.' He's one of those true-blue southerners." Free's laugh is cracked, sad. Her curls fall around her jaw in a dark hood that makes her eyes wider. "She loved to drink, Remy. And she did. Before you. After you. It was her thing. She was an alcoholic—your daddy was just the gateway to her depression."

"He's not my daddy."

She nods, once, smiling but not smiling. "No, he's not."

"Why'd she give me up?"

It's hard not to compact all my curiosity and fear and anger into those five words, five words I never wanted an answer to. I still don't think I do. But they're out, hovering between us like a giant spaceship waiting to crash-land into my chest.

Free pulls her hand back. She slouches, not looking at me. Maybe I shouldn't have asked. Maybe this is the one thing Free can't give me.

"Momma always said, 'He's better off where he's at.' Every time I asked, I got that same response. I was six when you were born." Her eyes fall on me, dark and full. "It ain't easy going from rubbing your mom's stomach waiting on your little brother to arrive to finding out you're never gonna meet him. That he's been taken in by another family. That your mother thinks all the things you have are too worthless to raise a new baby in. That your new brother deserves more, but all of this is good enough for you."

Anger lives in Free's voice, but it's not for me. I can tell. It's for Ruby. Most of it is for the guy who made her fall in love, then left. None of it's for me, but here it is: loud and fiery and smacking me in the face.

"I'm sorry."

Free tuts, shaking her head. "Don't be. My life, where I'm from *is* good enough. I'm damn good enough."

I don't know how to reply. I almost reach out to grab her hand. I sense she doesn't want me to. This isn't Free looking for comfort. This is Free rejecting Ruby's messed-up idealism.

"When I was younger—after you were born, I used to wonder about you. Wondered if your life truly was so much better without us," says Free. That hint of resentment still lingers. Even if her expression doesn't announce it, the tightness of her voice does. "I kept asking and asking about you. What you looked like. Where you were. Was your favorite color purple like mine? But Momma never would tell me."

And that's how we're different. Free wanted to know things about me. I never wanted to know anything other than my family: my parents and Willow.

She shrugs weakly. "Then I gave up."

I almost reach for her hand again.

"Until Momma died." She chews on her straw, traces the names on the table with her eyes. "I was eighteen."

I hiccup, hand over my mouth. *Eighteen.* I'll be eighteen in a year. How would I survive without my parents? I wouldn't.

Free says, "It's like curiosity reached into my chest, tore away all the muscle and bone, and reminded me, 'I'm not alone. There's someone else.'"

"Me," I whisper.

"You." She hums. "Luckily, Momma wasn't great with all her secrets. I knew her passwords. Did a little snooping in her e-mails. It was an open adoption, you know?"

I didn't. I don't really know what that means. I tell her as much. Free explains about how, in certain adoptions, the birth parents and the adoptive family come to an agreement that permits limited contact—e-mails exchanged, photos shared. She found a dozen e-mails from my parents to Ruby a few weeks after I was born: a timeline of updates and baby pictures.

"Your mom," Free's shaking her head, "I don't know her, but she seems pretty genuine. In every e-mail, she never stopped thanking Momma."

I grin at my hands. Abby Cameron, sweeter than a bowl of peach cobbler and vanilla-bean ice cream.

"Momma never replied to your parents. Not one single time. Eventually, they stopped writing her."

My eyes lift, and we share a long, sad stare. The *'and then she died'* is left to float in the ether between us.

"I was so angry at her for so long for keeping you from me," whispers Free, that latch shutting away her anger undone again. "Until I saw those e-mails. Until I realized the reason she couldn't say a damn thing back was because she didn't know if she'd done the right thing for both of us."

"Is that how you found me?"

"It's not hard to find people nowadays," she replies. "Social media makes it way too easy. Looked up your parents on Facebook—cute dog by the way."

"Thanks," I say, almost laughing.

"Clicked around and there you were." Free looks away again. "I saw your face and I was a little girl running around the house, shouting about my baby brother again." Her voice is even softer when she whispers, "I just wanted to know that little boy I never got to meet, to know I wasn't alone."

I bite my lip hard enough to taste something sharp, unpleasant. But I don't flinch in front of Free—only my hand, the one in the middle of the table, a few inches from hers. In my head, I hear a chant, set to my drumming heartbeat: *We are not alone. We are not alone.*

"God, why'd you let me go all Viola Davis in the middle of a coffee shop?" She laughs again, brighter. Her fingers brush under her eyelids. Maybe she's trying to disguise the tears. Maybe I'm rubbing my eyes too.

We finish our coffees. An old couple walks in holding hands. The barista seems to be coming down from an espresso high. The music inside Aurora is a little loud—this cool rotation of reggae versions of vintage songs. I like it. Free's bopping her head. It's a nice interlude in our awkward silence.

"Tell me about being seventeen in Dunwoody," she requests with a low sigh. I can tell she's pretending to be nonchalant. I wonder if she really wants to know, or if this is just our way of walking around the elephant plopped on the table between us. I'm okay with that.

I tell her about school, about the things she couldn't learn from Facebook. She tells me about her friends, about what she's studying—biochemistry, because, unlike for me, science is fun for her—and I tell her about Mr. Riley and about Lucy and Rio and my Zombie Café addiction.

"Do you want to know about my family?" I ask, because I'm high on caffeine. I'm cruising on this moment of sharing things about myself without having to set it to pretty little words in the Essay of Doom.

Free says, quick and sharp, "No."

And I come down from my high. "But—"

"I'm good," says Free, jaw tightening. "Maybe one day, but not now."

My mouth hangs open. Something guarded hardens Free's features, like a great wall protecting a castle. I don't understand it. Should I? She's shared so much about Rudy and herself. I want to reciprocate with things about my family. I stare and stare at her until she turns back to me, shrugging.

"Should I not have—"

"We've had enough heavy talks for the day," Free interrupts with a look in her eyes that's almost fond again. Almost.

"I'm sorry if—"

"It's cool." She rests her chin on her knuckles so just enough of her smirk is hidden. "Let's talk about you and dating."

I cough into my hand. Is it appropriate to Google-search "How to come out to your newly-found half-sister over coffee?"

"Single," I choke out.

She taps her fingers on the table. Her nails are painted aqua. I focus on that.

This whole coming out thing—it's always, *always* weird. "I'm gay."

"I guessed."

My head snaps up, eyes squinted. "What?"

"I guessed you were gay. I mean—"

"Was it the way I talk? Is it because..." I wave a hand around. "... my body language? My posture?"

"Your posture?" Free snorts so hard, I swear she's going to spit up iced coffee. "Damn. You have photos on your Facebook wall with some boy." Aha! So, this Facebook-stalking thing is a family trait. "He's cute. He's got RDF, though."

"RDF?"

"Resting Douchebag Face."

I almost fall out of my chair and brain myself on the table.

"Is he your boyfriend?" she asks.

"Ex." I hate how my skin crawls when I talk about Dimi.

"Ah." Free's wearing that same expression. The relaxed one that says she doesn't give a damn that we're talking about me dating a boy, that I'm gay. She says, "Should probably delete those cozy Christmas photos in the matching-sweaters, then."

She's right. I hate all this attention on my old scars. "What about you?"

"What about me?" She's deflecting, just like I do. Our similarities are showing in fluorescent colors.

"Come on," I try, eyebrows wiggling, "There has to be someone."

"Hell no!" Her scratchy outburst startles a young woman with glasses who's hiding behind her laptop. Free doesn't care. "I'm all about school."

"So, no one?" It's kind of hard to believe. Free is magnetic. She has an electric energy that could compel people to fall in love with her.

"No Tom, Dick, Harry, Caitlin, Jamar, Diego—"

"Caitlin?" *Hello, puberty-voice!*

Free tosses her head back, shaking that jungle of dark curls from her face. She points an eyebrow upward. "Remy, labeling sexuality is simply a way for closed-minded people to keep everyone in these neat, tidy boxes. Sorry, I'm not about to conform. I already have enough checkmarks on job applications. What happens in my bedroom isn't going to be monitored too."

I slump in my chair. My hand reaches for my cup. It's empty. "Wow." I breathe.

"I'm not saying I'm hooking up with Caitlin or Diego or whoever," she clarifies. "I'm saying I'm in a relationship with school. A good relationship. I plan to be somebody."

Be somebody. Those two words swirl in my brain. Free, like Brook, like Lucy, knows who she is, who she'll be.

I watch Free play with her phone and the way she chews her straw: confident shoulders, reckless hair and a curvy mouth, and focused. I have no clue how to tell Free that she looks a lot like a somebody to me.

Silently, we agree our time is over. Free has to study. And, unfortunately, the Essay of Doom hasn't written itself yet.

I grab my phone, zip my hoodie. She hauls on her backpack. Her head's cocked; she's watching me without being rude. More curious.

"Hey." It's the first time I've heard hesitation in her voice. "Are you sure you don't want to know about—" Her pause is heavy. I know where she's going with this, even if she hasn't finished. "Just his name?"

"I already know his name."

"You do?"

"Mystery Donor."

Free's laugh shakes every part of her. "Cute. It could use some work, though."

"I like it."

"Okay. Mystery Donor."

We hover by the door. New and departing customers maneuver around us. I kind of shuffle and she sort of smiles. It's not a goodbye.

"Next time," Free starts with that smirk, Ruby's smirk. "Don't wait so long to message."

"Next time?" I wish I was confident enough for it to not be a question.

"Yeah. Next time. I haven't told you everything yet." She hasn't. It frightens me. I'm intrigued, but I'm more afraid than curious. "Cool meeting you, Rembrandt."

"You too."

"Wow. I have a pretty awesome gay younger brother."

"Half-brother," I tease.

When she leaves, I hold on to the words crammed into my mouth. I might have a pretty awesome nonconforming older half-sister.

CHAPTER NINETEEN

MONDAY MORNING, LUCY STOPS ME at my locker before my fourth period anatomy class. I haven't seen her all weekend. Between the ninth draft of the Essay of Doom and Mr. Riley organizing the GSA club's Sunday bowling outing—some of the members had plans on Halloween and a few of the younger ones wanted a daytime event instead of facing curfew dilemmas—I only managed to FaceTime Lucy to help decide on an outfit for her Saturday afternoon date with Brook.

"Two words," she says, leaning against her locker with a grin. "Homecoming. Prince."

"I agree." I shoulder my locker closed. "No one says no to 'Purple Rain.' Ever." Yawning, I shove my book into my backpack. "Are you putting together a playlist for the dance?"

"Huh? No." Lucy huffs. She looks nice today: striped shirt, dark jeans cuffed at the ankles, red Vans to match her necktie. "Sara's in charge of music."

Obviously. Sara's too controlling to trust anyone with major tasks, even Lucy.

"You need to run for homecoming prince."

Both my eyebrows shoot up. "Me? No."

"Yes."

"That's not happening, Lucia." I shake my head and edge around her.

"It *is* happening, Rembrandt." She beams. Honestly, she looks as if she's possessed by the school-spirit demon.

I bet Aunt Sandra could pray it out of her. "You're bananas," I say, walking away.

The warning bell rings. I take longer strides. Mr. Khorram is a pretty laid-back teacher. Anatomy isn't an easy course, but he plays Pink Floyd while we study and prefers Q & A sessions to lecturing during lessons. I'm more anxious about getting a good seat than avoiding Lucy, though, the latter deserves extra emphasis, especially when Lucy catches up to me.

"You'd make a great prince. People love you!"

"They tolerate me," I mumble.

"You're popular."

"People find me affable and ethical and are content with my attentive manner," I argue. I've used just enough SAT Prep vocabulary to stun her silent—briefly.

"It'll be no contest," she says. "Who's more loved than you?"

"Jayden, Evan Coles, Armin Darvish, Alex *or* Zac." I list each guy on my fingers. "Silver—"

"Are you effin' kidding me? Silver?"

Mr. Khorram peeks at us from behind a stack of papers when we walk in. Sunlight glints off his bald head and softens his cheeks. I wave shyly. Lucy carries on.

"You're a front-runner, trust me."

I don't trust her. And I don't like that Asher Feige snagged the most coveted seat, the front-row window desk.

Lucy pulls me to the second row, the Pretend Geeks Row. We find desks, and she tugs a rolled-up poster from her bag. "I already have a game plan. I called in a favor and had this mock-up done over the weekend."

"'Called in a favor.' What're you, a mob boss?"

Lucy's hair is plaited into a neat braid. She flicks it over her shoulder and flutters her eyelashes.

I almost drop the poster. It's a drawing of me done up like a character in a manga: large eyes, small mouth, blushing cheeks. Manga-me is waving. Above my curls reads "VOTE 4 REMY" in rainbow colors. A glitter bomb exploded around the edges. And... "Is that a freaking unicorn?!"

Lucy smirks down at me.

I scowl back. If I glare long enough, maybe she'll catch on fire—or the poster will. I'm good with both.

"Ian drew it. Well, you. I added the unicorn and glitter. Muy en fuego."

"Obviously," I say, deadpan. "Did it have to be so..."

"Gay?"

I swallow the sharpness of that word. I'm not ashamed. But it's a label, and my mind drifts back to what Free said. Then a T. rex of guilt gnaws at my heart because I haven't told Lucy—anyone—about meeting Free, so I focus on the poster.

"We're playing to your strengths," says Lucy.

Perfect. I'm the Superman of gayness. Clearly Lucy's dubbed herself my campaign manager. Outside of the glitter and rainbow and ridiculous unicorn, the drawing of me is amazingly accurate. Ian nailed my smile and the brightness of my eyes, and my curls appear purposefully unmanageable.

I want to kiss him. Then, I remember. I already have kissed him— five times. Number six could be just around the corner.

I shake my head. "I don't want any part of this, Lucia."

"Too late, Rembrandt." Lucy's cockiness is in full swing. "You've already been voted onto the official ballot by a committee of your peers and constituents."

"You lie."

She puts a hand over her chest and says, "It's true."

I squint at her. "I'm telling Rosa Maria Reyes you're spending too much time watching CNN instead of Netflix like a normal teen."

Lucy pats my head before taking her seat. "Normal is overrated, Rembrandt."

* * *

"ALL HAIL PRINCE CAMERON!"

The hallways are empty after school, save for a few students running to a practice, a club, or detention. That doesn't stop my jaw and spine from instantly locking.

But it's just Brook. He leans against the locker next to mine, smiling smugly. A "VOTE 4 REMY" pin is fastened to his letterman jacket, rainbow letters and unicorn included.

I put away my Algebra II book and mumble, "Your girlfriend is dead to me." He chuckles. "No, seriously," I say, shutting my locker, "I've already planned the funeral. Open casket so everyone can see I had her buried in that stupid Sailor Mars T-shirt."

"She loves that shirt." Brook has this dreamy heart-eyes look. It's gross. "Come on, little dude. Join the parade."

"What parade?"

"The homecoming parade! You have to admit this place is kind of magical around homecoming." He still has that same dreamy expression. "Go Marauders!"

"Brook, the only parade I'm joining is the Pride parade."

"Like the button!"

I scowl. Lucia Reyes, aged sixteen. Maplewood junior class president and unbeloved best friend.

Brook is eyeing me with a new, serious look. His mouth is a thin line and the soft, concern in his eyes is familiar. "We don't have to talk about it," he says, "but—"

I hold up a hand. "You're right. We don't have to talk about it."

I've carefully tucked those five minutes from Friday night into a deep, dark part of my brain. They sit close to that one big fight Rio and I had in middle school when we didn't talk for three days and right beside that time I fell down the stairs and it took my dad five minutes to find me, bruised and weeping. Sighing, I lean on my locker.

Brook watches quietly, as if he knows the ice is fragile, already starting to crack.

"Thanks for," I pause, my breaths shallow, "for what you did at the party."

He shrugs halfheartedly. "I could've done more."

"No." I shake my head. "You did enough. What would've happened if you hit him? As cool as Chloe thinks her dad is, I doubt Lieutenant Parker would've given you a slap on the wrist. A black kid assaulting someone else at a party where there's underage drinking and weed? It's not a good look."

"Probably not." A sly grin crosses Brook's lips. "Let's hope Chloe's dad doesn't discover that I found out what car that dickhead was driving and had a little fun with Mrs. Cowen's beauty products all over that nice paintjob."

I gasp, and Brook, all broad eyes and relaxed expression, cracks up. Then silence. Brook waits; I settle my breathing.

"The whole thing sucks." I close my eyes. "It's not that he was coming on to me. It's *why*. All he saw was my skin color, something he'd never had. It's like, that's all people see sometimes? I'm not Remy; I'm Remy, the black kid. Or, sometimes, just the black kid."

Brook doesn't say anything but I can tell he understands. It's in his eyes.

"What kind of asshole does that?"

"A lot of them." Brook laughs, ironically. "Just another day in the life of being black, right? Our melanin attracts the unwanted. You're either Suspect Number One or every undercover racist's get-out-of-jail-free card because, 'Hey, I've got a black friend!' Or you're some exotic flavor they just have to try once."

"A piece of chocolate." I make a face.

Brook says, mockingly, "That warm piece of caramel. Black coffee for their side of cream."

"It's gross."

"It's *people*, little dude. It's what they're taught, either by example or by perception."

"It's effed up, Brook." I sigh. "All I am is a skin color."

"And that's all they love or hate about you too."

I whisper, "We'll always be a stereotype."

"Not to the good ones." Brook says it in that way that's all him: certain and full of hope. "To the important ones, we'll be an inspiration, a best friend, and the love of their life. Those are the labels that matter." He adds, firm but endearing, "And don't let others take pride in who you are—your race, sexuality, whatever—away from you. They didn't give it to you; they have no right to snatch it away."

The corners of my mouth twitch. Brook Henry is a universe of so many undiscovered stars. That little corner Liam is tucked into shrinks. It's still there—let's face it, things like that are always there—but it gets smaller and smaller.

"Now," Brook grabs my shoulder, squeezes, "get on the home-coming parade. It's happening. You're gonna win."

"I'd rather get mauled by a pack of mountain lions."

"Aren't they solitary animals?"

"I don't know."

"Either way, gruesome imagery." Brook makes a face. "We'll work on better campaign slogans later. I've got swim practice."

"This isn't happening, Brook."

"Can we fit that on a T-shirt?"

"I'm not running for homecoming prince!" I shout. Brook's already halfway down the hall.

"Positive thoughts, little dude!"

"I'm positive your girlfriend is destined for a freak accident!"

Mrs. Kowalski, the freshman English teacher, peeks her head out of her classroom, and gives me the stink-eye.

Brook howls. "My weirdo best friend wouldn't approve of such nocturnal activities."

My mouth clicks shut; my eyes must be wide, blue moons. Then I remember the poster.

"TRAITOR!"

Ian raises an eyebrow as he sits down across from me. He's on a break. Casually, he passes me a ceramic mug of steaming green stuff. I sniff curiously. It's not poisoned. Or, it could be, but not with anything I can detect.

"Matcha," he says.

"You're deflecting," I say. "This is a trap."

"It's matcha."

I sip while squinting at him. It's not bad. It's odd, like all green things, but not terrible. I refuse to tell him this. He owes me answers. And kisses. In no particular order.

It's torture to look at him today: The way his hair peeks out of his beanie. Glasses slipping down his nose. Black apron contrasting with his loose red sweater. Stupid hoop earring and fingers snapping along to something rhythmic with synthesizers. Obviously, Trixie has given Ian control of Zombie's playlist again.

"You let Lucy corrupt you into ruining my life," I accuse.

"It was a paid gig."

"Paid with what?"

Ian's mouth upturns. "A supersized bag of candy corn."

I groan, then sip more green stuff. "She's playing dirty."

"You didn't like it?"

I pretend the disappointment in his voice and the wounded look on his face don't exist. This is a war. Ian's sided with the enemy; casualties are expected.

"It's nice," I force out. "Okay, it's sick-as-eff. You're crazy talented." Defenses are crumbling. The heat level in my cheeks has reached radioactive levels.

"Cool," he whispers.

"Cool."

"I mean, thanks."

"You're not welcome."

Our laughter is a harmony only dulled by the guy on the speakers singing about a woman named Eileen. Some girls wearing matching Georgia State sweatshirts join in, crooning into the straws of their iced coffees. This is what makes Zombie great. It's the aura; even Trixie's behind the bar dancing. Maybe it's the music or the way Ian's Adam's apple bobs when I catch him staring at me, but I'm feeling good—brave.

"Hey." I wait until our eyes meet. "Do you wanna hang out Thursday, after school?"

"Hang out?"

"Go somewhere."

"Somewhere?"

I'm helplessly addicted to the shine in his eyes when he says that, as if it's our word. No-Dating-Remy is a poser. "Yeah, somewhere," I confirm.

One side of his mouth lifts. Then something passes over his face, like a reminder. "I can't. I have to—" He pauses, frowning.

Eileen's song fades. I wait in the odd hiccup of silence. "What?"

"It's nothing."

I doubt that. I nudge his foot, and he shakes his head. "I need to spend time with my dad. Thursday's my parents' anniversary—well, what *was* their anniversary. My dad gets all quiet and standoffish. He pretends he's good. But he's not. That first year, he went to church, ate dinner alone. Then, around midnight, I heard him crying in the kitchen."

Coach Park crying? It doesn't compute. Coach Park is silent unless he's talking to a swimmer. He's an android, incapable of emotion.

"That's ironic, right?" Ian laughs hollowly. "My mom used to dance alone in the same kitchen my dad cries in."

We stare at each other. Nothing else exists: just me, searching for a way to comfort, and Ian, pretending he doesn't need it.

He looks away first. "Anyway, I plan to crash on the couch with him and marathon sci-fi movies."

It's the sweetest, nerdiest thing ever. "Sounds like a good plan," I say.

Ian bites on his lower lip; his dimple is fully exposed.

I stand to leave. I have homework and the Essay of Doom and I'm desperate for some Willow-Clover sofa time. I don't get far.

"Hey," Ian says, two fingers brushing my knuckles. "What about Saturday morning?"

On cue, my voice cracks. "Saturday morning?"

"Yes. Saturday."

Everything inside Zombie is brushed tangerine by the sinking sun, everything including the small space between our hands where Ian's fingers still hover. My skin itches for the warmth.

"Okay. Saturday," I finally say.

And No-Dating-Remy spontaneously combusts.

CHAPTER TWENTY

FIVE MINUTES BEFORE SIX A.M. is an unreasonable hour for any teenager to be awake. But this is tradition. Our yawns are contagious. They start with Lucy, then Rio. I'm next. We're this band of yawns and sighs and impatient exhales. We're parked outside the Krispy Kreme, waiting for the hot light to illuminate the window.

"Why do we do this to ourselves?" I ask.

"Tradition," Lucy mumbles, eyes closed, reclined in the passenger seat. A nearby street lamp's amber glow brightens her almost-peaceful face.

"Because I've had a hard week," says Rio from the backseat. She's been rambling about homework and lab projects and *The Leaf* since I picked her up twenty minutes ago, but nothing about the Mad Tagger. We haven't returned to our talk about Ian being on the Suspect Wall. I'm still frustrated about it. I still can't tell her why I *think* Ian can't be the Mad Tagger.

I yawn loudly. The driver's seat is semi-reclined; my arms are folded behind my head. Last night was another marathon of working on the Essay of Doom.

Correction: I stared at a blank Word document, then Mrs. Scott's list of potential colleges next to my newly-printed map of all the cool coffee shops around Emory's campus and the list of Creative Writing workshops offered. I've circled all the ones I want to take in red marker.

I also stared at my latest message from Free:

Message from Free Williams
Is your favorite color purple? Momma's was yellow. What are your other favorites? Food? Drink? Weather? Celeb crush? ☺
Sent Nov 6 10:31 p.m.

My eyes danced for thirty minutes until tears blurred my vision. Everyone wants to know who I am. I don't have an answer. Eventually, I got sucked into a YouTube vortex of bears swimming in pools and corny '80s music videos. Seriously, what drugs were those bands on?

At 6:07 a.m., there's still no hot light.

"I need this," says Lucy. "Committees, anime club, presidential stuff, Brook. I need a break."

"A break from Brook?"

"No. Well, yes. But not a bad break."

"Any break from a relationship is a good break," says Rio.

I roll my eyes. Rio doesn't date, ever. It's, like, her religion. The Church of Love is for the weak. On Valentine's Day, she sacrifices giant teddy bears while blasting grunge-rock to appease her heartless god.

"One day, Rio, you'll find The One," I say affectionately.

"'The One' doesn't exist. This isn't a Kate Hudson movie," says Rio. "We're not all falling madly over a crush like you."

"What?"

"Oh, come on, Rembrandt." There's a look in Lucy's eyes that's completely uncalled for. "We've seen it."

"Seen what?"

Rio sighs impatiently.

"Dude," Lucy punches my shoulder, "the way you *look* at Ian."

"Every day at lunch," Rio adds.

"Ian?" My voice is Prince-levels of high. "I don't—"

"You do," interrupts Rio. "Constantly."

"It's kind of obvious," Lucy says.

"Obvious to who?" I ask, eyes narrowed.

"Jayden, Chloe, Sara—"

"That's bullshit." Sara is like a shark; she can smell blood. If Sara Awad knew anything about Ian and me, she'd hold it over my head like a dog treat. Besides, I can totally appreciate the way Ian dresses or his nerdy glasses or a little dimple action without having a crush. It's completely acceptable. "It's not true. You have no proof to back-up these insidious accusations."

Lucy snorts. "Insidious?"

"Shut up."

"SAT Prep looks good on you, Rembrandt."

I ignore her. "I'm not crushing. There's no crush. Crushing is sixth grade."

"And these are the gays of our lives," Lucy says.

I hate them. I thumb through the playlists on my phone. I need POP ETC. But Lucy steals my phone and finds some random power-pop song.

"It's not like this is the first time this has happened, Romeo. If there's a cute boy, you fall over your feet—more than usual—while the rest of us cease to exist," says Rio, a hint of something in her voice. I can't name it. After another yawn, she adds, nonchalantly, "We don't care."

A balloon of guilt fills my lungs, because I am keeping secrets. Not the Ian thing—his sexuality isn't mine to share.

But there's Free—the fact that she exists.

"It wouldn't be the worst thing, you know," says Lucy. "You liking someone new."

Rio snorts. "It would. Infatuated Remy is the worst."

"He kinda is."

"*He*," I say through my teeth, "is right here."

"Remember the Elijah thing?" Rio continues as if I'm a ghost.

"Remember the Calvin Ingraham thing?"

In the rearview mirror, I can see my cheeks have reached neutron star levels of bright—just like the neon red "HOT NOW" sign that's finally illuminating Krispy Kreme's storefront.

I hop out of the driver's seat. "I'm getting a dozen." Rio does this happy shoulder-shimmy dance until I say, loudly, "For me!"

Lucy and Rio respond with twin middle fingers. It's all the confirmation I need that we're okay.

I can keep some secrets.

CHAPTER TWENTY-ONE

No one should spend a Saturday morning at school for any reason—unless that reason involves Ian Park. We're outside Maplewood's aquatic center. Ian's fumbling with a set of keys and the chain lock on the side entrance. I yawn. It's too early.

An overnight rain has left a thin reef of fog and mist around campus. The sun is a pale glow behind lumpy gray clouds. It's chilly outside, enough that I'm wearing a sweater for reasons other than fashion choice.

"This is Somewhere?" I ask.

Over his shoulder, Ian says, "Somewhere new." Ian and his infinite amounts of Somewhere.

"But it's not new," I say around another yawn. "I've been here."

"Not with me."

Good point. But a Saturday morning breaking into school property will land us in a Somewhere called jail. I'd love to explain that to Mrs. Scott while she shreds that list of dream colleges for me. The door snicks open. Ian smiles roguishly. I don't bother to ask how he has a set of keys to the aquatic center. Perks of being the head coach's son, I guess. The swim team is away for a meet. It's just Ian, me, and the pool.

Scratch that—this is the best reason to spend a Saturday morning at school. Ian doesn't bother turning on the overhead halogens. The lights at the bottom of the pool splash teal and aqua and turquoise against the walls and the tiles framing the water. The air's warm but damp. It smells of chlorine and possibility. Everything is quiet, except the whispering music coming from Ian's phone, propped on a diving board.

Tiny ripples disrupt the water's perfect blue surface. We're dipping nothing but our toes in. Our shoes are piled by the ladder to the high board. My sweater's in the bleachers. Ian's cardigan is near the door. We're two boys in jeans and geeky graphic T-shirts, nervous, but calmed by the water.

Simple Minds is playing. I'm learning his music. I'm learning the little curves of his mouth that launch that dimple.

"This is kind of cool," I say to interrupt the quiet. I hate the way my voice echoes.

"Is it?"

I shove him gently. "You know it is."

"I used to hate this place. The water, the smell, the stupid drenched towels piled in the locker room that my dad would tell me to pick up." He wrinkles his nose. "I used to think this is all my dad was. And this," his arms spread out, hands shaking, "is what made my mom leave."

"It's not the reason?" I ask, soft and unsure.

Ian sighs. "No."

His arms to drop to his sides. I give him a look—a question with my eyes. *Can I hold your hand?* He nods slowly, and I grab his hand.

"My mom didn't love being away from her family. She didn't love this place," he whispers. Blue hues dance across his nose, his sad eyes. "She loves me, but I don't think she loved him anymore."

We stand quietly again. The song changes: "Alone" by some band named Heart. Another Max Cameron instant-like. I'm not into it but it's bearable because I'm with Ian, with his shy smile and hand tucked in mine.

"Sorry." He shakes his head. "Word vomit." The coiled tightness of his jaw says he needed to talk about his parents, his mom.

I squeeze his hand because words aren't forming. It seems good enough for him.

"Can you swim?" he asks.

"Kind of."

"Kind of?"

I can float. I can hold my breath underwater. I have strong leg muscles, but my coordination between kicking and moving my arms is incredibly amateurish. Clover can outswim me, Willow too. But I don't tell Ian all of this. I say, quietly, "I'm a willing learner if you're a capable teacher."

He laughs at that. Head tossed back, sharp Adam's apple bobbing, he's a wonderful canvas of skin to touch, to kiss.

"Maybe," he says.

"Maybe," I repeat; the promise rests deep in my spine.

"The water's warm," he says with too much confidence. "I promise."

"We're not getting in there."

"We're not?"

I know better than to trust that dimple. His eyes are bright. His fingers are knotted too firmly around mine. I know what's about to happen. But I jump first, pulling him with me. We sink right to the bottom; soaked denim weighs us down.

It's not terrifying, fighting to crack the surface before water fills my lungs. Maybe that's the adrenaline. Maybe it's the muscle memory guiding me up. Maybe it's Ian's excited shouts echoing against the walls when I emerge. Maybe it's because we're still holding hands.

"Asshole."

"You started this," I yell, grinning. He smiles back; his hair is stuck to his forehead. I wade closer. We're halfway between the shallow and deep ends of the pool. I'm breathing hard, but I ask, "Are you mad?"

"Do I look mad?"

"You look wet."

"Funny." He splashes me.

I retaliate with a bigger wave. We sway and thrash and never move too far. We float closer. Cold fingers intertwined; our palms kiss until our heartbeats intersect at that one point of contact.

Ian's cheeks are ruddy; his skin is pale. Quick breaths push his lips apart. My breathing syncopates. He swallows, then says, "Can I—"

"Yes."

He kisses me, softly at first, then, with a loud gasp, a curious tongue. I sink into it, sighing. My fingers thread into his soaked, dark hair. Our knees knock as we tread water. Our skin is cold. I focus on the heat of our mouths, on the taste of chlorine and matcha and something new happening. On Madonna singing about being crazy for someone.

Then, in silent agreement, we dunk underwater. We're swallowed by blue-green and silence. For once, I can't hear anything: not my thoughts, not my fears, the person I'm not or possibly am. I only hear my thunderous heartbeat, and it's the most calming noise ever.

* * *

IT'S THE STRANGEST THING, LYING in someone else's bed, gradually learning the shape of their pillow. The newness of wearing their athletic shorts and Pokémon socks as you stretch. Or adjusting to the way their Maplewood swim team hoodie with sleeves so long they bunch over your knuckles feels.

Face-to-face, we're so close our noses touch. Our foreheads bump whenever one of us shifts. Our quiet breaths are underscored by the rain falling outside Ian's bedroom window.

I could compare all this to days with Dimi in his bedroom. I don't. Instead, my eyes roam from Ian's lazy expression to all the things I notice about his room. He has posters dedicated to weird anime and even weirder '80s musicians pinned at awkward angles on marigold-painted walls. In a corner is a piano-keys dresser, white drawers with thick black handles. Polaroids of palm trees, fresh oranges, the Pacific Ocean are taped everywhere. His black sheets are dotted with white stars. We're lying in the middle of a galaxy.

I push hair off his forehead. His eyes trace my face. I bite my lip. It's still sore from kissing, from his teeth. "You're quiet."

He shakes his head, which makes our noses nuzzle. That makes me giggle. His index finger repeatedly draws something against the inside of my wrist, letters, like an SOS, in pressure soft as a newborn's heartbeat.

"I'm not usually this affectionate," he says. "This is new. You're new." He hasn't met my eyes. I don't force him to. "This is strange and weird."

"Strange and weird?" I repeat nervously.

Nose scrunched, he says, "My dad's not really a touchy guy. I think that influenced how my mom was about affection."

"How?"

"Whenever I was in the room with them, my mom only kissed the top of his head or rubbed his hand, gave him a quick hug."

"That's not strange or weird."

"It is," insists Ian. "It is when you have someone like my halmeoni in your life. When she knows you, she hugs you like you belong in her arms. Sweet kisses to your forehead. She'd lay her head on my shoulder after a long day and tell me all her stories."

"Is everyone in your family like that?" I ask "Aunt Jilynn?"

The corners of his mouth twitch. I think he likes that I remember.

"Yes." His finger steadies on. "Whenever I Skype with mom's family back in California or the ones that live in Daejeon, they're always piled on top of each other, cheek-to-cheek, trying to talk to me. But my parents were never like that, in and out of public. So I'm not…"

When Ian goes quiet, I press my thumb behind his ear and wait until his heartrate slows. I let him squeeze onto those memories like a midnight that'll never end.

"This is new," he says. "You're new."

"New is good," I tell him.

"I should know what to do. Right?"

"Nope. We're strange and weird. No instruction manual needed."

He laughs; I do too. Because this is new, which is scary and exciting and unexpected. And I think we both like that.

Ian tells me more about his halmeoni and about his infatuation with *The Pirates of the Caribbean* growing up—the reason behind the hoop earring. I talk about Willow and about my obsession with Charlie Brown holiday specials. I almost tell him about Free. But I can't, not before Rio and Lucy, not before my parents.

"What're you writing?" I ask.

His finger pauses on my wrist. An outbreak of crimson tints his fawn skin. He clears his throat; his shy eyes roam my face. "Na neo joahae."

"What?"

"I like you." Then his finger traces a heart into my palm.

I can't stop myself. I whisper, "Can I kiss you?" and when he nods, I lean forward. I kiss him. Every soft, insistent feeling for him is in this kiss. Every "no, you can't" is erased by a loud, vibrant "yes, you will." My thumb finds his dimple and his leg wiggles between mine.

He touches my hips. I move into his grip. A small tug of war follows as limbs and hands and lips navigate unknown waters. I let him win, because I'm more experienced, because he needs to learn what he likes, what he's comfortable with. But we're both hard and needy.

We're both shaky and clumsy. I almost knee him in the groin. He almost rolls me off the bed. The pillows fall, as do our sweaters. He's breathless on his back under me. His eyes blink. I kiss a mole on his neck to settle him.

"Remy." His voice is tight, but happy. "Can we—"

"Can we *what*?" I interrupt.

He groans impatiently. It's the most exciting thing I've ever heard. But I get the message. I ask him if he's sure? If he has protection? If he wants his first time to be with me? Because that's huge. I wasn't Dimi's first. I've never been anyone's first.

But every answer is, "Yes, yes, hell yes."

And every answer comes with a kiss like a promise. What we're about to give each other, we deserve.

CHAPTER TWENTY-TWO

NOVEMBERS IN GEORGIA ARE BIZARRE. The weather is like a five-year-old in a candy aisle—perpetually undecided. Some days, it's a seven-layers-of-clothing deal. Other days, it's a light hoodie and shorts kind of thing.

Today, it's the latter, so after school Lucy and I sit at one the few outdoor tables at Zombie. She's studying fashion magazines. I'm scowling at my laptop screen. The Essay of Doom glares back at me. I have five hundred words written. Only ten of them are any good. Then again, two of the ten are my name, so I'm not sure that counts.

"Orchid or coral?"

I blink at her. Lucy's head is bowed. Her hair is piled messily on top of her head, surprisingly kept in place by four highlighters.

"Which color?"

I flinch. "What?"

"I'm trying to find the perfect color for my dress."

Her dress. Right. It's hard to forget homecoming is around the corner. Everyone's talking about what to wear. Advertisements are plastered everywhere, including the VOTE 4 REMY poster taped to Zombie's big, scenic window: rainbow and unicorn and my big manga-style eyes for every caffeine addict to mock.

Our drinks are sweating next to each other on the table. The sun's gradually descending. Dying light softens Lucy's features. She's glowing.

"Gold," I say. "Definitely gold."

She sweeps fallen strands of dark hair from her face. "Is that your gay-best-friend stamp of approval?"

I roll my eyes. She's only teasing. But it's been in my head lately: the GSA, the Ford Turner comments, the homecoming campaign posters.

Is this who I am? Am I too gay? Is that a thing? My brain's a mess. I set a new record getting ready for school this morning: forty-five minutes. I kept staring at the clothes in my closet: pastel this, neon that; pink and yellow and bright; so much gay and gay and gayer. Every shirt, every pair of jeans screamed, "Hey, look at me and my attention-needy self! I'm a rainbow! I'm a stereotype!"

I decided on a pair of black skinnies—of course—and matching pair of Nike Air Force 1 low-tops and a plain collared shirt Aunt Sandra bought for my last birthday. Black, obviously. Today, I just wanted to be average. No stereotypes. No declarations. Except, on cue, everyone noticed.

"Did someone sell you some bad product? Have you gone emo?" Alex and Zac asked.

Totally.

"You don't look like yourself," Jayden said.

Perfect! I don't feel like Remy Cameron right now.

"Who are you?" Sara asked.

I don't know.

"You're still helping me shop, right?" Lucy asks.

I cock my head. "You don't want to go with your mom?"

"Nah." Lucy sips her macchiato. It's no longer an Instagram-worthy aesthetic masterpiece. "She'll be too busy with work."

She casually leaves out the part where her mom probably can't afford anything new either. Paying rent and buying groceries and school supplies for four girls doesn't leave much money for homecoming dresses. I think Lucy's mom's secretly saving for a prom dress, anyway. But none of that bothers Lucy. She's happy using the money she gets from tutoring neighbors' kids to hit up a thrift store for something to wear.

That's Lucy—our rock, our foundation. All the things that make our table of friends cool extend from Lucy. I'm in awe of her. If I'm honest, I've always been in awe of her. I just don't say it out loud enough. Maybe that makes me a coward or a bad friend.

"Yeah, I'm still down," I say, my lips curved into a half-smile. We'll make a day of dresses and fitting-room selfies and pizza afterward. As much as I'm dreading homecoming, I'm looking forward to this.

"Thanks," whispers Lucy. Her eyes crinkle and her cheeks lift.

Sunlight reflects off my laptop screen. I haven't typed a new word in thirty minutes. The Essay of Doom is taunting me. "Hey."

Lucy barely lifts her eyes from dress-browsing. "What's up?"

A planet-sized lump clogs my throat. I scratch my eyebrow. "Do you think you know who you are?"

"Who I am?"

"Yeah." I hiccup. "Yes."

Lucy twists loose hair around her finger. Her eyebrows do this funny dance when she's thinking: wiggle-wiggle, up-down. "No," she replies coolly. "I know the things people see me as—Latinx, brown skin, seventeen, a girl whose dad threw her the deuces because responsibility isn't on his agenda."

I bite my lip hard. The skin around Lucy's eyes tightens. She doesn't look mad, more annoyed. I shouldn't have asked.

"I know who I'm going to be, though." She sits up straighter, shoulders pulled back. "A leader. A legend. I'm going to make Latinx people in political office the standard instead of an abnormality."

I grin. "SAT word."

She smacks my shoulder. Then, serious as ever, she says, "I'm going to kick down a lot of doors, Rembrandt. For my mom. For my sisters. For me."

This has always been Lucy: confident, groundbreaking, a superhero.

I slump in my chair. Pink and yellow spots crowd my vision like exploding pixies. My brain melts like a popsicle in mid-June. This is another confirmation, another reminder. Everyone around me knows who they are or are going to be. I know nothing.

"But what if—" I can't look at her. "What if you don't know who you're going to be because you don't know who you are currently?"

We're quiet. Cars cruise by playing music or talk radio. Kids run from an SUV to the ice cream shop. Traffic lights dance from yellow to red to green.

Lucy says, "But you know who you are."

"I don't. I mean, I did and this *thing*," I wave a hand at my laptop, "came along and now there are so many questions."

"Questions are good."

"Are they?"

"Sure." I can hear the smile in her voice, even though I still can't look. "Questions are how we start to discover things."

I don't tell her how I don't want to discover anything. For seventeen years, I've been Remy Cameron, a music junkie. I've been that boy who got hard when Dev Patel sneezed. I was the boy with a cute dog, a beyond-awesome little sister, and two marginally cool parents that everyone knows. A picture-perfect reality.

Now, I'm squinting at my world, discovering all the cracks. Mrs. Scott sees me as a gay, black teen she can guide to success. Everyone at school associates me with being the GSA president or Dimi's ex-boyfriend. The neighbors think I'm Willow's babysitter; not her brother. I'm a lost adopted boy instead of a boy in love with the family he was given. My world is filled with identities overshadowing who I am. Who I *think* I am.

Lucy folds her hands and rests her chin on them. "You didn't know who you were at eleven when we forced Wyatt Matthews to eat a mud sandwich."

I chuckle. "We were criminals."

"We were vigilantes. That asshole said Rio looked like a lumpy squash when she wore that epic sunflower dress. He deserved it." He did. "And you didn't know who you were the summer before freshman year."

I rub my curls. The age of BCO—Before Coming Out.

"You didn't know who you were last summer."

"I was a virgin. A relatively awesome virgin."

"You were passable on the awesome scale."

"True that. Dimi brought down my stock."

"You set the standards too high with him."

We crack up. My cheeks are damp, and I hope it's from the laughter. I hope Lucy doesn't notice.

When we stop, Lucy's voice is gentle, far away. "Point is, you found out a little more about who you are. You always do. Life is a journey, Rembrandt. You don't know all of it at seventeen. Or as an adult. In fact, I think when you finally do know all of who you are, the universe stops the clock and ends the journey."

"That's kind of morbid, Lucia."

"Shut up. I'm going through an emo phase, like your wardrobe."

"I still look great."

"You look like death."

"High-fashion death."

She rolls her eyes. "The jury's still out."

We slip back into comfortable silence, the kind that's existed forever between us.

Inside Zombie, Ian's shuffling around. I watch him hang a new menu he's doodled on, talk to Trixie, fix his glasses, sip a steaming matcha latte. I haven't said anything to him since lunch today. I asked him for a fry. Red-faced and stammering, he passed me the whole tray. And he didn't say anything after the last bell when he hooked a finger in my belt loop and tugged me into an empty classroom. He spoke in kisses.

Ian sees me through the glass. My smile feels never-ending.

"I've seen that look before," accuses Lucy.

"On yourself?"

Lucy gasps, then kicks me. "I have never."

Oh, but she has. It's true, Brook Henry's unbearable levels of puppy love when it came to Lucy started the second she stepped on campus freshman year. But peak Brook-infatuated-Lucy was scary: hardcore stares and notebook poetry and forcing me to watch endless YouTube videos of Olympic swimming events.

"I tried to ask Brook about it." I freeze. "But he says it's nothing. I'm seeing things," she says, and my limbs finally relax. Unspoken trust lives.

"It really is nothing," I say. She squints. "We're friends."

"A likely story."

We leave it at that. I know why I *can't* tell her, but that doesn't make keeping this from Lucy any less difficult. I used to tell her everything about Dimi, even when things were starting to fray, when I could tell she hated him. This is new for me, dating—or non-dating—someone who isn't out. I'm more aware of every touch or look because that might tip someone off. I can't walk up to Ian at his locker and kiss him in the middle of Maplewood's morning traffic jam.

Someone clears their throat. Standing over us is Darcy. While the rest of Maplewood's student population usually looks like the *Walking Dead* after school, Darcy always seems ready for another eight hours of social awkwardness and pop quizzes. In her peach sweater and khaki skirt and blonde hair strategically pinned up to show off her cheekbones, she's a preppy candidate for sainthood.

She shoots me a half-wince, then turns to Lucy. I guess I should be thankful she didn't publicly damn my sexual deviancy to passersby.

"We need to do something about this Mad Tagger situation, as a collective," she says, huffing.

"What about them?"

"He struck again."

Lucy raises an eyebrow. "Again?"

"Yes!" Darcy shrieks. Her skin's blotchy-red. "My posters for a prayer circle to be held before the dance were vandalized."

I quickly grab my drink to stop myself from snorting. Anyone could've defaced GTFO's posters. Darcy has a select group of minions and an army of non-fans.

"The class presidents should convene and stop this madness." Darcy makes a face like a disgruntled cartoon lion. "Clearly Principal Moon and Chloe's dad are clueless."

"O-okay," says Lucy, slowly, "but what're we, you know, *teens* gonna do to stop a criminal? We're not Dumbledore's Army."

"It's obviously a student. We could sniff out the culprit."

I guffaw. "Did they forget to wear deodorant?"

Darcy's glare is like a vampire on steroids. I raise surrendering hands. It's one thing to combat Darcy, President of GTFO and Queen of Cardigans, in the halls of Maplewood. I can guarantee a small measure of safety there. But public Darcy doesn't seem quite as determined to keep a clean slate with the law.

"Okay, Darcy," Lucy says. "Maybe we can plan something?"

"It's already being coordinated. We can't let homecoming be desecrated by..." She pauses, directs that venomous glare at me. "...people who don't understand the purpose of traditional values."

I bite my lip so hard, hints of coppery blood drip on my tongue.

"Fine. Text me the details," Lucy says, rubbing her temples.

Darcy nods curtly at Lucy. She doesn't spare me another glance. Good. I'd hate to ruin her day with my one-fingered response to her "traditional values." It might add a couple of years to her soulless life.

Lucy sighs. "What the hell?"

I shrug. I have enough to figure out about myself. I don't need to analyze who Darcy Jamison is too.

"I wonder if Rio knows about this latest incident?" Lucy's already texting.

Rio's been on radio silence. There was no morning meet-up on the steps outside school. She wasn't at lunch. I texted her twice after school—no response. Maybe she's knee-deep in this Mad Tagger stuff. Maybe it's nothing.

The setting sun peels blue from the sky. It's pinker, verging on rose-gold. Everything smells like ground coffee and exhaustion. Lucy texts, and people pass our table, and my brain implodes with more thoughts. I don't add a single word to the Essay of Doom the rest of the day.

* * *

"HEY." I FIND RIO AT her locker the next day before homeroom. "You've been hiding."

She tucks a lock of amber hair behind her ear. She's wearing this cool crossbones-print shirt under a denim jacket layered in enamel pins. And she's strategically not making eye contact with me.

"Rio?"

She sighs, nose wrinkled.

"What's up?"

"The sky," she says, her voice clipped.

"Okay, lame." I tilt my head. "What's going on? You've been missing."

"Busy."

"But you—"

"I'm gonna be late." She slams her locker shut and starts to move around me, but I catch her arm. Her face tenses.

"What's wrong?"

"I'm busy."

"With the Mad Tagger thing?"

Rio's eyes cut me like a machete. "Yeah, that whole 'Mad Tagger thing.' That *thing* you're too busy to help out with."

"I'm not—" I pause. I guess I have been busy. And maybe I've been devoting more time to Lucy because, well, Lucy doesn't think Ian's the Mad Tagger. Rio does. But that's not the only reason I've been too busy for Rio. I have homework and family time and an essay that's eagerly devouring my academic career like a snack. Oh, and that half-sister I still haven't told anyone about.

Rio glares, pouting impatiently. I don't have anything to say. I'm drowning in a sea of "who am I?" and I don't know how to scream loud enough for my friends to hear. "I'm not too busy."

Rio *pffts*, then shakes my hand off. I let it fall to my side. We stare and stare as students hustle around us on their way to homeroom.

I can't move. It's as if a thunderstorm is about to crack heaven open and flood the hallway. And my feet have decided this is where I'll stay.

"Lucy said you're going to the dance," hisses Rio.

I suck in my cheeks. "I mean," I wave my hand at the wall plastered in campaign posters, where mine is smack in the middle of ones for Jayden and Armin and Ford Turner and, surprisingly, Silver, "I kinda have to, don't I?"

"Nope."

"But—"

"This is so predictably you, Remy. Pretending to hate the social hierarchy. The rebel who's only rebelling because he doesn't know what else to do," Rio spits. "You don't hate the system. You *fit in* with it. You're popular."

"So are you."

She laughs harshly. "By association. I'm popular with an asterisk. With a disclaimer." Her voice breaks. "And I don't give a damn about it."

"It's just a dance."

"It's not just a dance, Remy."

"For fuck's sake, what do you want of me, Rio?"

"I want you to be a *friend*." Her face is crimson, and not because she's supporting Maplewood's athletic department. There's this little tremble to her bottom lip. It's scary. "I want you to stop being a friend when it's convenient. Be a friend instead of always, *always* being caught up in a new boy. Elijah. Dimi freaking Antov. And now Ia—"

"Don't," I plead. The hallway is relatively empty now, just us and two lost freshmen. But still, I don't know who might hear. I can't out Ian. "This isn't a thing."

Rio rolls her eyes. "It's such a thing."

"Jesus, Rio, I'm sorry, okay? It's been…" My throat closes. The words can't escape. "It's been tough."

"Really? Tough? You look fine. Content."

"I'm trying here."

"*This* is trying?"

There's something about her voice. I've always been pro snarky-Rio, but not today. The late bell rings, and I'm done. "Forgive me for, like, finding other ways to deal with stuff instead of being bitchy and a loner. Geez, it's not like Lucy's been around either," I say, venom burning the roof of my mouth. "She's busy too."

Rio yanks her phone out of her back pocket. "No, it's just you," she says, wiggling her screen in my face. Her thumb swipes through the camera roll. Photo after photo. Rio and Lucy at the movies. At a park. At a damn pet shelter. Photos of Rio with Alex Liu too. A lot of Rio and Alex.

"Is he replacing me?"

Shock dilates Rio's pupils into black holes with pale green rings. "No," she says, quietly. "It's not like that." Something in her tight shoulders and nervous eyes says it's *something*.

"So, you've been chilling with everyone but me?" I try to dilute the hurt in my words. "You haven't posted anything about this." I'd know. Rio's timeline has been nothing but a collage of Mad Tagger artwork.

"Seriously?" Rio's exasperated. "Plot twist: I don't post every little aspect of my day on Twitter or Instagram or whatever social media platform to give my life validation. Likes don't make any portion of my life more significant."

"Rio." I close my eyes. An intense veil of red—anger—forms behind my lids. "It's a lot. The essay. My family. I have a—" The words almost fly out. "It's a lot."

"It's always a lot, Remy."

"Freaking hell, Rio. For once, let this be about me. Quit acting as if you're the only one alone in this world because your parents are never around," I say with a growl. "You have no clue what I'm dealing with."

She winces. Then, with a tight voice, she says, "You're right. I wouldn't know. I'm only the friend you talk to about boys and meaningless romance."

I hear her walk away. I hear the pain in her voice and the static of my heart and the world ending. I should've told her. She's my best friend.

"Mr. Cameron?"

My eyes blink open. It's Principal Moon. She's a few feet away, standing with Mrs. Scott, who's wearing a red-and-gray floral dress and a disappointed expression. There's so much school spirit around here nowadays—crimson and steel streamers and pirates painted on classroom doors and homecoming posters *everywhere*—that I want to vomit.

"Remy?" It's Mrs. Scott's "concerned" voice.

I ignore her, glaring at some art kid's banner advertising the dance, the stupid, friendship-dismantling dance.

Principal Moon clears her throat. "Would you like to add attending detention to your class schedule today?"

"No, ma'am."

Ma'am is a southern thing. Principal Moon is all grassroots. I guess I'm trying to impress her so maybe she can write me a recommendation to Emory, since clearly Ms. Amos won't be after I fail AP Lit.

"Are we going to homeroom today?"

I whisper, "Yeah."

"Yeah?"

"Yes, ma'am."

"Good."

I push off the bank of lockers I've been leaning against. My heart's raging louder than one of Zac's EDM playlists. My nails have left deep crescents in my palms.

I'm not even halfway down the hall when Mrs. Scott yells, cheesy as a kitten poster, "We're on the road to success, Mr. Cameron!"

I successfully stop myself from telling her to shove that "we" up her tight ass.

* * *

MESSAGE FROM FREE WILLIAMS
Tonight's date: Physical Chemistry of Biological Systems. Let me tell you. She's a boring date. I think I have Momma's poor taste in romance ☹
Sent Nov 13 8:02 p.m.

Message from Free Williams
BTW I've been thinking. Are you sure you don't want to at least see what Mystery Donor looks like? Momma kept a lot of photos.
Sent Nov 13 8:05 p.m.

I stare at my phone for a long time. I shouldn't be on it. The deadline until I turn in the Essay of Doom—until my dreams of attending Emory bite the dust—is getting closer and closer. But I need the distraction.

I consider Free's question. The more we message, the more I wonder if Ruby was anything like her: refreshing and curious. The more I think about my fight with Rio, I wonder if I'm anything like

Mystery Donor: selfish and oblivious and angry. I'm angry with Rio. But I'm mostly angry with myself.

I FaceTime Lucy. She picks up immediately. Her hair is a frizzy mess, and she has heavy shadows under her eyes. She's finally registered to take the SAT in early December. She's been possessed by panic for two days.

"You look scary," I tell her, half-serious.

"It's a good thing you're gay and not my type," says Lucy, rolling her eyes.

"Hey," I say, then sigh. She squints at me. She can tell I'm not myself.

"Spill it, Rembrandt. You're eating up my study time."

"If you had the chance to see your dad again, would you?"

"You know he lives in Texas, right? I could visit."

"Hypothetically. If you could." I feel my throat closing up. The hand not holding my phone is trembling. "Please, Lucia."

She twirls her hair around her index finger, eyebrows pinched. A faraway look passes over her eyes. Again, I shouldn't have asked. Maybe a real reason why Lucy and I don't talk about these things exists.

"No. I wouldn't."

"Why?"

Lucy pushes hair out of her face. That look returns. Then she says, "There are some people who leave our lives and it's not our job to hold on. To ask, 'what if,' even if we want to. We're supposed to let them leave."

I bite my thumbnail. We're on each other's screen, backlit by bedroom light and matching laptops, but we can barely make eye contact. "What if it means there's a part of us that's hollow? Or always curious?"

"We're not empty without them, Remy," she says, like a reminder, like a vow. "What they take with them, we didn't need. They only leave behind that 'what if'—but so does everything else in life."

We exhale together. Maybe those doors we're afraid to open in friendship need to be cracked just a little. Maybe we need to see what's on the other side.

"Is this about the Rio thing?" she asks tentatively.

"No."

"I don't want to…" Lucy chews her lip; her eyes dance in the light. "I shouldn't get involved."

"Good," I whisper. "It's for the best."

"Is something else wrong, Rembrandt?"

"Too much shit to unpack, Lucia," I reply, returning that same weak grin she's been sending.

"I hear you. One day?"

"One day," I confirm.

She tells me she has to go. Her mom needs help with her sisters. I hang up. Clover's pacing my floor. I missed our evening walk. I never miss our walks. I never fight with Rio. I'm someone new. Or this is who I've always been. Was Mystery Donor this confused at seventeen? The thought wipes a cold film across my brain. Then I remember Free's message. And I remember Lucy's words.

Message from Remy Cameron
No. I don't need to know what he looked like. Who he was. He's gone.
I'm not him.
You're Free. I'm Remy. We're not them.
Sent Nov 13 8:39 p.m.

CHAPTER TWENTY-THREE

"It's been six days. Our longest fight was three. This feels like it's gonna be an eternity."

"Have you tried texting her?"

"No."

"FaceTime?"

"Nope."

"Have you sent her parents an e-mail?"

I chuckle, shaking my head. Ian's such a nerd. He's the kind of person that would walk up to a friend's parents, shake their hands, and ask for permission to go on a walk with their child. At least, that's what he's done with me. We've looped around my neighborhood twice. It's extra chilly today, but I don't mind. Clover doesn't either. She's chaperoning us—according to Mom. Truth is, she needed a walk. And I needed Ian time.

Outside of school, we haven't seen each other much. He's been busy, I guess. There's that word again: *busy, busy, busy*. Except Ian hasn't been at work—not that I randomly popped up at Zombie the other day. Mom wanted caffeine and Willow wanted a muffin. That's it. I didn't casually suggest the café in hopes of seeing him. And Ian hasn't been with Brook, who picked up extra shifts at Regal Cinema to pay for a rental tux for homecoming.

We've texted. One night, we FaceTimed. It was a bunch of yawning and sleepy smiles and my ramblings about Adult Swim. But nothing else: no hidden soft touches; no dark-classroom kisses; no happy, clumsy sex in the back of my car, which might've happened once a week ago. My lower anatomy likes to remind me of that last detail.

Mostly, I've missed Ian's glasses, his stupid little topknot, his word vomit, and the way he looks in sweaters. He's wearing mine today, the one I left at his house after our unplanned, fully-dressed swimming adventure. I'm wearing his hoodie. None of this escaped Mom's intensely keen observation skills.

We pass Mr. Ivanov's house a third time. We always stop to admire the lawn. It's not even Thanksgiving yet, and he's already piled the grass with reindeer and elves and plastic candy canes. The big white oak is dressed in twinkle lights.

Clover barks. Then we're walking again. Ian's quiet. More than usual, at least.

"Everything okay?" I ask.

He's studying the neighborhood. It's after six p.m.; the sun is a bruised peach in the distance. November looks good in Ballard Hills. The trees are on fire; gold and crimson leaves everywhere, hardly any green left. Election signs fight for lawn turf. Pumpkins and paper turkeys guard front doors. The cooler weather gives the scenery a new gloss.

"I'm good," he finally says.

"You seem distracted."

He sighs. It's not a good sigh.

Clover's ahead, marking another tree. Her kingdom is expanding.

"My mom came to visit," says Ian, like a whisper on the wind. "A quick visit."

I lazily step closer. Our fingers almost brush, but Ian maintains a distance, an invisible wall.

"We talked." He pushes hair behind his ear.

"About?"

"Me." That one word is underlined, highlighted, and the font is huge. I already know what he's going to say.

"She talked to a few family members about me... being gay. They're not okay with it." His nose wrinkles and, under my tight sweater, I can see his muscles contract but not release. He says, "I try not to let it bother me. It could be a lot worse. It *is* a lot worse for other kids. It's not as if she disowned me. She still... loves me. I'm not trying to impress her. I'm not trying to impress anyone with my sexuality. But it's family. They're all I've had for a long time."

We pause at a curb. Three orange leaves fall between us. There's a space and I hate it. I hate what it represents.

"But family can be a lot of things," I say. "Friends and support groups and..." One word hangs in my throat. Ian tilts his head. We both know what it is. Neither one of us says it aloud.

It's not my word to claim. It should be given. It's another thing that should come with permission. Instead, I say, "Family isn't always what we're born into."

Ian smiles at that. It's small, but genuine. "It's just been on my mind, that's all." His smile endures, but it's weakening. "No big deal. Back to you and Rio."

But I don't want to talk about Rio. I want to tell him it's a big deal. That all of this matters. And I want to reach out, touch his hand, but I can't. Not because I don't have permission, but because words hang in Ian's throat too.

"I don't know." I start to walk again. Ian and Clover follow. "We're just... I don't know. It's stupid."

Ian hums noncommittally.

"Now I don't have a date to the dance." I try to make it sound like a joke, not an invitation. I fail.

We've paused four houses down from mine. Willow's *Family Circus* curtains are visible from here.

"I can't," he mumbles.

"Sorry. I wasn't— I mean, I *was*, but…"

"I'm not comfortable yet."

"Okay." That entire word tastes like a lifetime of lies. He's not comfortable. He's comfortable enough to flirt and kiss my neck and unbutton my jeans and fall asleep on my shoulder in his bed while his dad is gone, but not enough to go to a silly dance. I know that's not fair. It's an asshole conclusion, but I can't help it. I wasn't in the closet long enough to know what being "uncomfortable" meant.

Ian's staring at his shoes when he says, "I need time. I like you."

"I like you too."

"This is good."

"Good," I repeat, numb and vacant. "It's no big deal."

I wonder if he wants to tell me it is. But he doesn't. Clover barks, then trots off to our yard.

Ian turns the other way. "I need…" He sighs. The Bad Sigh. "Just not now."

"Okay," I whisper.

He doesn't kiss me goodbye, doesn't promise to text. I think he will, though. Then again, I kind of don't want him to. I don't want to miss him. I don't want to think of Ian as another missing piece from my half-put-together puzzle. And there's no one to talk to about this. Not Lucy. Definitely not Rio. Brook might take Ian's side. I can't go babbling this in a GSA meeting. It's only me.

I stare at Mr. Ivanov's yard, at all these wonderful pieces coming together to create this epic scene, this fully-imagined idea, even if it's a month early.

"Where's the Thanksgiving-love, Ivanov?" I say to the wind, to the white oak.

Suddenly, a voice beside me says, "Jonathan used to love Thanksgiving. It was his favorite holiday."

I whip around, and next to me is an old man with a tired face, sad brown eyes, and a plaid shirt. He's staring at the tree, too, with tight shoulders and a slight hunch to his stance. I've never seen Mr. Ivanov outside of his house.

"He loved watching the parade," Mr. Ivanov says. "He was an interior designer, so things like this..." He waves an arm at the lawn. "...were his pride and joy. We'd decorate it together every year until he couldn't, until he didn't want to get out of bed. Then he'd let me decorate our bedroom and pretend that was good enough."

Something aches in his cold voice. It's the way I talk about Dimi, the way Free talks about Ruby: hollow resentment mixed with longing.

I finally get my voice to work. "Jonathan?"

"My husband." A brief tremble passes over him. "My late husband."

I manage not to appear shocked, but I am. I shouldn't be shocked that Mr. Ivanov had a husband. I shouldn't have assumed he was straight or peculiar or anything but a man who's missing a piece of himself and unable to navigate through that.

He clears his throat. "It's been seven years. Seven years since the chemo stopped working. And I still can't decorate for Thanksgiving."

The wind shakes the remaining leaves until they fall. More color to the lawn. Another piece of life ending.

"Maybe I'll try again next year," he adds

We exhale in unison. Mr. Ivanov's gaze on me is heavy; his head is cocked. He's not as old and withered as he looked peering from behind his curtains.

"Everything okay?"

Instinct tells me to lie. This is the first time I've been in the same breathing space as Mr. Ivanov. He's always been a ghost with a whimsical yard. But I reply, "No," because something tells me he knows what it's like to not be okay.

"Most of us aren't okay," he says. "We're simply good at hiding it."

"I guess."

We leave it at that. I watch Mr. Ivanov walk shakily toward his house. Then, over his shoulder, he says, "Tell that dog of yours this land is sacred. Jonathan might've loved dogs, but I don't need her shitting on my lawn," with a grin, a full one.

After he's back behind the safety of his blood-red door, I stand there wondering why Mr. Ivanov shared all that with me. Is it because he doesn't have anyone else to talk to? Do we find that safe space in strangers, people who don't know us well enough to judge our flaws?

It hits me. I tug out my phone, pull up Facebook messenger, and type away. I find the one person who doesn't know me well enough yet to consider me a failure.

* * *

"So, this is about boy problems?" asks Free, picking a leaf of spinach from her pizza slice. "Fine. You're buying."

"Deal."

We're at Savage Pizza. It's one of my favorite places in Little Five Points. I love all the comic book memorabilia on the walls and the action figures hanging from the ceiling. Bright pops of yellow and blue and red are everywhere. The scent of oil and fresh parmesan on the New York-style pizzas is blissful. We've been here thirty minutes and haven't talked much.

Correction: *I* haven't said much. Free's talked about classes and a party she went to where they played *Clue,* as in the board game. She's talked about the cute waiter at the Vortex she's totally not going on a date with. But we haven't discussed Ian at all. Until now, I guess.

"I'm ordering more pizza and you're gonna pay with that fancy credit card your parents probably gave you," she says.

"I don't have a credit card," I say with bite. "I'm not some spoiled kid, you know. Living in the suburbs doesn't mean I get a BMW and a trust fund."

"Yeah, sorry. That was whack."

"It kinda was."

"My bad," says Free. She tilts her head. "I guess I'm a little jealous sometimes."

"Of what?"

"Gee, I don't know, little bro." Her lips pucker. "Maybe it's the whole 'our momma gave you up for adoption because she took one good look at our lives and thought you'd be better off' thing? Maybe she was right?"

"She wasn't," I mumble. "My life isn't so great."

"Shut up." She chucks a pizza crust at me. "It is."

"It's not." I sigh. "I'm one of five black kids at school. My freshman year, I was the token gay kid until others finally came out. I've been the token everything. I'm like a dragon in a city of unicorns."

"Wow. That's a visual."

"It's not so great."

"Just because things suck in this one moment doesn't mean they'll always be shitty. It doesn't mean they've always been shitty." She sips ginger ale from a mason jar—another cool quirk about this place. "It's temporary. Shit's not that serious."

I rub my temples. It is that serious, isn't it? It feels that way. In fact, it feels as if I'm the only one who sees how epic all this is. Because, a month ago, I was Remy Cameron. Now I'm Remy Cameron—insert six different labels to describe me.

Our silence hangs. Free orders another pizza. I don't complain. Her choices suck—spinach, jalapeños, and pineapples—but I'll survive. A headband holds back her forest of curls. Her shirt says, "Moody Judy," and gold hoop earrings match all eight of her rings.

My half-sister defines cool. I want her to hang with Willow. I want her to *know* Willow, so I ask, "Are you sure you don't want to meet them someday? My family?"

It's bizarre to ask. *My family*, as if Free isn't family too.

"Remy—"

"It's just that..." I bite my thumbnail. "...you said you wanted to find me because you wanted to know the little brother you never got to meet, because Ruby took that from you. And I get that—to have a missing piece. But you found me, and they're part of me. I'm not asking you to fall in love with them, though that'd be pretty cool."

Free purses her lips.

"I'm asking you to know me. And to *know me* is to know who helped me get to where I am."

"Bro." She sighs. "Don't you get that that's part of the problem? Our mother made sure you could *get somewhere* while I've had to do it alone. Just me."

"But it doesn't have to be that way. Not anymore."

She leans back, studying me.

"You don't have to," I whisper, "but it'd be cool if you'd at least gave it a shot. Gave me a shot."

Free smirks—that Ruby smirk—and says, "Are you sure you want to go to Emory? You'd have a pretty good career as a lawyer."

A halfhearted version of her smirk tugs at my mouth. "That might be my only option unless prayer gets me a passing grade in AP Lit."

Free laughs so hard the bored waitperson behind the register turns to squint at us. Then I ask Free if she's religious, what she believes in. She tells me about Ruby and her issues with organized religion. After Ruby died, Free found friends that prayed with her and took her to church. Now, she finds solace believing in *something*.

I like that. Tension melts away from my muscles, my bones. I feel loose. So, I talk. I tell Free about coming out, about Dimi. I babble about the Essay of Doom for ten minutes: my questions, my uncertainty, everything.

"Do you actually believe all these things define you?" she asks.

I shrug. Or, I try to, but suddenly my shoulders are too heavy again.

Free says, "You think because you like corny indie music and live in the 'burbs, you're not black enough? Because you have dope-ass taste in clothes, you're too gay? Because you're adopted, you don't think you know yourself? You date an asshole and that defines you?"

"I mean—"

She holds up a finger. "Yes, these things are a *part* of you, but they don't *define* you. Don't let *them* define who you are. Know your history, Remy. Know the struggles. Know the victories. Understand why people marched and protested and fought for you. Martin Luther King Jr. existed for a reason. Stonewall happened for a reason. NWA saying 'Fuck the Police' was a statement. For us."

Her hand covers mine on the table. I hadn't realized it was shaking.

Free's speaks gently: "I love thoughtful hip-hop with messages about who we are, who we've been, who we *will be*. But I can jam to folk-singer-songwriters, too, and still be black. Still be me." Her fingers squeeze mine. "There's no such thing as 'black enough.' You can't be 'too gay.' Adopted doesn't mean you're not whole. There's just you. And that's pretty dope."

New pizzas come out. A family of eight crams into a corner booth. This girl outside sings showtunes. But we're in a bubble.

I blink hard until my eyelashes unstick. I breathe, shallowly at first, then clearer. "Am I anything like her?" I ask.

Something in Free's smile changes. She's in an alternate universe where smiles are sad. "I don't know. Maybe? You love hard, I can tell. She did too."

"Why'd she give up?" It's not the first time I've wondered. It's the first time I wanted to know, though.

"Easy answer: the alcohol." Free watches the bubbles in her ginger ale. "Long answer: She loved him too hard. He left, and then she didn't want anything. Or, she did. She wanted something better for you. And then nothing. She wasn't my momma; she was a shell."

Across the table, Free's eyes shine. Maybe it's the lighting. Maybe it's something else.

"They say you can't die from a broken heart, but Ruby did." Free looks away, smiling that alternate-universe smile. "A broken heart and alcohol and painkillers. Ironic, right?"

We're quiet. So very quiet. We're giving each other space—me to absorb and Free to release.

"Maybe you are like her," says Free. I turn my hand over to cup hers. "Maybe the better parts?"

"The best parts," I say.

"The parts that refuse to use men or anyone as a reason to breathe. As a purpose to live. The parts that don't let any one thing give him validation."

I absorb that. Then I grin, sad but hopeful. "Hey." I nudge her foot under the table the way Lucy would, the way Rio does when

I'm spaced out and need direction. "What do you do for the holidays now that... you know."

Free leans back. Springy curls brush her shoulders. "Mom's been dead since freshman year of college. I've managed. I've got friends. I house-hop and go bowling. I'm good."

"Maybe you could, I don't know, add another house to your plans?"

"I'll think about it."

"You'll think about it?" I squeak. Pizza and vocal disruptions of the puberty kind—my favorite kind of afternoon.

Free rolls her eyes. "It's being considered." She orders another ginger ale. "I haven't had any family to want me around during the holidays in forever. Not even my dad."

I think about that for a moment. About what Free's said about Ruby's e-mails. "She never told them, did she? She never told my parents you existed?"

A small tremble moves across Free's mouth. She shakes her head. "It's not that I don't want to meet your family, little bro. It's that, after she died, part of me wished I was given that same opportunity. That they should've known I was there."

"But they didn't."

She shakes her head again. "It's messed up, right? For me to think that way?"

"No." I squeeze her hand. "But our future family therapy sessions are going to be wild."

"Damn right." She giggles, then pushes the pizza aside with her free hand. Leaning on the table with her chin on her knuckles, she says, "Okay, tell me about this boy."

CHAPTER TWENTY-FOUR

WHEN I WAS NINE-YEARS-OLD, MY dad brought paint buckets and brushes and sheets into my bedroom. "We're going to do something cool," he said, beaming. "Cooler than watching TV." I didn't believe him. Cooler than *cartoons*? No way. He wanted to paint my ceiling, which was way more complicated than HGTV made it seem. It was a lot of work, but it was also the most adult thing I'd ever done. I painted swirls and zigzags. My dad held me in place.

The result: a mural. The sea and clouds and stars intertwined. Full moon yellows and ocean blues and minty green. I love this mural. I love lying under it, on my bedroom floor, after a bad day, listening to music, letting Clover rest her head on my stomach. Under a hurricane of colors, I'm at peace.

Today wasn't great. Yesterday either. Lucy had SAT stuff and boyfriend stuff. Rio and I are still on radio silence. Ian's quiet too, extra quiet. So, it's just me, Clover, a POP ETC playlist, and a view of the clouds, stars, and sea.

My laptop is opened. A finished draft of the Essay of Doom awaits editing. I refuse to read it over. Every word seems as if it's not good enough. It's trash. It's a Welcome to the Failure Parade anthem, sung by Mrs. Scott.

I should finish it. I should eat dinner. But I stay here, drowning and floating simultaneously.

"Hey." I turn my head. Mom's leaning in the doorway. A half smile twists her mouth.

I try to smile back and fail. There's a theme here.

Mom sighs. It's either disappointment or concern. Maybe it's exhaustion. She's still in a black and white striped, tie neck blouse and slightly wrinkled rose slacks from work. Her hair's gradually come undone from a bun. Something passes over her eyes. "Is this about a boy?"

"What?"

"Your mood lately, Remy. Is it a boy? Is it your friends?"

I don't answer, peering at a blue patch on my ceiling.

"Is it school?"

"Mom, I just—" I pause, words unable to pass through the dryness in my throat. Frustration has built a lake of fire in my chest. And all the days without Ian and Lucy, the resentment I still have toward Rio, are like kerosene. "I don't want to talk about it."

"Remy." Her shoulders fall. "That's not healthy. I wouldn't—"

"No, you wouldn't," I finally snap. "You wouldn't get any of this, either. You wouldn't get why I'm feeling like this." I glare at her. She's stiff, arms folded. "Maybe I'm not like you. Or like Dad." My voice trembles like my hands at my side. "Maybe I'll never be like either of you."

For a moment, Mom's stunned. She closes her eyes, whisper-counts to ten. And then the firestorm inside of me subsides. Regret douses the flames.

"I'm... I'm sorry, Mom."

"No," she says, hoarsely. "Don't apologize. Don't..." Her eyes are wet. "This is part of growing up."

There's those two words again.

We're so quiet. Clover's breaths are as loud as my heartbeat. Then Mom says, "'You Make Loving Fun' by Fleetwood Mac" with this fondness in her voice.

"What?"

"I don't know what you're going through or when you'll want to talk about it," she says, "but that song helped me through tough times when I was younger."

I squint at her. My mom, younger? What a wild concept!

"We've all been there." She clears her throat. I hope she doesn't cry. I hope I don't either. "Maybe not the exact same situation or the same results, but… just listen to that song, and I'll be downstairs with hot chocolate and a shoulder when you're ready."

"And your world-famous peanut butter brownies?"

"World-famous?"

"Moderately well-known peanut butter brownies," I compromise with a shy lift to my lips.

"If this is you baiting me, you're terrible at it." Then, as she's closing the door, she adds, "But, yes, that can be arranged."

After she leaves, I reach for my laptop. My music app is already up. In less than ten seconds, my bedroom is filled with rhythm guitar and something dreamlike. I can't help it. I dance. Clover barks at my feet, but I ignore her. The music and the voice singing about miracles and magic seeps into my blood. Breathless, I dance off the regret and confusion. I shake away the image of what my words did to Mom. On one foot, hands in the air, head tossed back—from my hairline to my toes, I feel light.

Like the clouds.

Like the song of the ocean.

Like the stars at night.

ALONG THE WALLS OF DAD'S office is a photographic walk through our family history: Mom in the kitchen, beaming over a peach pie,

Grandpa holding me in a rocking chair, Dad in his varsity football uniform, Willow's toothless grin on her fourth birthday. My favorite one is from the first day my parents brought me home. I don't know why. But there's something about Mom's glassy eyes and Dad tentatively cradling me like a balloon that might pop; their smiles, identically wide, almost too big for their faces; and my tiny fingers curled into Dad's shirt—just the three of us.

That's messed up, right? Willow's the best sister ever. But there are moments where I miss being all my parents could think about. Maybe it's selfish. Maybe we shouldn't rush to grow up and make our own choices. Maybe you can't really get those days back.

I wonder what Free's childhood home looked like. Did Ruby have any photos of a toothless Free? Any birthday pictures? Did she keep any photos of me that my parents e-mailed her? I quickly ditch that thought. I don't care. I don't want to know anymore.

"Hey, kiddo?"

I startle. In the doorway, Dad's watching me. He's backlit by the hallway light, gauzy yellow across his rust-colored hair, against his stubble and warm blue eyes. He looks tired, happy but tired.

"Everything okay?"

I stare at him, unblinking.

When I was younger, I'd come stumbling into this office and crawl into Dad's lap. I'd go on and on about whatever was on my mind: cartoons and the sky and kids at school, the new baby growing in Mom's tummy. Everything. Just me and Dad. Now it seems like a hundred million years ago, like I can't be that kid anymore, like I can't tell Dad everything.

"Kiddo?"

"It's nothing."

"Really?"

I can almost hear it in his voice—the doubt. Maybe Mom told him what happened. "It's nothing, Dad."

"But—"

"I'm fine." It's such a lie. It tastes sour, like drinking Coke after brushing your teeth.

"Come on." Dad motions to the hall. "Let me show you something."

"What?"

"Something cool."

PEANUT-BUTTER-AND JELLY-STUFFED FRENCH TOAST, THE end-all of breakfast-bread meals, the Godzilla of French toast. It's Dad's favorite recipe—mine too—and he only breaks it out for special occasions: New Year's Day, my parents' anniversary, my birthday. It's a rigorous process; precision is key. There's a rule that no one can talk to Dad while he's creating. We're not even allowed in the kitchen. But, this time, he's teaching me the recipe. This time, I'm a part of creating something cool.

Bobby Flay, eat your heart out.

It's after nine p.m. Willow's already asleep. Mom's in the living room binge-watching grim crime shows to exorcise the life of a wedding consultant. It's Dad and me—and Clover, but she's the exception to every rule, as all good dogs are.

Dad walks me through all the steps. He lets me do everything. Sometimes, he stands over me, guides my hand or directs with his words. Mostly, he leans against the island, observing. And every time I look over my shoulder, he's smiling.

We eat at the island instead of the table. One plate, two forks. We don't say much, but I don't think either one of us knows what to say. There's a mystery between sons and fathers. It's a universal rule that they can be in the same space and never be able to say things—stupid rule.

"Tell me," Dad says.

"Tell you?"

He digs into the fluffy bread until creamy peanut butter and sticky jelly spews from both sides. "Whatever. Anything. Tell me, kiddo."

I stare at him. His soft features are happy and tired. It's the same dad who held me in his lap while I talked for hours. He's still him. And I'm still... I think I'm still me.

Dad nudges my elbow. "It's just me." It's just my dad.

"I have a birth sister. A half-sister."

I wait for his reaction. Surprise. Anger. Disappointment in me for hiding this. But he does this little eyebrow lift, chews quietly, and then says, "Tell me, kiddo."

My brain and heart are moving in two different directions, stretching my insides like a rubber band. I don't know where to start, how to start. But I try—from the beginning.

I start with the essay. Facebook. Messaging Free. Meeting Free. The thing with Ian. Fighting with Rio. My dead mother and Mystery Donor. My fading dreams of Emory. It's as if a dam inside me splinters before shattering, and my thoughts are the flood. I talk so much, so long, that I'm hoarse. But it's out. All of it.

Dad doesn't say a word. Periodically, it looks as if he wants to, but he doesn't. He lets me talk. He lets me finally breathe.

Afterward, his thumbs are on my cheeks, catching tears. I don't know when I started crying. I'm not sure I'll stop.

"Kiddo," he says, sadly.

"Don't." I try to shake my head, but I realize I'm trembling all over. "I'm fine."

"You're not."

"I'm not," I whisper.

"But you don't have to be," he tells me. "You don't always have to be fine."

I let him pull me in, wrap his arms around me. Tears dampen the cotton of his UGA T-shirt.

"When you were younger, I was terrified. I've always wanted to protect you. All parents want to protect their children. I tried so hard when you were little. But I knew, one day, there were things I couldn't protect you from. Things that I'll never face."

He doesn't name those things, but I know what they are. I'm black and he's not. I'm gay and he's not. I'm adopted and he's not.

Dad kisses the top of my head. "You're amazing, kiddo. You're so strong." There's a tremor in his voice. "Maybe I can't protect you from everything, but I feel so blessed knowing you're strong enough to face some of it by yourself."

"I'm not."

"Not fully, but you're much braver than you give yourself credit for." We breathe together—inhale, exhale. "I know you'll ask for help when you need it. When you're ready."

Will I? I want to ask him. It took so long to tell him.

"I should've been a better dad." He's sniffling.

I hide in his chest a little longer. "You're great."

He guffaws, wet and broken. "If I am, it's because of my son. Because he's hashtag cool-as-eff."

"Dad, no." I pull back with tear-stained cheeks.

Dad's nose is red. His eyes are shiny jewels. His grin is a sunrise—comforting and renewing. "Talk to Rio," he tells me. "If the Ian thing works out, great. If not? That's okay too. And this essay…" I groan. "Write what feels right. Yes, your mom and I would love it if you aced AP Literature, but it wouldn't be the end of the world if you didn't."

"It wouldn't?"

"Your mom coordinates real-life Anne Hathaway romcom movies. I tell people how to power their Wi-Fi on and off. We're doing okay without AP Literature."

"But what about Emory?"

"What about it?"

"Dad." I exhale shakily. "It's all I've dreamt about for the past two years. Emory. Writing. It's my path. Where I should be."

Dad squeezes my shoulders and laughs, not condescendingly, but amused. "Kiddo, Emory is a wonderful place, but it doesn't have to be *your place*. You don't have to commit yourself to one dream."

"But you did."

"You think UGA was my dream?" Of course, I do. It's all he bleeds: black and Bulldog red.

Dad sighs heavily. "UGA wasn't my dream school. It was the school closest to home. That's why I chose it."

"Why stay?"

"I had a younger brother who was going through things that I didn't understand, and he didn't explain. Grandpa wanted me to go across the country, be the ultimate tech geek, but I wanted to be nearby just in case Dawson needed me, because he'd do the same for me. Do you understand?"

I do. It's why I chose Emory in the first place. I can't imagine living on the west coast. Or even somewhere like Florida. I can't be that far from my family. From Willow... in case she needs me.

In case *I* need *them*.

"And that path I chose at eighteen didn't look anything like the one I wanted at sixteen," says Dad, eyes brighter. "But it's the path that introduced me to your mom. To a job in Dunwoody. To your birth mother who introduced us to you."

New tears kiss my cheeks, but not from frustration, not from the unknown, from the love I could feel in my dad's voice and in the way he held me.

"Your path isn't determined by an essay. Or a grade. You will find your place only one way—by continuing to walk. Keep walking, kiddo. You'll get there."

"And the rest?" I ask.

"The rest we'll talk about another time. Me, you, and Mom," says Dad.

"I hurt her," I whisper, eyes lowered in shame. "I said some awful—"

Dad cuts me off. "It's okay. She's okay." His hand brushes my curls back. "We'll talk about," he hesitates, blinking, "your half-sister. We'll go through all the adoption stuff. The things we know about your birth mother. Together. Just the three of us. If you want?"

I still don't know if I do. This is my life. This is my dad. I don't know if I need the rest. But I whisper, "Okay."

Dad tosses the leftover French toast scraps on the floor for Clover, then walks to the sink. "Talk to Rio," he says again. He starts washing the dishes.

I pull out my phone and text her:

I miss you.

A lot.

Third grade levels.

And I'm sorry.... Really sorry.

I wait. I see the text bubble appear, disappear. And then nothing. Nothing until my phone lights up. It's Rio on FaceTime. I answer, and there she is, eyes as green as the face mask she's wearing: nose scrunched and that Rio smirk.

"It's about time, Romeo."

CHAPTER TWENTY-FIVE

THE THING ABOUT REVEALING SECRETS is, your mind is always anticipating six million scenarios of how it'll go before the secret is ever out: the good, the bad, the zombie apocalypse version. It never goes the way you're expecting. Sometimes it's worse. Sometimes it's not a big deal. I'm not sure which of those this moment is.

Lucy's wide-eyed, jaw agape. I'm certain she hasn't blinked for a solid two minutes. Rio's studying me. It's almost like her detective face—squinted eyes, pinched mouth, lowered eyebrows—but gentler. It's her journalist face, her compassionate face. I've missed that face. I'm glad I apologized. I'm glad she apologized too.

We're sitting on a blanket in the field behind Maplewood Middle. Memories are stamped onto every inch of our surroundings. The playground's see-saw is where Lucy had her first kiss. The brick of the building where Rio shoved a kid—the first and last—for making fun of my eye color. The fence we've climbed. Yellow-green grass where I watched Elijah play football. Deep blue sky and clouds we've laid under, on our backs, and watched for hours. I thought it was the perfect place to tell them about Free and my birth mother.

"Wow," says Lucy.

"You have a sister," Rio says for the third time.

"Half-sister," I say.

"You have a half-sister," repeats Rio.

I nod. She continues to scrutinize me.

"And your parents know?" asks Lucy.

I nod again. She finally blinks.

"Wow."

I want to laugh. None of this has been funny. Life is funny in that super-ironic way no one likes. It's catastrophes and tragedies, and there's just something so hilarious about how emotions guide the ship instead of anchoring it.

Talking to Mom about this was weird. She was super calm. She held Dad's hand, then mine, and listened patiently. Mom did all the things you're supposed to when someone is telling you something big. Even the "I love you, thank you for talking about this" part. Somewhere inside me, I knew she wanted to cry: for me, for not knowing what to say, for not knowing.

But she did say something. She said, "You might not ever want to know her. That's okay. But know this: Your mother gave us a wonderful gift. She gave us a beautiful boy who is strong enough to carry the world on his shoulders. But you don't have to, not always. Even when you think you're supposed to for the sake of others, *you don't have to.*

"Remy, we don't get to decide who other people think we are. What labels they want to attach to us. But we get to show ourselves who we know we are. You know yourself better than anyone. You're a gift. You're you, no explanations or labels necessary."

Then I cried. But it was a good cry.

Mom combed my curls back. She whispered, "You know who you are," and I do. I know, I know, I know.

"So," Rio says, tapping her chin, "what now?"

"Nothing."

"Nothing?"

"Nothing," I repeat happily. "I have a half-sister. She's really cool. And, I don't know, we'll probably hang out. We *will* hang out. But this doesn't change me."

Lucy's eyes brighten. She grabs my hand. "This doesn't change you."

Something swells inside me, forcing its way up through my chest, to my throat. "I'm a Cameron," I say. I can't stop beaming. "I'm a Cameron!"

"You're a loser with an unhealthy Reese's addiction," Rio says. "And poor wardrobe choices."

"You're a coffee addict," Lucy chimes in.

"You're incapable of making smart love life decisions, Romeo."

"And you're a future homecoming prince without a date," says Lucy.

I groan. Seriously, I need to spend less time on the Essay of Doom and more on my intricate, indisputable—thanks PSATs—plan of revenge on Lucy. "I don't need a date," I say with the confidence of a virgin liar.

Rio side-eyes me. Lucy cracks up. She grabs a glazed donut from the Krispy Kreme box I brought. Guaranteed reinforcements were needed.

"You could go stag." Lucy sighs disappointedly. Lucy, the anime-infatuated secret romantic. "Or," the corners of her mouth curl, "you could go with a certain cutie in glasses who loves *Yuri!!! On Ice* and is totally friends with my boyfriend."

I glare at her. Cool best friend loyalty aside, Lucy's annoying about these things. She's obsessed with taking two people she thinks will be great together and trying to make magic happen. But Ian and I aren't characters in one of her fanfics. We can't just... happen, as much as I want us to, as much as I miss that geek.

"No." I shake my head. "It's not... It's not like that, Lucia." I shove a donut in my mouth and leave it at that. I'm not outing Ian. I'm not feeding her fangirl dreams.

"Or," Rio starts, "you could go with me."

Lucy's head snaps up. I've got this goldfish-face thing going on. *Is Rio Maguire going to homecoming?* No. That's ridiculous. She's not.

Except Rio has this determined look. She says, "I'm not going to the game, Lucy. That's beneath my antisocial heart." She turns to me. "But I'm your best friend." To Lucy, she says, "And I'm your best friend. Promises were made in third grade over juice boxes and *Adventure Time.* I'm not bailing on that."

"You don't have to," whispers Lucy.

"I know."

"But you are?"

"Hair appointment made. Mom is skipping a trip to New Orleans for the whole manicure and make-up thing. Dad is documenting the entire ordeal for future family reunions." Rio gags. "Sacrifices are being made."

I reach out to squeeze Rio's hand. It's sweaty and shaking.

Secrets—they're a son of a bitch.

Lucy leaps across the donuts to hug Rio, knocking her over. I join. We're a dogpile of laughter and grass stains and friendship.

CHAPTER TWENTY-SIX

I NEVER COME TO MAPLEWOOD High football games. I don't do the whole football thing, period. Not unless it's required, like Dad and UGA games. Even then, it's only bearable because of Willow and Clover. The first half is almost over. I'm sitting on the hood of my car in the parking lot outside the stadium. I'm not sure who's winning. Judging by the constant echo of frustrated yelling, I'm guessing it's not us.

Lucy's inside. She's texted me seven times. Jayden has too. Brook sent me a video message from the stands, surrounded by the boys' swim team, whose faces are painted crimson and steel. I wonder if Ian's inside. Then I frown. We still haven't talked.

The bright stadium lights create this cool lavender tint to the sky. It's chilly tonight. My nose is tingly, and I really should've brought a heavier hoodie, but I don't know. I'm wearing Ian's hoodie. Why? Because pathetic is in my DNA—probably on Mystery Donor's side.

My fingers ache from the cold. I squeeze my phone. It lights up: 8:02 p.m. Half-time is soon. That means the homecoming court presentation and the crowning and everything I'm avoiding. Well, everything superficial.

My phone screen brightens again. A text from Free:

Big nite!!!

I snort. We had another meeting at Savage yesterday. No big family stories or heavy questions. Just us, shooting the shit.

I text back:

Yep. Potentially Maplewood's first openly gay HC prince. Yay!!!

I hope she gets my sarcasm. She texts a string of emojis that are either cheering me on or calling me on my cynical bullshit, probably the latter. Then, for whatever reason, I think about our mother. I almost visited her grave today. Free gave me the address. She had to coordinate the entire funeral and the burial at a cemetery in Decatur; her father helped. To bury your mother at nineteen—Free's stronger than I'll ever be.

What would I say to Ruby?

Why?

What made you so sure I'd end up happier than with you and Free?

Would you love me if you knew I was gay?

I have nothing to say to her. Not because I'm angry or because I'm hurt. Because I have a mom. I have a family. And Ruby gave me that gift, so I guess the only thing I could say is, "Thanks," but I'd still feel weirded out talking to a headstone.

The thing about curiosity is, it never really goes away until you have an answer. It stays quietly curled up in a dark corner of your mind. Always there.

I text Free again:

Do you think she'd be OK w/ me being gay?

It takes a minute before her reply chimes in:

She would've loved you for being you. She was dope like that.

I tip my head back, smile at the lavender sky. That's good enough.

The cheers from the stadium boom. A few people mill about in the parking lot. It's time for bathroom and smoke breaks. It also means it's time for that thing I'm hiding from.

BY THE TIME I MAKE it to the side of the football field where the homecoming royalty and their escorts are crowded together, the seniors are marching onto the green to the band's sick rendition of Fall Out Boy's "Thnks fr th Mmrs." At the back is a pouting Ford Turner. He looks like playing dress-up instead of competing in the big game is killing him. Good.

The juniors are a talking, cheering, disorganized mess. Sara's at the front. She looks amazing, all deep reds and hints of gold. Her hijab is crimson. She has this perfect winged eyeliner, like the ones in YouTube tutorial videos. It's kind of stunning. Differences aside, I can admit Sara deserves to be chosen Homecoming Princess. And not just because Lucy—the traitor—opted out of the ballot, but because Sara truly is junior class royalty.

I spot Jayden in the chaos. It's the hair—flawless and super tall. He's wearing his cheerleader uniform, but with a bowtie: classic Jayden Blue. He's being escorted by both his moms. They're in matching bowties and suspenders. Nancy's hair is swept up with flowers, and Tori's sporting a gel-stiff faux-hawk. It's clear where Jayden gets it from. Chloe, as star quarterback, has to focus on the game instead of walking him onto the field. It's awesome his moms are here, though.

He waves me over. I pause. It hits me: I don't have an escort. I'm not even dressed-up like everyone else. I look out into the stands, where hundreds of faces are blurred by the bright lights. This isn't what I want. This isn't who I am.

I shake my head at Jayden and try not to drown in guilt when he frowns. Then he nods, as if he understands. Homecoming court isn't my scene, just like GSA isn't his.

I backtrack. I speed-walk to my car. Maybe Rio's free. We could drive to downtown Decatur, get hot chocolates and stroll around. Be anti-homecoming together. I'm only halfway to the parking lot when I hear, "And Homecoming Prince is… Jayden Blue!"

Perfect. Jayden deserves it. It feels like a victory for both of us. I turn right, then left and collide with someone.

Aerosol cans clatter against the cement. They roll aimlessly between our feet. I stumble out an apology to whoever I crashed into.

It's Darcy—pink-faced, wide-blue-eyed, perfect-blonde-ponytail Darcy. And she's scowling at me.

"Sorry."

"Whatever."

I squint at the cans. Spray paint. Darcy's fingers are red and pink and black. Her hoodie is a mural of colors too. She's breathing heavily, and her backpack hangs off one shoulder, opened. A tattered copy of *Alice in Wonderland* peeks out.

"Holy shit. You're—"

"Could you just, like, *move*. Go away."

"Darcy, you're—"

"I'm not," she screeches, then flushes when an older couple passing by gawks at us. "You don't know what you're talking about."

But I do. The panic in her moon-sized eyes says we both know I do.

Darcy Jamison is the Mad Tagger.

She bends down to pick up the cans. She's scrambling, hands shaking. I help. When her eyes meet mine, I ask, "Why?"

She sighs, then sits on the cold ground. Knees to her chest, she wraps her arms around herself. Her jeans are worn at the knees. I don't think I've ever seen Darcy in jeans. I don't think I've ever seen Darcy sit on the ground. She looks so small.

"Because," she closes her eyes, "everyone labels you a Jesus freak because you went to Christian summer camp as a kid, because praying before every meal makes you a religious dictator. Those same girls who played dolls with you as a kid whisper behind your back now."

Her damp eyelashes begin to flutter. I consider touching her arm, maybe her shoulder. Then I think about Ian, about his halmeoni teaching him to always ask for consent before touching anyone and I don't. But I scoot closer, so she knows I'm there, so she can borrow some of my warmth.

"Because, one day, your little brother comes into your bedroom crying. All the kids at school tell him his sister loves God and no one else." She exhales shakily. "He thinks I hate him because…"

Our elbows brush. Darcy tucks her chin. I nudge her shoe to tell her to continue. I think she needs to say it, say everything.

"Because he's demisexual. He thinks I hate him because he's demisexual and not straight. 'Not what God wants' is what those kids told him." She giggles, but it's wounded. "But I don't care that Cody's demi. He's my brother."

Cody. Not Silver.

Her nose twitches. "Despite what everyone tries to preach, God loves Cody for Cody. You can still believe in a higher power and not be heterosexual. They're not mutually exclusive."

"I know," I whisper.

I know Aunt Sandra loves me. I know I can be me and still have faith in something greater. *I know, I know, I know.*

"But why?"

Darcy's eyes finally blink open. They're fiery blue. "I'm tired of living like every label they give us matters. I'm not a label. Cody's not a label either."

Wow! Darcy freaking Jamison—straight A's and perfect hair and a rule-breaking legend.

Darcy cocks her head. "I treated you like crap because I was too afraid to admit I was jealous."

"Of what?"

"Of you. You live your life loud and proud. You're always yourself. You don't give a shit."

I'm speechless. I've never heard Darcy swear. Not even a "damn."

She blinks at me. "That was a lot, right?"

"Word vomit," I say, face happily scrunched. I shake my head. "That was... perfect."

Our elbows are pressed together. People step around us, staring and whispering, but I don't care. I'm used to it.

"Darcy Jamison," I whisper. "The Mad Tagger."

"Yeah. Surprise!"

"Now what?"

She puffs out her cheeks. "I'm done. Finished my last one."

"Really? Can I see it?"

Darcy turns this sweet, cotton-candy pink from cheeks to neck. We stand, and she leads me down a path behind the stadium, across a half-finished sidewalk, and over the crosswalk that leads to Maplewood's student parking lot. And there it is. It's massive—a giant mural stretching over at least ten parking spaces. In huge red and black letters: "Popularity = 'It is better to be feared than loved.'" And, in pink lettering so small I have to squint: "His name is Cody."

I turn to her, mouth open. Chilly wind sweeps blonde hair loose; strands blow across her cheeks and her chapped lips. She's happy. Darcy looks free.

"You're not scared they'll know?" I say.

She shakes her head. "Cody should be free to be himself. No labels."

I nod. That little piece of me that wants to grab her hand, for support, remains. But I don't. We stand closer, though. We stand together against whatever labels they've tried to tag us with.

"I won't say a word," I tell her.

Gratitude passes over her face. Rio's going to kill me if she finds out. That's okay. This is one more secret I can carry. For Cody.

Darcy tucks her hair back into place; her self-conscious smile is directed at me. "Is it bad?"

"No," I say. "It's perfect. Darcy, you're perfect."

CHAPTER TWENTY-SEVEN

By Saturday evening, my life is a disaster.

Okay. That's an exaggeration. But I'd rather jump headfirst into a pool of ice than pick out something to wear to the homecoming dance. I don't have many options. Formal wear isn't my thing. I own a battleship-gray suit from two Christmases ago, courtesy of Aunt Sandra. There's also, this cool navy button-up with white polka dots from a date with Dimi for our five-month anniversary. We went to the Cheesecake Factory. My parents paid. I should've donated the shirt to charity. Maybe I can get away with a sweater? A dope red one with a gray beanie. All school spirit.

"What about this one?" I hold up a pastel blue button-up. The zigzag pattern on the fabric shines in the right lighting.

Willow shrugs. It's her response to every option. But it's better than Clover's snoring and Bert's empty stare. They're my panel of judges for this fashion shitshow. I rifle though my closet and drawers. Honestly, why can't jeans and a T-shirt without stains be the official attire for all high school events?

"You're going to a dance?" Willow asks.

"Uh huh." I tug out a plum sweater. Seriously, what the hell was I thinking with this one?

"With that boy?"

I whip around. Willow's blinking at me, head tilted. I raise an eyebrow. "What boy?"

She's sitting on my bed in a Wonder Woman T-shirt and Superman socks pulled up to her knees. These days, Willow's making strong fashion declarations about her allegiance in the Marvel vs. DC debate. I don't know if I approve.

She loops a tie from Mount Clothing Rejection around her neck. Then she wrecks her strawberry blonde hair with tiny hands. It sticks up everywhere. And I get it. She's supposed to be Spike Spiegel. She's supposed to be Ian.

I cross the room to her and sit down. My neck and ears are hot. *Willow knows I have a thing for Ian.* I kiss her forehead and loosen the tie so it doesn't choke her. I say, "No, I'm not" with a small voice.

"Are you sad?"

Yep. I pat her hair down. "I'm good, Willow."

"He's fun."

"A little bit, yeah."

"You're funner."

I don't have the heart to correct her. Instead, I wrap her in a hug, mash her face to my chest, and we giggle as if this is all we're meant to do—Willow the Rockstar and me.

I settle on a plain white oxford and a forgotten scarlet varsity cardigan from the back of my closet with the suit's gray slacks and pair of red-and-white checkered Vans. Dad shows up with a tie. He stands behind me, looping a perfect Windsor knot.

"It was your grandpa's."

My lips twitch upward.

It has a rainbow pattern. "It was his favorite," Dad says, smiling with somber eyes. "Thought you'd like it."

I admire my complete outfit. It's a perfect mishmash of all these pieces that somehow fit together. "I love it."

Rio and Lucy arrive just before eight, which is strange, since the dance starts soon. Not that I live far from Maplewood. But Mom insists we do the picture thing. It's not as lame as people complain about. We master the *Charlie's Angel* pose. Then the *Mean Girls* one. And a bunch of goofy ones too. This is only homecoming. I can't imagine prom.

Lucy keeps shooting me looks. She's blatantly admonishing me with her eyes.

"What?"

She sizes up my outfit. Whatever. *This* is me trying.

"Leave him alone," says Rio. "At least there's no way he'll upstage us."

It's true. Lucy found a vintage strapless gold dress with a ballerina skirt during our shopping trip. Her hair's knotted on her head; her cheekbones are softened by rose blush. And Rio's a dream in the D.D. dress. Her hair is purple—deep and beautiful as the night's sky blessed by wakening stars.

"If I'm going to do homecoming, I'm at least going to wear the opposing team's colors," she explains as we walk out the door. Leave it to Rio to be so terminally anti-Maplewood that she'd dye her hair the color of a rival high school.

Brook's minivan is parked at the curb. A giant bowtie is tied to the front bumper. It's so corny. It's so Brook Henry.

"Nailed it, little dude." He fist-bumps me when I crawl into the back. He's wearing a rented tux. "Nice tie!"

I blush. "We're gonna be late."

"We won't be late," Lucy says while fiddling with Brook's iPod. She puts on something soulful.

"We won't be late," Brook confirms, stealing the iPod back to switch to a country song.

They squint at each other, wink, then agree on old school Lauryn Hill.

"We *are* late," I argue. I fasten my seat belt, slouching.

"Chill, Romeo," says Rio. "We're making a stop."

"A stop?"

"Yes," they say in unison.

"Fine. Whatever." I pout, kicking the back of Brook's seat. "But I refuse to endure the wrath of newly-elected Homecoming Princess Sara Awad for being tardy to this social-pariah celebration."

ZOMBIE CAFÉ ON A SATURDAY is sparsely populated. The writers are still pretending to craft new novels. The geek squads with their cappuccinos read graphic novels or watch anime on their laptops. The old man in an armchair has his decaf coffee and a newspaper. College kids with dead eyes have overpriced textbooks piled in front of them. But it's still mostly empty, not that I'm complaining. I'll take Zombie any hour when there's a free corner table and Trixie behind the bar.

She marches over to us the moment we're through the door. "You're late."

"Exactly!" I say.

Her attention is directed at Lucy and Brook. "I'm not getting paid to talk anyone off a ledge. I had to cut off his latte consumption after three."

"Wait," I say, confused. "You're not talking about the dance?"

Trixie sizes us up. "You look great, but no."

"Where is he?" Brook asks before I can interrogate Trixie.

"Bathroom."

"I'll go talk him down."

"I'll handle our other problem," says Lucy. Brook kisses her cheek, then punches me in the shoulder. He walks off, humming.

"What in the actual fu—"

"There are chairs already set up," interrupts Trixie. She nods to a corner of the café usually inhabited by hipsters and stoners needing caffeine to come back to Earth. I hadn't noticed the two stools, an amp, someone's used guitar, and a microphone.

"Um."

"Sit. Cold Body's on the way," Trixie says to me. "Go."

"Come on, Romeo," Rio says, hooking her arm in mine.

I'm dizzy and extremely confused. Nothing's adding up except that my best friends are really good at keeping secrets.

We're seated in this semi-circle in front of the stools. The house lights are dim. A string of orange fairy lights hangs on the wall behind the stools. Obviously, this secret comes with ambiance.

Trixie drops off the Cold Body and iced lattes for Lucy and Rio. They're whispering to each other. I keep checking my phone. It's after eight-thirty. We're missing Alex's EDM music and bad dancing. I'm not mad about that. But I kind of want to hang with Chloe and Jayden. Sara's probably already plotted a fail-safe plan to murder us without anyone finding the bodies.

Brook slides in next to Lucy. "Mission accomplished. That dude has zero chill."

"Duh." Lucy smirks. "Look at his romantic choices."

"True that."

"What are you talking about?" I ask. Rio's mouth pops open to answer—or to snark—but then Trixie's tapping the microphone.

"Okay. This is a new feature at Zombie. Or a one-time thing. It depends," she says.

"On what?" some girl shouts from across the café.

"On whether I earn more tips from this or y'all walk out," replies Trixie.

Rio snorts.

"Anyway." Trixie winks at someone behind us. A guy with arms stained in tattoos and a ridiculously groomed beard sits at one of the stools. He grabs the guitar, tunes it. Then someone else sits down, playing with his glasses, one knee bouncing nervously.

Ian.

"Welcome to Saturday's first open mic night-ish at Zombie," Trixie announces. "Pending." She gives Ian one quick, concerned look. "Welcome Ian Park to the stage!"

Brook whoops. Lucy claps loudly.

Everything's blurry, then perfectly in focus, perfectly centered on Ian.

"Thanks," he says when Trixie steps away.

"Sing!" Brook shouts.

Mr. Tattoos-and-Guitar strums a few chords, and Ian grips the mic. His voice is... terrible. It's squeaky, and, honestly, singing isn't his calling. But Ian's really going for it, eyes closed, mouth way too close to the mic. It's seriously one of those out-of-body experiences, a disaster you can't prevent. And I love it. Ian's singing that one song about letting love open the door, that one song I love. Except it's slower and chill and probably the best version I've ever heard.

Rio and Lucy get up to dance. Brook is a hot mess of yelling and clapping. The geek girls sing behind us. The old man leaves. But the college zombies order more coffee and ditch their textbooks to drag their chairs closer. And no one gives Ian hell about his voice.

It's epic.

When he's done, Ian's a violent shade of red. But he's smiling at me.

Mild confession: I'm hardcore smiling back.

WE'RE STANDING OUTSIDE ZOMBIE, IAN and I. Our friends' version of giving us privacy means they watch intently from inside with their faces pressed to the glass.

We're quiet for a long time. It's chilly, but I don't mind. I'm standing close enough to absorb his heat, but not too close to be obvious, just in case. In case what happened ten minutes ago wasn't what I thought it was.

"Was it too extreme?" Ian finally asks, so soft.

"Extreme?"

"Too over the top?"

"Depends."

"On what?"

I stare at my Vans. "What was it for?"

His feet shuffle in front of mine. His hand closes the gap. Our pinkies link. "For you," he whispers.

My brain overdoses on endorphins. I can't deal with the blush overload. "It was great," I say.

"Really?" There's something electric in his voice.

"Perfect. Weird." I knot my ring finger around his. "Perfectly weird."

"Thanks." I can hear his relief but still can't look at him.

It's so easy to be cynical about romance. I'll admit, after Dimi, I thought love wasn't worth it. All those big romantic gestures in movies? In books? Unrealistic. They're always so lame and corny and it never happens like that. But that's bullshit. It happens. People do wild, over-the-top, certified mushy things for the ones they care for. And it's not bad. It's epic.

"So," I finally lift my eyes, "Brook knows, obviously. And…"

Ian bites his lip. "I came out to Lucy and Rio. And Trixie."

I nod.

"And Aunt Jilynn."

My breath catches, a sharp noise.

"She was…" I wait, then he finally says, "She was great. She told me she loved me and how incredible I am. And that I better visit soon. She was so Aunt Jilynn."

Our shoulders relax simultaneously. Our breaths come in hushed puffs; the toes of our shoes touch.

"A few friends back in Arcadia know too." His nose twitches. The cold spreads pink into his cheeks. "Not a lot of people. I'm still… I'm taking it slow. Testing the waters."

"And?"

"Mostly good."

"Mostly?"

"Yeah." The dimple appears as his mouth upturns. "We'll leave it at that. That's all I want to focus on."

Somehow, all my fingers have claimed his. He squeezes.

"Coming out is," he pauses, making a face.

"A lot."

"A lot," he repeats.

It really is. It's this secret that's all yours for so long. Then you suddenly have to share it for whatever reason and hope people are okay with it, or not. You suddenly have to prepare for the good, the bad, and the zombie apocalypse. Coming out is freeing. It's terrifying. It's monumental and amazing and draining. But it's yours.

"I'm not ready to march into school on Monday and tell everyone," he says.

"You don't have to tell anyone."

"I know. But I want to. I can. I will."

"Okay."

He looks away for a second, then steps closer. "I did this because I know who I am. I'm okay with me. And I want you to know I'm okay with us."

"With us?"

"Yes," he says, earnest and happy. "I did this because I deserve to be happy with a boy. I'm ready to tell the world that."

There's that word again: *Deserve*. My favorite word.

"So," I swallow and grin, "can I kiss you?"

"No." I flinch. But he smiles so wide, his glasses are touching his eyebrows. "I'm going to kiss you."

He does. Ian's chilly fingers brush my Dopey-ears, and his thumbs frame my jaw. He kisses me. His nose bumps mine, we re-configure, and I kiss him back. He tastes like matcha, and he feels like nerves and excitement.

Like a rollercoaster at night.

Like a boy who knows he loves me.

CHAPTER
TWENTY-
EIGHT

"Well, that was quite the presentation today, wasn't it?" Ms. Amos is sitting on her desk, short legs and tiny feet swinging. She smiles in that way adults do when they're presenting a rhetorical question. I'm at a desk in the front row. School's over, and the last GSA meeting before Thanksgiving break starts in five minutes. But, after my essay presentation, she asked to talk. I can't exactly turn her down.

"Um."

She lifts a hand. "It wasn't bad."

"It wasn't great."

"Well, it wasn't all flashy like Sara's. It certainly didn't have the soundtrack Alex's did." She giggles. "Is that how you felt about it?"

I bite the inside of my cheek, almost shrugging.

She folds her hands across her lap. She's holding an essay—probably mine.

"I tried really hard," I start to explain, because it feels as though she wants one, or I owe her one.

I stayed up all night. Started from scratch. I wrote from the heart. My heart. Because that's what writing is—your heart. It's not what will impress others. What sounds trendy or cool. It's what already exists in you. Your truth. What others take from it is just a bonus.

I thought about who people *think* I am. I thought about the boy I see in the mirror, who receives strange looks for wearing pink T-shirts or fitted sweaters. My brain focused on the boy who wants to attend a college that sees him for more than his sexuality or skin color. There are so many labels I wear—voluntarily and by force.

I said, "Fuck it" to every little piece of Remy Cameron that doesn't fit a pretty little mold. The Remy scared of his past. The Remy that was anything but a Cameron, an older brother, a best friend, and a boy who loves to dance around his bedroom to POP ETC. I'm not a few checkmarks on some administrator's diversity checklist. I put it all in my essay—without the colorful language Mrs. Scott isn't fond of.

"I can tell you tried, Remy," Ms. Amos says, her tone genuine. "I can tell you worked really hard on this." She holds up the paper.

"But it wasn't enough." I frown.

She shakes her head. "Do you feel it was enough? This is you, on paper. Right? Do you feel good enough?"

"I—" My eyes lower. My heart growls like the center of a thunderstorm. Then I say, "I am good enough. I'm me, and that's good enough" with my chin lifted.

Ms. Amos claps. "Exactly. You're good enough."

"I am?" On cue, my voice cracks.

"Yes!" She hops down. "The purpose of this essay wasn't for me to judge whether any of you know yourself. It was to open a door. To start a conversation. For some, writing something so introspective and personal injects confidence. It reminds them that, like all great heroes of literature, they've overcome monsters and heartbreak and family indifference. They've fought all the odds stacked against them. Discovery is in the journey, not the destination."

"And the others?" I mean the Ford Turners. The Andrew Cowens.

She sighs. "The others see this as an opportunity to get a better grade. To write what they *think* sounds good. They wear their masks to look like heroes in their own story, but they've yet to truly see the truth. And so, they'll continue pretending."

"How can you tell the difference?"

She points at her chest. Her heart. "Instinct. A little thing called teacher's intuition. Also, I've met my own challenges. Tragedies. I've asked myself this question for decades. Over and over."

"Have you found an answer?"

"Yes and no." I make a face. "Are we really looking for the answer, Remy, or are we proud to know we *can* ask the question?"

That "we" thing again. But Ms. Amos doesn't use it in a patronizing way. She doesn't use it like other adults. It's sincere. It's comforting.

"Your essay wasn't perfect," says Ms. Amos, serious, "but it's a start. A beginning."

I play with the zipper of my red hoodie, the one I love, the one I wore while walking Clover and seeing Ian for the first time.

"A beginning to what?"

"The journey to asking yourself the right questions," she says. "To rejecting the labels and accepting it's not all in your control, but what is in your power—it's beautiful. It's magical. It's yours. Don't let others take that from you."

I think about my family—my true family. My friends. About Ian. Then I think about Ruby—the woman who gave me a gift. I don't know her as a mother, but I know her as selfless, as someone who took what little power she had and did something amazing with it.

Ms. Amos is still holding the essay as I stand, grab my backpack.

The Essay of Doom.

No—the Essay of Me. Sincerely, Remy Cameron.

"Enjoy your Thanksgiving break, Mr. Cameron," Ms. Amos says, eyes twinkling. "I look forward to us working on something similar to this next year."

"Next year?" I choke out. *All that and I still failed?*

"Yes. You want to go to Emory, correct?"

I nod.

"Then we'll have to perfect this little essay of yours for admissions." She turns to her desk, then stops. "Until then, just be Remy."

I run to Room 302. Electricity surges through my blood. A smile pulls at my mouth. I can't help it.

I passed, I passed, I passed.

My Vans squeak against the terrazzo floor. I'm almost there. I nearly collide with three people loitering outside Mr. Riley's classroom.

"You're late," says Sara. Alex and Zac are behind her.

I'm breathless and sweaty. "Um. Sorry?"

"Whatever." Sara rolls her eyes, but her mouth twitches. She's anxious.

"What's going on? Is this official *The Leaf* business? Student council stuff?"

"We're here because…" Sara trails off, eyes lowered.

Zac steps forward. "We're here for the meeting. For the club." He fiddles with a seashell bracelet around his left wrist. "To join. As students who belong." A careful emphasis is put on that last word. *Belong.*

Alex raises a hand. His hair's exceptionally blue today. "I'm here as an ally."

I give him a thumbs-up—message received. Then, I glance at Sara. She swallows, nodding gently. I don't need to ask more. I don't need her to identify or wear a label. I realize I only want Sara to be Sara, whatever that means.

"Cool." I step around them, opening the door. "We're just about to get started. Would you like to meet the others?" I'm still holding Sara's gaze.

Her mouth pinches. Thick, beautiful eyelashes flutter. Finally, she gives me the one answer we've both waited for: "Yes."

"OKAY," FREE TAKES A GIANT swig of Cold Body, "this place *might* be cooler than Little Five Points."

"I know. Right?" I wave a hand around the air. "It's the ambiance."

She rolls her eyes. "SAT Prep doesn't give you an excuse to toss words like 'ambiance' into our conversations."

"No," I grin slyly, "but being gay does."

She spits out her coffee over the table we're sitting at, snorting. I mop it up with a stack of paper napkins.

"Jesus. Little bro, you're not some silver fox on a queer makeover show. You're only seventeen."

"Yep," I say. "But I'm crushing this adulting thing."

Free reaches over to scrub my curls. We share a smirk, the Ruby smirk. Zombie is so chill today. Maybe because it's two days before Christmas. The city is pretty dead. Only the local college kids crowd the prime real estate inside with hot cocoas while a happy rotation of music plays in the café—all '80s Christmas tunes. I know who's responsible for that.

Ian's at the bar, talking to Trixie as she prepares his latte. Matcha— the green stuff his kisses taste like.

"He's cute," Free mentions, nudging my foot. "It's the glasses."

"Yeah."

"And the dimple."

I shake my head. It's a thing, okay?

"He's nervous about meeting you," I tell her. I've caught at least five panicked stares whenever I peek at him. I'm nervous too. Not about him meeting Free. Ian's mom will be in town next week for New Year's. I'm having dinner with them, meeting Ian's mom.

Ian insisted on it. I gladly held his hand, kissed that dimple, and promised I'd only spill one drink the entire time. Something relaxed in his eyes. Something relaxed in my heart too.

"He *should* be nervous." Free fixes her curls; they're big and wild and fierce today. "I plan to give him The Speech."

"The 'I'll kick your ass if you break my brother's heart' one?"

"Nope. The 'wear protection every single time because diseases are real, I don't care where you put your thing' speech."

Coffee spews from my mouth this time. Seventeen's not too young for a heart attack, right?

I kick her foot. She cackles. Half-sisters are the worst. I'd rather get The Talk from Aunt Sandra than live through this. She's coming tomorrow, with Uncle Dawson and Gabriel. *Uncle Dawson's fiancé Gabriel.* I can't wait to celebrate that.

"I like his style." Free's still studying Ian. He's wearing a denim jacket—because it never gets too cold in Georgia until January—and that one hoop earring and a plain black beanie. Why do I love this boy?

"It's okay. Can't top mine."

"You're a walking advertisement for American Eagle," she deadpans.

I sit taller, prouder.

"Speaking of that," Free leans closer, "who tops and who bottoms?"

Just that fast, I'm in full-fledged blush meltdown. Luckily, I don't have to talk to my older sister about that—not that it's any of her damn business. The jingle bells over Zombie's door rattle and in come three familiar faces. It's my family.

Free freezes. My parents do too. Willow bops around like the little unbothered badass she is. Today isn't just about introducing Free and Ian. It's about her meeting my family, about them getting to know my half-sister.

Free fiddles with her curls, then tries to fix her ripped sweater with all the safety pins on it. Mom brushes her bangs back and straightens her peach cardigan. Dad's picking invisible lint from his UGA sweatshirt. It's this epic two minutes of 'do I look okay?' motions.

I swallow a laugh. Willow runs over; my parents slowly trail behind. Free stands.

Ian meets my gaze across the café. I finally crack up. All these strong, caring forces of nature in my life. All in one room. Finally. All these important parts of me colliding. No. Intersecting.

All the pieces in my puzzle finally fitting into place.

ESSAY

I VISITED MY BIRTH MOTHER's grave for the first time today. It was cold and windy; every inch of the earth was covered in either leaves or mud from yesterday's storm. I had to kneel to wipe the dirt from her headstone. It reads:

"Breathe in art; exhale life."

I didn't know exactly what it meant but, for some reason, I knew it was important. In a few ways, it defined who she was.

Her name was Ruby Williams. She loved art and jazz and old-school movies. She died when I was too young to know she existed.

She named me Rembrandt, after the painter. According to Wikipedia, Rembrandt is *"generally considered one of the greatest visual artists in the history of art."* That's a lot to live up to, even at seventeen. I like to think my mother knew I wouldn't disappoint her.

My full name is Rembrandt Joshua Cameron. My middle name is from my parents, who named me after my grandpa. I don't remember much about my grandpa, just as I don't remember much about my birth mother. But I know my grandpa loved to sing to me and rock me to sleep. He was a good man. Sharing his name means another weight for me to carry—to be a good person, to be loving to others, even if they weren't my blood.

Some people in this world would want me to clarify that my *adoptive parents* named me after my *adoptive grandpa*, but I try not to live in that world, a world where we not only use labels to clarify and identify, but also to remind people of what we are not.

From an early age, I learned to carry those labels as an indicator, a definition. When I was five-years-old, a classmate taught me a new label: different. We were drawing portraits of our families and, unlike my other classmates' portraits, I was not the same color as my parents.

I was *not* my parents' birth son.

And even though my parents have always taught me to be myself, I began to only know myself by the labels other people gave me: Black. Best friend. Adopted. Clingy. Popular. Gay. I wasn't always consciously aware of these labels unless others pointed them out, unless others defined me by what I'm not.

I let them taint how incredible it is to be Black, a best friend, confident, a part of a loving family, the president of the Gay-Straight Alliance in high school.

When I was ten-years-old, I received a new label: older brother. At seventeen, again, I found another label: younger brother. I discovered I had an amazing older half-sister, who loves music and ginger ale and studies biochemistry at Agnes Scott College, who continues to teach me that labels stretch beyond basic definitions and how labels do not encompass the entirety of who we are.

Part of me wants to believe I already knew this, back when I was five-years-old and being given my first official labels. But who are we without our labels? Do our labels define us, or do we give definition to our labels? I think it's the latter. I'm still learning.

A lot of what I'm learning is being shaped by my family, including my birth mother, who was a woman living outside the lines of definitions. My mother, who loved art and jazz and old-school movies, who loved me enough to give me to my parents, to give me the beginning of my story and the questions probing who I am. And though I may not ever have all the answers, I have one:

We have no control over what labels others give us, but we can define who we are by the ones we choose to give ourselves.

THE END

ACKNOWLEDGMENTS

THE JOURNEY TO WRITING A second novel was far from easy. But it was worth every moment of doubt, fear, and joy. Fortunately, some great people walked beside me for at least part of this journey.

Deepest and sincerest thanks to:

C.B. Messer, rockstar cover artist and Remy enthusiast from day one. I'm so grateful for all our conversations throughout the process of publishing this book. Thank you for your words of strength, understanding, and excitement and for listening to me when I didn't feel confident. I still firmly believe you are made of magic.

Annie Harper, editor extraordinaire. Thank you for challenging me. You always believed Remy was special and that I had it in me to show that to others. You helped me find the heart of this story. Every month should be Hallmark Holiday Movie month for you.

Candysse Miller, marketing genius. Thank you for the laughs, the encouraging phone calls, the chats in California traffic, and the hockey. Every day, I hope I make you proud.

To the early readers who helped shape Remy's story: My "OMG" twin—Jude Sierra, you're seriously inspiring—C.B. Lee, Taylor Brooke, Tiffany Chapman, and C.B. Messer and to my incredible sensitivity reader, Axie Oh, who helped bring Ian and his family to life.

My copyeditor, Nicki Harper, who continues to teach me the power of words.

My wonderful Interlude Press family—Pene Henson, Jude Sierra, Laura Stone, C.B. Lee, Julia Ember, Alysia Constantine, Killian B. Brewer, F.T. Lukens, Lilah Suzanne, S.J. Martin, Carrie Pack, Lissa

Reed, Naomi Tajedler, Rachel Davidson Lee, E.S. Kariquist, Michelle Osgood, Mia Kerick, Taylor Brooke, Tom Wilinsky, Jen Sternick, Charlotte Ashe, intern Will, and many more.

Becky Albertalli, I will never be able to thank you enough. You've made a lot of my dreams come true and you've been a true friend. French toast is on me next time!

Adib Khorram, you're my favorite nerd, the Picard to my Riker, and the most unexpected surprise in this journey. "You're simply the best."

Nic Stone, you intimidate me in the most inspiring ways. Thank you for always standing in my corner.

Simon James Green and Cale Dietrich, your support, jokes, and epic storytelling inspire so many of us.

Adam Silvera, my comic book geek twin—thanks for knocking down so many walls for me. Mark Oshiro, you always make me cry in the best ways. Shaun David Hutchinson, you're best of the best even when you don't believe it. Bill Konigsberg, your courage and love keep a lot of us going.

The G Squad—Adam Sass, Phil Stamper, L.C. Rosen, Caleb Roehrig, Tom Ryan, Alex London, Cale Dietrich, Adib Khorram, Shaun David Hutchinson, I hope we live loud and proud so that others will hear our voices and do the same.

My agent, Thao Le—thanks for your patience and geeky heart.

The incredible people continuously inspiring me: Angie Thomas, Nic Stone, Tiffany D. Jackson, Dhonielle Clayton, Patrice Caldwell, Kacen Callender, Jason Reynolds, Jay Coles, Brandy Colbert, Camryn Garrett, Sierra Elmore, Alyssa Cole, Karen Strong, Ryan Douglass, Justin A. Reynolds, Kimberly Jones, Kosoko Jackson, Brittney Morris, Ibi Zoboi, L.L. McKinney, Elizabeth Acevedo, Claire Kann, and more. I love our magic.

The awesome people in this amazing community I'm fortunate to be a part of: Dahlia Adler, Zoraida Córdova, Heidi Heilig, Eric Smith, Natasha Ngan, David Arnold, Samira Ahmed, Claribel A. Ortega, Kelly Loy Gilbert, Kiersten White, V.E. Schwab, Mason Deaver, Sandhya Menon, Sarah Enni, Arvin Ahmadi, Roshani Chokshi, S.J. Goslee, Terra Elan McVoy, Sabina Khan, Aisha Saeed, Sara Farizan, Kat Cho, Julie Murphy, Laura Silverman, Vanessa North, Susan Lee, Tara Sim, Claire Legrand, Jeffrey and Jeremy West, Sophie Cameron, Randy Ribay, Abdi Nazemian, Kevin Savoie, Ben Monopoli, Ryan La Sala, TJ Ryan, Michael Barakiva, Saundra Mitchell, Angelo Sumerlis, Preeti Chhibber, Roselle Lim, Natasha Díaz, Greg Howard, Jennifer Dugan, Ashley Herring Blake, Sam J. Miller, J.C. Lillis, Diane Capriola, Little Shop of Stories, Read It Again Books, YATL, and countless others. If I've missed your name, it's not because I've forgotten you. It's because my heart is overflowing with love and gratitude for all you've done.

The librarians, booksellers, teachers, bloggers, booktubers, artists, agents, and publishing professionals who have made my dreams come true. DJ DeSmyter, Rachel Strolle, Fadwa, Mina Waheed, Charlie Morris, Robby, Kav, Cody Roecker, James Tilton, Shauna Morgan—you're all amazing.

Mom: This book is a big hug to you. You've always known who you are.

My family: Dad, Sonya, Tamir, Piper, Lindsay, and the extended Indiana loved ones. My friends: Tamica, Angela, Jason, Ahmad, and Tony. S.A. McAuley, to whom I owe the biggest hug for starting me on this path. All the fandom peeps: you light up my world like... well, you know the rest.

Zeke, Daniel, Malachi, Jael, I hope each of you know you're my world.

And for all the queer teens of color: No single label can define you. You're more than the box they use to contain you. You're made of stars; let the world see you shine!

ABOUT THE AUTHOR

JULIAN WINTERS IS A BEST-SELLING author of contemporary young adult fiction. His award-winning debut, Running With Lions (Duet, 2018), received accolades for its positive depictions of diverse, relatable characters. A former management trainer, Julian currently lives outside of Atlanta where he can be found reading, being a self-proclaimed comic book geek, or watching the only two sports he can follow—volleyball and soccer. *How to Be Remy Cameron* is his second novel.

Content Warning:

This book contains discussions of racism, homophobia, past minor characters' death, and alcoholism, as well as depictions of homophobic bullying, and a scene involving brief sexual harassment/racial fetishism.

For a reader's guide to **How to Be Remy Cameron** and book club prompts, please visit duetbooks.com.

an imprint of interlude **press**

🌐 duetbooks.com
🐦 @DuetBooks
ⓣ duetbooks
🛒 store.interludepress.com

also from duet

Running with Lions by Julian Winters
IBPA Benjamin Franklin Gold Award Winner

When his estranged childhood best friend Emir
Shah joins his team, star goalie Sebastian Hughes
must reconnect with the one guy who hates him. But
to Sebastian's surprise, sweaty days on the pitch,
wandering the town, and bonding on the weekends
sparks more than just friendship between them.

ISBN (print) 978-1-945053-62-7 | (eBook) 978-1-945053-63-4

Not Your Backup by C.B. Lee
Sidekick Squad series, Book Three

As the Sidekick Squad series continues, Emma Robledo
and her friends have left school to lead a fractured
Resistance movement against a corrupt Heroes' League
of Heroes. Emma is the only member of a supercharged
team without powers, and she isn't always taken
seriously. But she is determined to win this battle and
realizes where her place is in this fight: at the front.

ISBN (print) 978-1-945053-78-8 | (eBook) 978-1-945053-79-5

Monster of the Week by F.T. Lukens
The Rules, Book Two

Spring semester of Bridger Whitt's senior year is looking
great... until a monster-hunting television show arrives in
town to investigate the series of strange events from last
fall, and Bridger finds himself trapped in a game of cat
and mouse that could very well put the myth world at
risk. Again.

ISBN (print) 978-1-945053-82-5 | (eBook) 978-1-945053-83-2